A
BOOKSTORE
IN BERLIN

A
BOOKSTORE
IN BERLIN

Joseph W. Michels

A BOOKSTORE IN BERLIN

Credit for cover art photo (Street scene in Dresden):Copyright © 2012 Joseph W. Michels

Credit for maps: Mitte District: Copyright © 2012 Joseph W. Michels, Rev. 2018; NATO Eastern Flank: Copyright © 2019 Joseph W. Michels

Credit for author photo: Copyright © 2019 Dina L. Michels

iUniverse books may be ordered through booksellers or by contacting:

iUniverse
1663 Liberty Drive
Bloomington, IN 47403
www.iuniverse.com
1-800-Authors (1-800-288-4677)

ISBN: 978-1-5320-7841-5 (sc)
ISBN: 978-1-5320-7842-2 (e)

Print information available on the last page.

iUniverse rev. date: 07/19/2019

Acknowledgements

I wish to thank my wife, Elizabeth S. Sweetow, not only for her thoughtful editorial input but also for her unflagging enthusiasm and support during the many months of writing. This is the thirteenth work of fiction to receive her editorial attention—a gift I gratefully acknowledge.

I also wish to thank my good friend, Colonel Dick Bergson, U.S. Army, Ret., for lending his considerable expertise in ensuring my use of military language and terms of address conform with currently accepted norms. In addition, Col. Bergson's careful reading of the manuscript contributed considerably to the clarity and consistency of the final product—a service I gratefully acknowledge.

Also by Joseph W. Michels

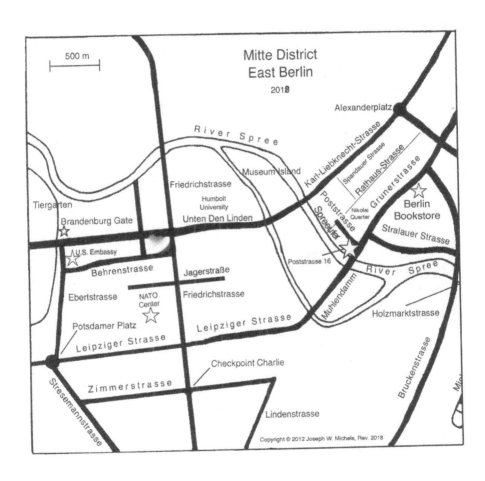

Mitte District
East Berlin
2018

500 m

Alexanderplatz

River Spree

Karl-Liebknecht-Strasse

Spandauer Strasse

Rathaus-Strasse

Grunerstrasse

Museum Island

Friedrichstrasse

Humbolt
University

Poststrasse

Nikolai
Quarter

Berlin
Bookstore

Tiergarten

Unten Den Linden

Spreeufer

Stralauer Strasse

Brandenburg Gate

U.S. Embassy

Poststrasse 16

River Spree

Behrenstrasse

Jagerstraße

Ebertstrasse

NATO
Center

Friedrichstrasse

Muhlendamm

Holzmarktstrasse

Potsdamer Platz

Leipziger Strasse

Leipziger Strasse

Checkpoint Charlie

Bruckenstrasse

Zimmerstrasse

Stresemannstrasse

Lindenstrasse

Copyright © 2012 Joseph W. Michels, Rev. 2018

Chapter One

It was the way he browsed that caught Elliott Stone's attention. He'd pull a book from a shelf—almost at random—appear to look at it then put it back and move on. It was almost as if it was meant to reassure anyone happening to notice that his movement down the aisle of books was a normal, everyday kind of thing.

The man had passed Elliott on the aisle before taking up the charade and seemed reassured Elliott was too deeply absorbed in examining the book he was holding to notice anything about the man's presence.

Elliott's interest in the man's behavior increased as he surreptitiously watched him pull down a book—this time with some care—open it, then take an envelope from his breast pocket and slip it under the inside flap of the book jacket before returning it to its place on the shelf.

Elliott turned away, still feigning interest in the book he was holding, as the man headed for the front of the store. Once he'd passed, Elliott studied him until he stepped through the entrance and out onto the street. He was young—maybe late twenties—and wore brown slacks and an unbuttoned dark gray sport jacket. Elliott guessed he was of average height. What most struck Elliott was the man's unkempt appearance: he was unshaven and wore his hair long in some sort of tousled style.

Elliott was tempted to search for the book the man had chosen, but just as he was about to move towards the spot along the aisle where the man had been standing, the check-out counter clerk stepped into the aisle and walked determinedly past Elliott, stopping briefly to retrieve the book, open it, remove the envelope, then return the book to its shelf.

Elliott expected the clerk to return to the check-out counter but instead he continued further along the aisle—to the far wall where there was a doorway. He opened it and stepped through, closing the door behind him. Moments later, he reappeared, walking briskly up the aisle, giving Elliott an unfriendly look as he passed, before heading back to his place behind the counter.

The unfriendly look nagged at Elliott as he continued browsing. It seemed a gratuitously unbusinesslike gesture, especially since he hadn't noticed any other customers during the time he'd been in the store.

Finally, he felt he'd idled away enough time and headed for the entrance. Once he was back on the narrow cobblestone street, with its awning covered cafes, he tried to make sense of what he'd observed. There was a straightforwardness about the handoff—if indeed that is what it was—making the modest gestures at concealment seem contrived, almost proforma, as if undertaken not out of conviction but merely in accordance with procedural rules taken from some out-of-date manual. As Elliott thought further about the incongruity of the act he began to wonder whether there was something about the setting—about the bookstore itself—that might possibly lend some rational basis to the otherwise amateurish way the envelope was passed.

Elliott observed that the bookstore, like many shops in Berlin, possessed a deep but narrow footprint, widely popular because it made rent affordable by limiting the property's street-front presence. However in this case, as Elliott had discovered, the retail floor space was noticeably foreshortened by the presence of a dividing wall that allocated an unusually generous amount of the property's footprint to back room activities. The decidedly unbusinesslike use of available space could perhaps be justified, thought Elliott, if it was part of a strategy for making the store less inviting, though this would, itself, pose new questions. But putting those questions aside, he thought it helpful to review other aspects of the store beginning with why he'd been attracted to it in the first place.

It wasn't because he'd known about the bookstore and had made a point of searching it out. No, he'd simply been out on an early evening stroll in a part of Mitte with which he was not familiar—an area not far from where he lived in the Nikolai Quarter. As soon as he came upon the narrow cobblestone street lined with charming sidewalk dining venues, he knew he had to explore it. And there—stuck between two cafes—was where he discovered this rather unpretentious bookstore whose window display featured books in various European languages that seemed to be limited to titles dealing with contemporary European politics. Being in a profession that required knowledge of European military issues, Elliott understood why he had been drawn to the store, but realized others not so enamored of that topic and in the market for fiction or for other more popular themes might, quite understandably, be expected to pay little attention to the shop as they walked down the street or dined at one of the cafes.

Elliott smiled to himself as he realized the less than hospitable conduct of the bookstore clerk, a dour middle-aged man in his sixties who wore a dark nondescript suit, was probably intentional—a way to reinforce the message echoed by the store's limited inventory and narrow range of offerings that casual browsing was not to be encouraged.

But was that really true? he asked himself. To check, he chose a sidewalk table at one of the nearby cafes—a location where he could monitor the bookstore's entrance. "Einen Kaffe, bitte," he said to the waitress who took his order, then settled in to watch.

* * *

During the hour Elliott sat there he observed a number of couples approach the entrance, spend a few moments studying the published works on display, give a peek inside, then choose to give the shop a pass. He was about to leave his observational perch and head home when he noticed one man actually entering the store: also a young man like the one Elliott had spotted doing the handover. But this one was even younger—maybe early twenties—clean shaven, hair long but well-combed, wearing straight blue jeans, a black peacoat-styled jacket and sneakers. Elliott couldn't resist, he dropped some money on the table, got up and quickly reentered the bookstore.

He caught sight of the man about mid-point along the far left aisle and followed—remaining back just far enough to avoid being overtly intrusive but close enough to hope he'd recognize the book ultimately chosen by the young man if, indeed, there was to be another handover.

Then it happened. The young man selected a volume from a shelf at about shoulder height, carefully opened it up, then slipped his left hand into his peacoat pocket and pulled out an envelope. As he carefully inserted the envelope underneath the book jacket flap at the front of the book, Elliott took a number of furtive glances in his direction, intent on seeing something distinctive in the book's cover design that he could use to locate the volume once the man had left. Finally, as the man was returning the book to its place on the shelf Elliott caught a glimpse of the distinctive seal-trident on a blue background that he knew served as the coat of arms of the modern state of Ukraine.

Mindful of how quickly the counter clerk had appeared the last time, Elliott began moving towards the point along the aisle where the handoff had taken place even before the young man had made it out of the store. Fortunately the Ukrainian national symbol had also been reproduced on the jacket's spine, enabling Elliott to reach for the work without hesitation. He opened the hard cover, reached under the book's jacket flap and retrieved the envelope. Wasting no time, he opened the envelope, took out the single sheet of folded paper, then closed the envelope and slipped it back underneath the flap. He shoved the book hurriedly onto the shelf then began walking towards the front of the the aisle just as the clerk turned the corner and headed towards him.

Again, the clerk gave Elliott a disapproving look...but one that almost instantly turned to suspicion as he sensed the American-looking man had somehow involved himself. Elliott knew his suspicion would turn to certainty once the envelope was opened in the back room.

* * *

Elliott, impatient to learn what was written on the folded paper, stopped once he reached the end of the block-long cobblestone street—an intersection where the thin autumnal sunlight could better penetrate the narrow lane hemmed in by five and six story buildings. Glancing around to reassure himself no one was nearby, he unfolded the paper and began to study it. With some relief he found it readable, but only because he was fluent in Ukrainian. Rereading it a second time gave him the impression that it was some sort of transcript—most likely a transcript of a conversation captured using a remote audio receiver of some sort. Most alarming, in Elliott's way of thinking, was what was being talked about, and by whom. He'd need to contact Col. Lawrence Appleton, the defense attaché at the U.S. Embassy.

Preoccupied with such thoughts, Elliott walked doggedly towards the Nikolai Quarter where his apartment was located, keeping to the narrow back streets of Mitte to avoid the traffic and the crowds. He'd only gone about three blocks when he sensed someone following him. He glanced back and spotted a man approaching at a fast pace. Resuming his forward progress, he quickly searched his memory, hoping to recall having encountered the man earlier, but no one came to mind. He could hear the man's footsteps drawing closer and realized he'd need to deal with the situation one way or another. He stopped and turned to face the man.

The stranger seemed emboldened by Elliott's stationary presence and rushed forward, a knife suddenly appearing in his right hand. Elliott's hand-to-hand combat training immediately kicked in. Elliott stepped back, encouraging the man to lunge forward, aiming for Elliott's midsection, then Elliott moved in for the attack, deflecting the knife thrust with the blocking action of his left arm while simultaneously smashing his right fist squarely into the man's face. Keeping his left arm firmly against the man's arm holding the knife, Elliott used his height and athletic strength to put downward pressure on the attacker, leveraging the take down with his right arm locked around the man's head. With the man now on his back, Elliott kneeled on his chest and leveled repeated blows to his face until he sensed the man had dropped the knife. Elliott pushed the knife away, then while still kneeling on the man's chest he searched his pockets, pulling out a wallet. "I'll be keeping this," said Elliott as he stood up, "now get the hell out of here!"

As the man painfully got to his feet, Elliott studied him. The man was of average height, wore tight dark jeans, and a blue denim shirt under a padded hunting jacket with the collar turned up. Like so many European men, he favored the unshaven look and wore his hair short on the sides, long on the top. Elliott figured him to be in his mid-thirties. "You're from the bookstore...right?" said Elliott.

The man didn't reply, just gave Elliott an angry look, then limped away.

Elliott nodded to himself as he watched the man leave, pretty certain he'd guessed correctly. What surprised him wasn't the likelihood the bookstore people had sent someone to retrieve the paper, but that there'd been a deliberate intent to kill him in the process. That smacked of desperation: whatever these people were involved in, the stakes were perceived to be high enough to warrant maximum precaution on their part in dealing with possible leaks.

* * *

When he reached Nikolai Square he looked up at Villa Marckwald, the petit palais where his apartment was located, reviewing in his mind its security vulnerabilities in the off chance the man who attacked him, or some other agent or agents of the organization behind the attack, somehow found out where he lived.

Despite the fact he lived in a ground floor apartment he wasn't particularly worried about himself—it was his wife, and the other residents in the building that he worried about, several of whom were elderly, including his wife's grandmother.

He knew from past experience that the building's primary security weakness was the circular aluminum staircase attached to the rear of the building—installed some years ago as a fire escape precaution. Landings on the grand interior staircase that rose to the top floor were connected to the exterior aluminum staircase by double French doors of wood and glass. Anyone managing to access the aluminum staircase could quickly reach a set of these easily forced French doors and gain entry. The other glaring weakness were the windows of the ground floor apartments—windows easily reached from the ground and large enough to accommodate a swift break-in.

After an earlier break-in Elliott had arranged for bright floodlights to be installed aimed at the base of the aluminum staircase and activated by motion sensors.

As for the front ground-floor windows, so far he'd been satisfied with the protection provided by streetlight coverage during night hours, and exposure to the busy Nikolai Square during daylight hours. Until he had some solid evidence that he was being further targeted, he felt these circumstances continued to offer an adequate level of security.

As he unlocked the thick wooden entrance door leading to the building's interior hallways he felt some relief knowing his wife was back in the States visiting her parents and sister, and wouldn't be returning for another week. After a moment's hesitation, he walked slowly through the front hallway then into a second hall where the palace's grand elliptical staircase was located and where the door to his apartment was to be found. He put his key in the lock, then with a sigh he unlocked it and stepped inside.

The apartment consisted of three large interconnecting rooms along the front. And at the back: a hallway, large kitchen, two bathrooms and the apartment's modest interior entrance area.

After pouring himself a glass of single malted scotch, Elliott removed his sport jacket and shoes, and settled onto the deeply cushioned couch in the farthest of the three large rooms—the one he and his wife had chosen to be his study. She had her own office on the second floor which she used in connection with her management of the apartment building, and in pursuit of her freelance crowdsourcing business.

Elliott, 33, was an aspiring author—working on his first novel—who labored diligently at his new craft. But he was also a graduate of West Point and a lieutenant colonel, now in the U.S. Army Reserves, with eleven years of active military service in various elite units. More importantly, he was frequently brought back into active service to lead critical missions in counter-intelligence within eastern Europe—a prospect that now seemed all too imminent given what he had observed earlier that evening.

Chapter Two

"Lay it out for me, Elliott, what do you think is going on?" asked Colonel Appleton once Elliott had described the events of the previous evening. They were sitting in Appleton's office on the third floor of the consular wing.

"It's hard to tell, sir, but a reading of the transcript I retrieved from the second handover at the bookstore would suggest that persons attached to the NATO Planning Center on Jagerstraße are being surveilled."

"How could that be?" Appleton asked. "Hell, the Center is barely weeks old and we've made every effort to keep its existence a military secret!"

Elliott shrugged, "Maybe it's just these men who are being monitored, sir…maybe whoever's ordering the surveillance doesn't yet know about the Center itself."

"So, there's nothing in the transcript that mentions the Center, or points to its existence?" asked Appleton, seeking assurance.

"Nothing obvious, sir, but somebody like myself who knows of its presence here in Berlin would probably be able to connect the dots."

"Christ, the whole reason we set this thing up was to get planning for the Eastern Flank out from under the glare of NATO headquarters!"

"I understand, sir, and the plan you put together in setting this thing up is solid. No one would imagine NATO would entrust leadership of such a critical planning operation to a US Army colonel who's riding a desk in Berlin as the embassy's defense attaché," said Elliott.

"Hmm...so, these two men...the men whose conversation was being overheard...they were Ukrainian?" asked Appleton.

"Not necessarily, sir; they were speaking Ukrainian so I suspect at least one of them was, but the other...he could have been Russian or Polish," replied Elliott, who then added, "If the surveillance operative had identified them by name, or in some other way, we could be sure. But the fact the operative didn't supply such information leads me to believe that surveillance was triggered by something else...maybe some visual association with an embassy under watch, or observed proximity to NATO brass back at NATO headquarters in Belgium."

"So, their identities remain unknown?"

"Maybe not, sir...whoever ordered the surveillance might know...but just didn't tell the field operative."

"That's a hell of a way to run surveillance," said Appleton disgustedly.

"We're just grabbing at straws, sir," said Elliott soberly, "I'd recommend we initiate a counter-intelligence operation focused on the bookstore—see where this all leads."

Appleton nodded, "I'll arrange to have INSCOM cut orders reactivating you, Elliott...you okay with that?"

"Yes, sir," replied Elliott. "I take it you want me to lead the effort."

"Hell, yes! You're the man who spotted the activity and you've logged in years of counter-intelligence work...especially on opps involving eastern Europe. Who do you want on your team?"

"If you can get him, I'd like as my second in command, Capt. Perez from one of the SOCEUR Delta teams based in Stuttgart. I've worked with him on two recent opps—both in eastern Europe—and know he can do the job...I'll let him select three men from among his teammates...that should be enough."

Appleton shook his head, clearly perplexed, "I don't get you, Elliott...you'll be on a counter-intelligence opp, going up against a sophisticated adversary...why the hell wouldn't you want a team of intelligence specialists...maybe even civilian types... rather than a bunch of elite combat operatives?"

"I know these guys, colonel...was one of them myself. They're not just warriors, they're also trained observers who are often tasked with intelligence gathering. And from what I experienced yesterday it's likely we'll be coming up against a crew who won't hesitate to use lethal means to protect their operation...I want a team that can handle that kind of situation."

"Tell me about the substance of the intel these guys collected while listening in on the conversation," said Appleton wearily.

"Ironically, most of the chatter had to do with personnel issues...you know, who was being assigned...what share of

13

staffing would be made up of military types, what share civilian types."

"So, there was talk of a new Center! Dammit, Elliott, you said there wasn't any such talk."

"The way the conversation went, sir, seemed to point to NATO's newly established counter-intelligence center in Kracow, Poland, not to your Center here in Berlin. I didn't find that worrying. What I did find worrying were references to the existence of a "New Paradigm". That's terminology directly linked to our plans for strengthening NATO's eastern flank—the Baltics, Poland, Romania."

"Did they get into specifics…you know…deterrence strategies, chain of command, early warning capabilities—that sort of thing?" asked Appleton, somewhat mollified.

"No, but it's not surprising that staffing issues would monopolize conversations this early in the build-up of personnel attached to the Center. But with substantive meetings being scheduled for this week at the Jagerstraße headquarters off-premise conversations among the Center's personnel could become an intel bonanza for our adversaries."

Appleton nodded resignedly, "When I think about it, I know—sure as hell—I'm going to be raked over the coals for not referring this whole issue to the counter-intelligence center in Kracow…this is just the kind of thing that Center was intended to handle."

"You're right, sir, but we've a chance to fold up this intelligence-gathering outfit before they even determine with certainty the Berlin-based NATO Planning Center even exists, much less acquire a clear picture of what the team you lead is actually intending to do," argued Elliott.

"Okay, I'll buy it, Elliott, but you're going to have to act fast...I should be able to secure orders for you and your team by the end of the day...meanwhile, I'll call in some favors to get Perez and his Delta buddies flown up here while the paperwork is still in progress."

"I'll call Perez and give him a head's up, sir," said Elliott, who then added, "It might be good if you alerted your contacts at Berliner Polizei headquarters that you've ordered a NATO counter-intelligence operation in the city. They'll need to know the operation involves five armed US Special Forces personnel."

"Will do," replied Appleton as he rose from his desk chair, "I suspect they'll take it upon themselves to pass the information on to their federal counter-intelligence services so don't be surprised if the Germans try to get a handle on your identities, and who it is you and your team are attempting to interdict."

"So, you won't be giving our names to the Berliner Polizei?"

"They'll understand it's a covert operation, Elliott...but if there's some sort of violent disturbance where your team's involvement can't be concealed they'll be banging on my door demanding to know."

"I read you, sir," said Elliott as he stood up.

As they shook hands, Appleton asked, "Where do you plan on putting your men up?"

"I thought I'd have them bunk with me at Poststraße 16," replied Elliott. "I've got plenty of room...especially since my wife Claire is away. That'll also make it a bit harder for the

Germans to identify the team since there won't be any suspicious guest listings on hotel registrations, and there's no need for Perez and his men to register as my guests given the short time frame we're hoping will suffice for this mission."

"Good thinking…well, good luck, Elliott…keep me informed," said Appleton briskly as he opened the door to his office and gave a brief parting wave to Elliott as he walked out.

* * *

Elliott left the US Embassy and headed east on Behrenstraße, intending to walk the 2.6 km to his residence. During the half hour it would take him, he intended to think through some of the early steps he'd need to take to get up to speed. While he walked, he pulled out his cell phone and put a call through to Capt. Perez in Stuttgart.

"Capt. Perez, this is Lt. Col. Elliott Stone," said Elliott once Perez picked up. "I've put in a request for you to assist me with a counter-intelligence mission here in Berlin…an operation not too different from the previous opps we worked on together. The paperwork will probably take most of the day, but my commanding officer, Col. Appleton, thinks he can get you flown up here sooner. Any problem with any of this?"

"No sir…glad to be part of the mission," replied Capt. Perez.

"Good to know. Also, captain, I've arranged for you to select three men from among your Delta team to accompany you."

"Should we come armed, sir?" asked Perez.

"Affirmative, captain."

"Very well, sir."

"Once you know your ETA at Tegel give me a call…I'll pick up the four of you at the Arrivals exit."

"Will do, sir!"

Elliott broke the connection and continued walking. He smiled to himself as he thought about having agreed to giving up his convertible for a more practical sports utility vehicle once he and Claire married. At the time, it seemed to symbolize a shift to a more domestic lifestyle, but now, he realized, it also meant he'd be able to transport his newly assembled team around the city and wherever else within the state of Brandenburg the mission might take them.

Logistics continued to absorb his attention. He recalled seeing a collection of furniture in the basement of his building left behind by previous tenants, and thought it likely he could find sufficient beds with which to set up a barracks-like arrangement in the first of the three large rooms along the front of his apartment. They'd be able to use his study as a meeting room, he reasoned.

Not relishing the idea of cooking for five men, Elliott thought about various options for takeout. He knew there were at least a half dozen restaurants within a couple of blocks— either bordering the river Spree—along the Spreeufer—or on Poststraße itself. He wasn't sure how many offered takeout, but figured at least a few probably did. He sighed as he resigned himself to the fact that eating out, despite its obvious attraction, wasn't really a viable option—at least by the team as a whole—since the presence of a bunch of young athletic American males seated among an essentially European crowd would bring undue attention. If a member of the team did wish to eat out, he thought, it would have to be alone or at most with one other teammate.

He was just crossing the Spree on Rathausbrücke, where the Mitte district began, when he realized he'd also need to reassure the other tenants in the building that the presence of Perez and his men was nothing to be alarmed about. He'd have to ask Claire's grandmother, Alice, who lived on the second floor, how best to explain their presence in his apartment.

A moment's sudden inspiration drove him to turn right once he reached Spreeufer, that two-block long paved promenade along the Spree that led to Mühlendamm Brücke and on which most of the restaurants were located that Elliott hoped would offer takeout. He'd check with each one of them as he headed home.

Chapter Three

Capt. Perez and his three teammates emerged from the Arrivals baggage area of Tegel International Airport at three o'clock that afternoon, each carrying a European-brand duffle. Elliott, who was standing next to his SUV, gave a wave.

He watched them approach. All were wearing civilian clothes—some combination of tight jeans, dark T-shirt under a black leather jacket and cross-trainers.

"Good to see you again, sir," said Capt. Perez as he shook Elliott's hand. "Let me introduce the team: Sgt. Dan Farrand out of Newark, New Jersey, Sgt. Leroy White of Staunton, Virginia, and Sgt. Nick Hernandez who hails from Albuquerque, New Mexico."

"Pleased to have you on board, sergeants," said Elliott, shaking the hand of each. "Let's get your gear stashed."

As the four of them began stowing their duffles in the rear compartment, Elliott studied them. Sgt. Dan Farrand, probably of English/German stock, was fair skinned, about six feet tall and built lean. He'd fit in easily on the streets of Berlin. Sgt. Leroy White was African-American, maybe 5' 10" in height with a very pronounced muscular build. He'd stand out not only because of the color of his skin, but also because of his somewhat intimidating build. Sgt. Nick Hernandez, Mexican-American, was about 5' 8", agile and lean. He could maybe pass for a Filipino in a pinch.

And Capt. Emilio Perez was about the same height as Hernandez, but with short legs and a broad, solid torso. He might be taken for someone from the Basque region, but more than likely he'd be typed as Mexican-American, which is what he was.

Add all of that to their military bearing, short haircuts, and "can-do" attitude and you've got a team that's not high on anyone's measure of anonymity, thought Elliott a bit ruefully. But hell, he reflected, they'd just have to make it up in street smarts and observational acumen—something he felt confident they could do.

"Okay, let's roll," said Elliott as he gestured for Perez and his men to climb into the SUV. Doors were opened and all four men followed Elliott's lead. Perez took the front passenger seat, the three teammates climbed into the back seat. Elliott started the engine, put the vehicle in gear and pulled away from the curb.

"What have you lined up in the way of accommodations, sir" asked Perez as Elliott maneuvered through the heavy airport traffic.

"You'll all be bunking at my apartment," replied Elliott. "I've located four extra beds in the building's basement that can be brought up, and there's a large room right off the entry you men can set up as a make-shift barracks. The two bathrooms should easily accommodate the five of us."

Perez nodded, then settled back as Elliott turned onto the A111 highway that would take them towards the center of the city.

"It's about a half hour's drive," said Elliott, anticipating Perez' next question.

* * *

Alice, Claire's grandmother, had come downstairs to watch as the three sergeants carried up the beds from the basement. "Will they need extra linens and towels?" she asked Elliott.

"No, I think there's enough," he replied, then added, "You sure you're okay with my having taken them in?"

"Of course, Elliott," she replied dismissively, "though I suppose it's good that Claire is away…managing meals for five hungry men wouldn't be her fondest wish. By the way, what have you planned in the way of dining arrangements?"

"We'll eat takeout most of the time, I imagine," replied Elliott. "It turns out that several of the nearby restaurants are already geared up for that kind of thing, and a couple of the others assured me they'd be happy to accommodate us knowing Claire and I are regular patrons."

"Have you talked with any of the other tenants about your unexpected guests?" asked Alice.

"Not yet," replied Elliott somewhat pensively, "I was hoping you'd clue me in on which ones you think might object…give me a chance to reassure them before they get all riled up."

"Oh, I suppose you can guess who just as well as I can," she replied offhandedly. "It'd be your neighbor across the hall,

Wolfgang Hartmann. He's older and set in his ways, and it doesn't help that he's in ill health…I'd speak with him first. The only other tenants I can think of who might object are Klaus and Ines Meier who live directly above you. Like Hartmann, they're a bit older than the other tenants and might need reassuring…if you want, I can talk to them for you."

"I'd greatly appreciate it, Alice," said Elliott. "Be sure to tell them my guests will only be here for a week or so…nothing long term."

Alice nodded, then noting the fact that the sergeant named Leroy had closed the door to the basement said, "Well, it looks like they've finished up…please extend my welcome to them once more, Elliott."

"I will, Alice…thanks for everything."

Alice smiled, placed a hand on Elliott's arm as a sign of affection, then began climbing the grand elliptical staircase up to the second floor where her own apartment was located.

Elliott watched her for a brief moment, letting his emotions get the better of him, then, shaking his head, returned to his apartment to see how Perez and his men were getting on. As he stepped into the room set aside for the men he discovered that all of Claire's parlor furnishings had been carefully pushed against the room's interior walls, leaving a large open space at the center where the four beds were now positioned—arranged in a two-by-two pattern that allowed for generous spacing between them. The men themselves were busily occupied with making up the beds with sheets taken from Claire's linen closet. He watched with some bemusement as they gave the sheets a military tuck and fold.

* * *

It was six o'clock that evening. Elliott, Capt. Perez, and the three sergeants were seated around the large wooden table in the kitchen, eating takeout from an Italian restaurant on the Spreeufer promenade, when Elliott pulled out the wallet of the man he'd subdued and tossed it on the table.

"Give me your thoughts on who this guy might be," he said.

Dan, a non-commissioned officer with an enlistment pay grade of E7, picked it up, opened it, then shook out the contents, "Carries a Belarus identity card with the name, Vadim, showing his home town as being Minsk," said Dan laconically.

"Anything else?" asked Elliott.

"Looks like he's staying east of Bruckenstraße...in the Friedrichshain district," replied Leroy, an E6 who'd picked up some of the other papers that had fallen out of the wallet.

"It might help, sir, if you could describe him for us," said Capt. Perez.

Elliott shrugged, "About average height, mid-thirties, dressed casually like most other young men here in the city... fashionable jeans, collared shirt, rough jacket." He paused for a moment then continued: "He had dark hair...I remember that... worn long on the top...and sported what you might call an "unshaven" look. So, all in all, nothing really noteworthy in his appearance...certainly nothing that would give us a clue as to his circumstances, or why he chose to attack me."

"But you're pretty sure the assault had something to do with your retrieval of the transcript left behind at the bookstore," said Perez.

Elliott nodded, "It's the only plausible explanation."

"You were on target with the guy's age," said Dan, changing the subject, "his identity card has him being thirty-two years old...and the photo on the card pretty much matches your description of the man...so it doesn't appear he was carrying someone else's I.D....but if that's not the case, and the card has been tampered with, then I'd have to say the work is of pretty high quality."

"What about his decision to use a knife in the attack?" asked Nick, also an E6. "That say anything about him?"

"That he's probably not a professional hit man," said Leroy, shaking his head. "According to the colonel...here...killing was his intent. So why come at an able-bodied man with a weapon that requires close contact...where there's a risk of things getting messy should the victim resist...why not use a silenced handgun? Or if a knife is to be used, why not maneuver ahead of the victim and take him suddenly...without warning. No, this Vadim guy is probably simply muscle for hire...used for security gigs like enforcement or punishment, but this time tasked for a job far out of his skill zone."

"So, what's that say about the intelligence-gathering operation I stumbled upon at the bookstore?" asked Elliott.

"Well, for one thing," said Dan, "it's likely the operation is not being run by an arm of the state...like Russia's GRU or FSB. There's an amateurish quality about it...not only in connection with the attempted hit on you, but in the way you describe the hand-off."

"Yeah, but whoever it is that's mounting this operation isn't dumb or unsophisticated," argued Perez. "The transcript the colonel retrieved demonstrates that real intelligence data is being collected…and from actors linked to the newly formed—and top secret—NATO Planning Center on Jagerstraße. It'd be real nice to know how the surveillance was carried out, and whether it presumes our adversary actually knows about the Center, or is just picking up intel fairly indiscriminately—hoping maybe to sell it in bulk rather than piecemeal."

"Let's say Capt. Perez' wish list is high on our agenda…how might we go about answering those questions?" asked Elliott.

"Put a continuous watch on the bookstore…noting each time a hand-off occurs," volunteered Leroy. "That would at least give us a handle on who's doing the surveillance. Those identified could then be followed, and when they went into action the next time we could observe what methods they employed."

"It's a good idea, Leroy, but would it tax our manpower resources? We don't know how many hours the bookstore is open, or how many days in the week, and we don't know how many operatives are in play," argued Dan.

"I can help out there, gentlemen," said Elliott. "A sign in front of the bookstore indicated that the place was only open from 1600 hours to 2000 hours, Monday through Friday."

"If the interval of about an hour between hand-offs that you observed, sir, is standard operating procedure it might suggest the involvement of perhaps no more than four surveillance agents…that's assuming, of course, that other agents aren't checking in on alternate days," said Nick.

"Yeah, but we've got to keep in mind the possibility, sergeant, that we may be dealing with surveillance teams," argued Perez. "That's how I'd set it up…two-man teams…to ensure at least one agent stays on the target even if the other is blown or loses access to the target…for technical or other reasons."

"Or simply to watch the other's back in case somebody becomes suspicious," added Leroy in support of what the captain said.

"But that shouldn't actually matter," protested Nick. "Sooner or later, whichever agent executes the hand-off will eventually have to hook up with his or her teammate, so the possibility we're dealing with surveillance teams rather than solitary agents shouldn't add to our own surveillance burden."

"What about the conversational transcripts being handed over at the bookstore by the surveillance agents," asked Elliott, "should we intercept them, and if so, how could it be done without having our operational presence become known?"

"Haven't we already blown it, sir? It sure looks that way to me, given the attack on you by this Vadim character," said Dan.

"You're probably right, sergeant," conceded Elliott, "but in the oft chance that they judged my interference to have been a one-off kind of thing, and not knowing who I was, there's the possibility they're not ready to shut down the operation…not until they see whether I show up again, or someone else does who also attempts to intercept the hand-off document."

"That argues for us not attempting to interfere during the hand-offs," said Capt. Perez.

"I don't know, sir," worried Leroy, "we'd be risking the possibility that vital NATO intel might get successfully passed on."

"Okay, Leroy's right, but that's also assuming the people being surveilled are in a position to possess critical intel, and that even if they were, that they'd be so careless in their conversations," argued Nick.

"Which brings us around to the question of who at the Center is being targeted, and how they were identified…as people spotted passing in and out of the Jagerstraße Center, or because they have a mole inside the Center?" asked Dan.

"All good points, gentlemen," said Elliott. "Clearly, we've got our work cut out for us. Tonight, we'll just run recon—get you all familiar with the bookstore setting. Then, tomorrow, Sgt. Farrand and Sgt. Hernandez—you two will be posted near the Jagerstraße entrance to the Center, looking for anyone who seems to be watching who comes in and who comes out. If someone is spotted, the two of you are authorized to follow the individual and attempt to identify him or her, or at least get an idea of where the person is based."

"While they're watching the entrance, Capt. Perez, I'd like you to spend the day inside the Center—getting a feel for the way it operates, whether there are discreet office teams or national-affinity groupings…anything that might help us get a handle on who the key players are. Hopefully, we'll get a chance to ascertain whether they're the ones being targeted by the surveillance agents."

"Sgt. White, I'd like you to monitor the alley behind the bookstore…see if there's foot traffic in or out of the rear door to the place. I've got to believe there's a rear door; we'll attempt to verify that during our recon this evening."

"Meanwhile, I'll secure from Col. Appleton a list of all authorized personnel at the Center and get an assessment from him as to what kind of intel, should we encounter it, might signify that whoever is sponsoring the eavesdropping is fully aware of the Center's existence."

"So let's get this kitchen squared away then ready ourselves for this evening's recon," said Elliott, getting up from his chair.

Chapter Four

Elliott had the men stop for a quick briefing a couple of blocks short of the narrow lane where the bookstore was located. "I'll use text messaging to alert the rest of you if there's something meriting special attention, but in general you should try to get the feel of the area...have a cup of coffee in one of the cafes... stroll up to the bookstore's window and peer in, but don't actually enter. We'll regroup back here in an hour. And Leroy, I'm counting on you to walk the back alley...see if there's a rear entrance...maybe check if its locked."

"Will do, sir," said Leroy.

"Okay, Capt. Perez and I will take the lead," said Elliott, "give us an interval of about a half-block, then Sgt. White you should proceed. Farrand and Hernandez—you men take up the rear."

Everyone nodded, then Elliott and Perez, dressed in casual street clothes of the sort common in Berlin's Mitte district, headed directly for the cobblestone street lined with cafes. It was about seven o'clock and the low angle of the sun meant the surrounding buildings cast deep shadows. Elliott was pleased with that, knowing it would make it difficult for anyone on the lookout to monitor the team's movements clearly enough to interpret the team's intentions. Or if they were somehow spotted, the shadows would most likely complicate any effort to capture a clear photographic image of his operatives, or even to prepare a usable description of him and his men.

When he and Perez turned into the street they found it busy with evening strollers, the cafes packed. Elliott guided Perez over to the cafe where he'd ordered coffee that first evening. "While I order us some coffee why don't you check out the bookstore...take your time...maybe I'll spot someone who seems to be taking an inordinate interest in you."

Capt. Perez nodded, then strolled lazily towards the bookstore. Elliott watched him study the books on display in the front window, all the while casting surreptitious glances into the store. Even from where Elliott was seated he could see well enough to conclude that if there were any patrons inside they were out of sight—deep within one of the aisles running perpendicular to the front entrance. Only the counter clerk he'd encountered earlier was visible from where Elliott was seated. Perez approached the heavy glass entrance door—as if to enter—stared fixedly through it at some random book on display inside, then shake his head before turning back towards where Elliott was sitting.

Leroy was not to be seen, having chosen to walk the back alley first. But Farrand and Hernandez were now visible; they'd just turned in from the cross street the team had used in its approach. Elliott watched them hang back, pretending to study the menu of one of the cafes closest to that end of the street—waiting, Elliott supposed, for others to approach the bookstore, thereby setting up a kind of screen separating Perez' visit from their own.

"There's one of them!" Elliott whispered sharply, nodding his head in the direction the man who Elliott had seen make the second hand-off the previous day. Perez watched as the man entered the bookstore.

"What do you want to do, sir?" asked Capt. Perez as he kept his eyes on the man through the bookstore display window.

Elliott put up his hand, signaling for Perez to give him a moment while he texted the others: *Hand-off suspect currently in bookstore. Come immediately to front of bookstore and observe.*

"Captain, when he comes back out I'll want you to tail him… see where he goes…and if at all possible secure his identity… where he lives…anything that'll help us…take one of your men with you," said Elliott quietly.

"Very good, sir. I'll take Hernandez…he and Farrand will soon have visual contact," replied Perez as he texted Hernandez.

They watched as the hand-off agent disappeared down the far left book aisle then, moments later, reappear, heading directly for the front entrance. Hernandez and Farrand had just come up to the opening between adjacent cafes that offered pedestrians on the street access to the shops along the sidewalk. They caught the man's hurried exit from the bookstore and acknowledged it to Elliott and Perez with a nod.

Perez left the cafe and sidled up to Hernandez, whispering instructions. As the two men fell in behind the hand-off agent Sgt. Farrand wandered over to the bookstore and casually studied it—much the same way as Capt. Perez had done.

Meanwhile, Leroy, who was approaching from the opposite end of the street, having already walked the length of the alley out back, was too late to spot the hand-off agent coming out of the bookstore, but observed Capt. Perez and Sgt. Hernandez walking towards him. Just before the two men passed they signaled Leroy with a nod that the man walking in front of them was the agent in question. Leroy managed to study the man using his peripheral vision, hoping thereby to avoid alerting the agent to the fact he was under scrutiny.

Leroy kept on walking, keeping to the center of the street, passing the access aisle leading to the bookstore, but making no effort to join Farrand who was standing out front, peering in. He also ignored Elliott as he walked by, keeping his attention tuned to the action in the cafes further ahead.

* * *

An hour had passed and Elliott's men had begun to reassemble at the recon debriefing point a couple of blocks away from the cobblestone street. Elliott was the first to arrive, followed by Leroy. Sgt. Dan Farrand was the next to make his way to the street corner—now garishly illuminated by street lights.

"Capt. Perez and Sgt. Hernandez might be a bit late," said Elliott, "so why don't we get started…Sgt. White, what did you find out about the alley behind the bookstore?"

"As you expected, sir, there is a rear entrance to the bookstore. I tried the handle and found it to be locked. However, I did notice a fair amount of activity in the alley owing to the fact employees of the cafes along the street use the alley to grab a smoke or to put out garbage. The alley isn't wide enough for motorized vehicles so it's pretty much limited to foot traffic."

"Anything else?" asked Elliott.

"Well, I took the opportunity to ask a couple of the cafe employees out for a smoke if they ever hung out with the staff from the bookstore…you know…during smoke breaks?" replied Leroy. "They looked at one another, then one of them said, "Hell no, man…those guys are way too serious…they come out and don't even look around…just head down the alley like they've got some place real urgent to get to." I laughed with them…like both my question and their answer were just some sort of foolish joke…hoping they wouldn't think about it later."

"So, we can probably conclude from what they said that there are probably at least a couple of different men using the rear door as they come and go…you concur, sergeant?" said Elliott.

"Yes, sir," said Leroy, nodding his head.

"What about you, Sgt. Farrand…any special observations?" asked Elliott.

"Well, it's a bit speculative, sir, but I did get the feeling the street tends to attract an older clientele…people, let's say, who've at least reached their middle thirties. I felt a bit out of place from that standpoint. And since both your attacker and this guy we've just observed are closer to my age I'm thinking we might be able to use age as a marker. It might help us single out anyone sitting in one of the cafes who's watching for signs the authorities have placed a watch on the goings-on at the bookstore."

"Interesting," mused Elliott, "it certainly bears thinking about...good work, sergeant."

"Here comes Capt. Perez and Hernandez now, sir," said Leroy, pointing to their two teammates who were just crossing the street after having approached from the east—from a direction that suggested they were returning from the Friedrichshain district.

"Sorry we're late, sir, but the hand-off agent was heading straight back to his apartment...a ground floor unit on Holzmarktstraße...about three-quarters of a mile away," said Capt. Perez.

"Do you think he spotted you?" asked Elliott.

"Don't think so, sir," replied Perez. "It was pretty dark... especially the closer we came to his neighborhood, and Sgt. Hernendez and I made sure to alternate as the visible tail... sometimes staying well to his rear and sometimes walking on ahead."

"So, what would you suggest we do with this intel?" asked Elliott.

"Sir, I think Sgt. Hernandez and I should stick with him tomorrow—with one of us following him when he leaves his apartment and the other gaining entry to his residence during his absence in order to conduct a search," replied Capt. Perez.

Elliott frowned, "I don't know, captain…I think it might be better to put a fresh tail on the hand-off agent…maybe Sgt. Farrand here…with you handling the forced entry to the man's apartment. We'll keep Sgt. Hernandez out front of the NATO Planning Center as originally planned. I'll try to expedite my morning session with Col. Appleton in order to make time for the planned assessment of NATO's office staff that was originally tasked to you, captain."

"As you wish, sir," said Perez.

Chapter Five

"So, Elliott, I take it you've got your team in place...any idea when they'll be hitting the streets?" asked Colonel Appleton as they took their coffees into Appleton's embassy office.

"They're already deployed, sir...we went operational yesterday evening...ran a recon on the bookstore that produced enough intel to put a two-man team on one of their agents."

Appelton nodded approvingly, "How can I help?"

"It would be helpful, sir, if you could supply me with an overview of the staffing structure at the Center," replied Elliott.

Appleton leaned back in his desk chair and took a moment to collect his thoughts, "Well, immediately below me are twelve military officers holding the rank of lieutenant colonel or its equivalent, each of whom represents a key NATO country involved in the planning operation. The countries represented include those on the Eastern Flank—Romania, Poland, Slovakia and the three Baltic states—as well as countries providing the bulk of NATO's military forces affected by the planning: the U.S., Germany, the U.K., France, Italy, and Spain. They'll collectively serve as the Planning Group, with each of the twelve being supported by a military aide of captain rank who's expected to provide day-to-day operational oversight."

"Then there's a pool of about a dozen civilian military planning specialists drawn from one or another of the participating countries. They're there to provide critical expertise in the various areas under review."

"Finally, there are seven office support personnel...again, drawn from among the participating countries...who assemble the working papers and prepare position reports as needed."

"What about security personnel?" asked Elliott who was taking notes.

Appleton shook his head, "None beyond the inner doors...all security is at the main entrance or along the building's perimeter and is staffed by the German Landespolizei of the city-state of Berlin."

"And the building at night...is there security?" asked Elliott.

Appleton shrugged, "Pretty much as it is during the day, but with fewer personnel...the thought being that the building cannot easily be broken into, and is equipped with motion-sensing and other unauthorized-entry detection electronics should such an attempt be made."

"So, I'm counting about forty-four persons—yourself included—whom you say have regular access to the Center...is that right, sir?" asked Elliott.

"That's right...though you'll also have to keep in mind the fact that on any given day staff from NATO's Belgium headquarters, or from one of the other NATO facilities, might be visiting," replied Appleton.

"Won't such visits risk compromising the secrecy surrounding the Center's existence?" Elliott asked, clearly concerned.

"It's a worry…one I don't dismiss lightly," replied Appleton, "but I make a real effort to limit access…and always insist that such visits, should they be essential, are arranged with sufficient advance notice that steps can be taken to mask the visitor's identity when entering or exiting the building."

"That go for me as well?" asked Elliott.

Appleton sighed, "It's tricky, Elliott…on the one hand there's every reason why you need to get inside and study the Center's operations…on the other hand, as the leader of a covert counter-intelligence team tasked with uncovering what we believe is an organized attempt at gathering highly classified intel the risk of having your cover blown is great. You'll need to make that call…not me…but if you're intent on gaining entry just let me know and I'll arrange it."

"Thank you, sir…now…if you don't mind, I'd like to turn to another topic…is it possible for you to clarify for me what tactical or strategic steps aimed at hardening our defenses along the Eastern Flank wouldn't necessarily imply successful penetration of the Center even if they show up in the transcripts we might recover?"

"I see what you're getting at, Elliott…let me think for a minute," said Appleton, rocking back in his chair.

Elliott sipped his coffee while he waited.

"I guess the best way to come at it is to regard any intel having to do with planned deployments…either of combat personnel or military equipment…as unrelated to the agenda at the Center.

I say that because the planning of such deployments leaves a long trail of clues, making it likely our adversaries have already got wind of them. I'm thinking of NATO's plan to deploy from Britain and Romania four battalion-sized battlegroups suited for combat along the Polish sector of the Eastern Flank. Or the deployment of the main components of a U.S. heavy-armored brigade in Poland. That goes also for any chatter regarding future deployments of the American SM-3 missile defense system…hell, we'd like to set up such installations all along the Eastern Flank and our adversaries know it."

"I'm not saying such intel isn't damaging to our defenses, and obviously it must be interdicted if at all possible, but it wouldn't necessarily imply this outfit you're tracing has knowledge of… and access to…the NATO Planning Center on Jagerstraße," added Appleton.

"What would suggest they have such knowledge," asked Elliott.

"It's the soft underbelly of military deterrence that we're attempting to strengthen, Elliott…things like upgrading our early warning capabilities, or updating contingency plans with regard to the Eastern Flank. Some of the planning is organizational, like subordinating NATO forces to a single chain of command, or adjusting operational level commands in NATO. So, if you capture intel dealing with military chain of command or organizational realignments…or issues of military infrastructure…then you'll have my wholehearted attention."

"I understand, sir," said Elliott, getting up from his chair. "I'll keep you informed."

"Thanks, Elliott," said Appleton, rising to shake Elliott's hand, "Please assure your men they're doing a vital job...even if it's on the streets of Berlin and not at the forward edge of some small Romanian village along the perimeter of the Eastern Flank."

"Will do, sir," replied Elliott before making his way out.

* * *

Elliott gave some thought as to how best to map out the rest of his day as he walked to his SUV, parked on the street about a half-block away. It wasn't likely his men would be texting him any urgent action reports this early—after all, it was only about ten thirty in the morning and they'd been at their posts for at most two hours. He gave a shrug, unlocked the door with his remote, then climbed in. As he pulled away from the curb he decided he'd work his way over to the Center's Jagerstraße building, some five blocks away. He knew it was a risk, especially if a hostile spotter made a habit of photographing the vehicles of drivers that slowed down or stopped. But he wanted to do a pass-by—maybe get a feel for how police security was deployed and maybe spot Sgt. Hernandez—there to check on whether, indeed, there was someone engaged in hostile surveillance of the Center's staff.

He turned onto Jagerstraße from where it began at its west end and drove at a sedate pace, careful to avoid any noticeable alteration in speed that might cause attention, especially as he passed the NATO Center. Only one policeman was standing outside the Center's entrance, though he spotted another patrolling the sidewalk a short distance away. Hernandez was nowhere to be seen, which of course he expected. What most reassured him was the apparent absence of any overtly conspicuous signage or architectural embellishments that would draw attention to the importance of what was going on inside. It just looked like any of the other bland institutional office buildings scattered throughout the city.

Elliott drove on, gradually making his way towards Mühlendamm Brücke—the bridge that crossed the Spree River close to where his apartment was located. Moments later, he turned left onto Poststraße, circled the small park, then passed through the arched gateway that gave access to the rear of the petit palais where he had an assigned parking place.

After locking the car, he walked around to the front of the building and entered through the main entrance. Elliott listened for activity, especially once he reached the spacious interior hall that accommodated the grand elliptical stairway, but found the building predictably quiet. Most of the younger tenants had already gone to work, and the few children in the building had been packed off to school. As for the more elderly tenants, they generally kept to their apartments during the morning hours, choosing to run errands later in the day. So, thought Elliott with relief, no unusual disturbances…no one hovering around his apartment door. He believed it meant the presence of his military guests hadn't yet caused any worrisome consternation among the tenants. For this, he mostly credited his wife's grandmother, Alice, who's quiet, diplomatic style could always be counted on whenever potential disputes threatened to present themselves.

He unlocked the door to his apartment and stepped inside. He almost called out to his wife Claire, but then remembered she was away, visiting her parents and sister. He headed down the hall towards the kitchen, checked to see he and his men had left everything shipshape, then proceeded on to the large room at the front of the apartment that opened onto the kitchen.

Elliott settled into one of the room's deeply cushioned armchairs. His wife Claire had insisted the room be reserved for his writing...she called it the "study". He wasn't sure he was in the right state of mind to work on his novel, but he'd try, he thought—anything to fill the hours until his men began to report.

* * *

Sgt. Hernandez was the first to call in; it was 11:30 a.m., "Sir, I've identified a single spotter," began Hernandez once Elliott had picked up. "He's positioned himself at a second floor window in the building directly across Jagerstraße from the Center. He came to my attention because I caught him opening the window, then watched as he raised a digital camera with a telephoto lens. I think he's preparing to photograph personnel from the Center as they step outside on their way to lunch."

"Good work, sergeant," said Elliott. "What I'd like you to do is to photograph any of the staff leaving in pairs or in groups... forget about any that leave by themselves. If I'm correct, it'll be such groupings that the spotter intends to photograph and to ultimately target. But how that information is relayed to the agents tasked with eavesdropping baffles me."

"I could follow one of the pairs the spotter has photographed and see if they pick up a tail, sir," said Hernandez.

"Yeah, but which pair or which group? That's the hard part…it's not likely they've got a bunch of agents poised to tail whoever comes out."

"Maybe, sir, the staff at the Center tend to take their midday meal at one of only a few places located nearby. If I follow one pair they might lead me to a restaurant or cafe where others from the Center are also intending to eat…so even if the two people I'm following don't pick up a tail, one of the other pairs showing up at the same place might have."

"Okay…let's do as you suggest, sergeant, "said Elliott, "but choose a pair leaving towards the end of the initial rush out the door…I'm guessing it's more likely it'll be one of the stragglers that's targeted by the agents."

"As you wish, sir," replied Hernandez. "I'll text you once I know how things are going down."

"Do that, sergeant…and good luck!"

* * *

"Damn!" he said under his breath, believing the spotter tagged by Hernandez was probably associated with the outfit based at the bookstore. He'd need to let Appleton know.

"Colonel, I've got bad news," said Elliott once Appleton's aide had connected him.

"What's that, Elliott?" asked Appleton.

"One of my men tagged a hostile spotter preparing to photograph Center staff as they leave the Jagerstraße building for lunch."

"You're confident the surveillance is linked to the bookstore operation?"

"I can't be absolutely certain, sir, but I've taken steps to check that theory out."

"If it turns out to be true I'd say that's a game changer, Elliott."

"Yes sir...agreed. We'll proceed on the premise that the surveillance is connected until we know otherwise."

"You do that...anyway I can help given this turn of events?"

"If we do observe a member of the Center's staff being targeted we'll need to text you a photo so you can identify the person."

"Makes sense...I'll keep my cell phone handy."

"Thank you, sir," said Elliott before breaking the connection.

Elliott checked his watch; he figured if he hurried there'd still time to make it over to Jagerstraße before all the staff left the building for lunch. He got up from his chair, grabbed his sport jacket and headed out, keying-in his pick-up location in his cell phone's ride app as he went.

The wait was less than four minutes. Once the driver made the circuit around the Poststraße parklet and had turned on to Muhlendamm Straße Elliott phoned Hernandez.

"Sergeant, I'm on my way over," said Elliott once Hernandez picked up. "Give me your position."

"Sir, I'm currently standing between two parked cars about one hundred and fifty feet east of the Center...I can see the spotter but he's not looking in my direction...his attention is directed at the Center's entrance. I'm acting as if I'm about to climb into one of the parked vehicles."

"I take it this is a new location...what happened with the earlier location, and where was it?"

"My original position was the shaded entrance alcove of a building adjacent to the Center. It was from there that I spotted the surveillance agent. Worried that he'd begun to sense my continued presence, I stepped out and walked over to where I'm now standing."

"I take it you're no longer able to get facial shots of the Center staff as they leave the building without attracting attention...is that correct?"

"Sir, yes sir. I thought it best to give priority to ensuring I could maintain a watch on the spotter while remaining undetected. From here, it won't be especially noticeable when I step onto the sidewalk and follow one of the couples. That would not have been the case from where I was concealed earlier. I didn't want to risk the spotter alerting whoever is being tasked to tail and eavesdrop on the Center's staff that he suspected the active presence of another surveillance agent...one most likely acting against the interests of his organization."

"I understand, sergeant. What I want you to do now is to remain at your present location, maintaining a watch on the spotter across the street. I'll take over the job of tailing one of the couples. I'll text you when I'm on site...let me know which pair seems to be of special interest to the spotter…those are the people I'll follow."

"Yes sir."

As Elliott broke the connection he glanced at the face of the driver in the rearview mirror, trying to gauge how much of his conversation the driver understood and whether he evidenced a level of interest in what was being said.

The driver saw Elliott checking him out, "Polizei…ja?" he said with a knowing grin.

Elliott nodded, then let loose with a flurry of conversational small talk in rapid, Berlin-dialect German meant to allay the driver's curiosity.

Chapter Six

"Okay, Hernandez, I'm at the corner...one block east of the Center," texted Elliott. It was just past noon.

"Roger that," texted Hernandez, who then added, *"Spotter engaged pointedly with a pair of men heading in your direction. Only suited male pair en route."*

"Understood...will follow," texted Elliott back.

Elliott had no difficulty identifying the two men. Both wore dark suits, held themselves with a military bearing, and were about the right age to hold the Army rank of captain. They were chatting in accented English with each other, not minding those around them, and didn't look up as they passed. Elliott fell in behind them, keeping a screen of several other pedestrians between him and the two men.

As he followed, Elliott tried to work out the accent. He felt it unlikely they were western Europeans given the nature of the accents; more likely they were from Eastern Flank countries, like Slovakia or Romania. He'd know once he sent Appleton their photos.

Once the two men reached Friedrichstraße they crossed the street and turned right. It was then that Elliott spotted someone who might be a tail. She was a tall, attractive brunette, with long hair, dressed in stylish jeans and a tan T-shirt under a black leather jacket. It was the dark sunglasses she wore that had caught his eye. Looking back, he realized she'd been part of the screen of people shielding him from the two men for at least a block. It was only after she'd crossed the street and turned— following the men—that he'd had a chance to glance at her face.

He couldn't be sure, of course, but his instincts told him to keep an eye on her. He thought the feeling might have been triggered by her body language—a confident, purposeful stride that didn't lag behind or overtake the two men.

The men eventually entered a nearby restaurant. Elliott stepped over to a shop window, as if to study the display, keeping the young woman in his peripheral vision. Sure enough, she also entered the restaurant. Elliott let ten minutes pass before following. When he finally stepped inside he glanced around. The two men had been seated at a table towards the back of the room.

The young woman had somehow managed to be seated at a table less than ten feet away. It was a table for two, with the two chairs placed at right angles to the back of the room, meaning the young woman could maintain surveillance with her peripheral vision, augmented by an occasional side-glance. Given the noise level in the room, Elliott was sure she was too far away to hear distinctly anything the two men might be saying, especially if they spoke in a quiet, conversational tone. But then he noticed she had her cell phone out—was it because she'd taken their photo?

What he felt was more likely was that she was using the audio receiver on the cell phone to capture the conversation between the two men. The stored digital recording on the cell phone would need to be stripped of all extraneous noise, but he knew the technology for that was easily available. And his own tests had demonstrated the latest smart phones had receivers sensitive enough to capture a conversational voice up to a distance of almost twenty feet, perhaps even further.

Once the head waiter had seated him, Elliott pulled out his cell phone and, pretending to make a call, photographed the setting: the woman, her cell phone on the table, and the two men seated not too far away—busily engaged in conversation.

* * *

While he ate, Elliott studied the other patrons—curious whether the young woman had a compatriot seated elsewhere in the room. Despite his feeling that there must be one, he eventually concluded he was wrong—that it was unlikely there was anyone else tasked with eavesdropping on the two men. He hurriedly finished lunch, then urged the waiter to bring over the check, anxious to leave the restaurant before either the two men or the young woman got up to leave. He intended to tail the young woman to her residence, or to wherever she planned to go next, and didn't want to make it easy for the woman to associate him with the restaurant should she later spot him following her.

Elliott was uncomfortable standing on the sidewalk immediately outside the restaurant so he crossed Friedrichstraße and took up a position that would allow him to observe the woman from a distance once she made her exit from the restaurant. As he waited, he texted Col. Appleton, *"Observed agent involved in eavesdropping surveillance on two male personnel from the Center (photo attached). Believe them to be military, maybe of captain rank. Surveillance agent—a young female—appears to use smart phone audio receiver for eavesdropping. Will follow her, hoping to locate transcription editing hardware. Elliott."*

Eventually, the two men stepped out, then began to retrace their steps, clearly heading back to the Center. Moments later, the young woman emerged. She took a moment to watch the men walk away, then turned and began walking in the opposite direction—south on Friedrichstraße. Elliott followed, but remained on the opposite side of the street.

Elliott gave a quiet thanks for the fact most Berliners enjoyed walking the city's level streets rather than automatically hopping on an autobus or making a beeline for the nearest taxi pickup point. He knew ride hailing software had recently begun to undermine the practice, especially given the technology's ease of operation. So he expressed some relief as the young woman seemed content to continue walking as she made her way down Friedrichstraße.

But his relief turned out to be short-lived as the woman he was following turned east at the next intersection, then headed for a U-bahn station a half a block away. Elliott rushed to catch up, crossing Friedrichstraße despite a warning light signaling vehicle traffic was about to resume. Walking briskly, he made it to the U-bahn station just as a train on the rapid transit system arrived, then watched as the woman boarded. She'd chosen a car towards the front of the train, allowing him to board without betraying his presence by choosing a car a bit further back.

Thirteen minutes later, Elliott, who had made his way towards the front of the train, watched the woman get up from her seat in preparation for exiting at the next station. Worried she'd note his presence if they exited the station at the same time, he stepped off as soon as the doors opened, hastening to reach the streets ahead of her. Glancing around, he found himself in a neighborhood of Mitte just north of where the two channels of the River Spree came together.

Sensing her imminent appearance, he turned away from where the passengers were coming out, pretending to be engaged in a cell phone conversation, then watched as she began walking south, towards Stralauer Straße.

Elliott held back until she'd gone about a block, then followed, again keeping to the opposite side of the street from the one she'd chosen. When she reached Stralauer Straße Elliott saw her turn left. Not wishing to lose her, he ran forward. He reached the corner where she'd turned and caught sight of her about a half-block ahead. Noting the presence of more pedestrian traffic, Elliott chose not to hesitate in closing the gap further. He figured the presence of the other pedestrians would make his own movements reasonably inconspicuous. A few minutes later, he sensed she was about to make a move in the direction of a corner apartment building. By that time, the gap between them had lessened to about twenty feet. Elliott held back and watched as she opened the door at the entrance to the building, then stepped through, letting the door close behind her.

Elliott waited long enough to allow the woman to make it through the interior hall and onto the stairway, or into an elevator if the building had one, then pulled open the outer door and stepped inside. He heard the clicking of heels on stairs—a distinctive sound that resonated up and down the open stairwell—and listened for a change in gait that would signal she'd reached a landing. Knowing each floor in buildings of that age generally offered the climber an intermediate landing in addition to the floor proper, he counted the shifts in gait—two... then four...then listened as the shifts in gait stopped entirely after six. With a nod, Elliott satisfied himself that the woman had entered an apartment on the third floor above street level.

Elliott checked his watch; it was approaching 1:30 p.m.. Knowing the hand-off couriers tasked with bringing eavesdropping transcriptions to the bookstore appeared constrained by the limited hours the bookstore was open—four to eight in the evening—he figured one of two things would have to happen: either the woman would need to leave her apartment and take her digital eavesdropping file, together with her notes, to a place where the transcription could be prepared or she, herself, was the one who prepared the transcription and the hand-off courier would need to visit her apartment.

He ruled out an internet-based or cellular-based transfer owing to the risk of interception by counter-intelligence operatives. And besides, he thought, it would be blatantly at variance with the manual transfer protocol he'd observed at the bookstore on three occasions. Either way, he reasoned, something needed to happen at the building he was presently standing in…something that would most likely occur between then and four that afternoon. Reconciling himself to having to stand watch for the next two and a half hours, he left the building and began searching for a local cafe or park bench from where he'd be able to monitor activity at the building while remaining reasonably comfortable.

With evident relief, Elliott spotted a dark green awning no more than about forty feet away that held the promise of some sort of eating establishment. From where he stood he couldn't discern its actual nature given the tubs of waist-high evergreen shrubs that ringed the space beneath the awning, so he walked over. It turned out to be a small, neighborhood restaurant that served coffee and various light refreshments all through the day. At the moment, there were no patrons sitting outside, though Elliott did see one party occupying a table inside. He figured the choice to sit inside had nothing to do with the weather; it was cloudy but there'd been no rain forecast as far as he knew, and the air—although a bit humid—was pleasantly temperate.

He chose a seat close to the tubs of shrubbery lined up along the edge of the outdoor seating area facing the woman's building. Given his height, Elliott knew he'd have no difficulty looking over the top of the shrubs at the building's entrance, and that at the same time he'd be more or less concealed from unwelcome scrutiny by persons entering or leaving the building.

A waiter came out to take Elliott's order.

"Kaffee, bitte…das wird vorerst alles sein," said Elliott, reassuring the man that he'd most likely order something more a bit later.

Once the waiter headed back inside Elliott pulled out his cell phone and called Hernandez, "Sergeant, is the spotter still on station?"

"Affirmative, sir, but there's very little happening now...I suspect he'll be tempted to leave."

"Stick with him, sergeant," ordered Elliott. "If he leaves follow him."

"Will do, sir...any success with the tail?"

"We scored big time...a female operative followed the two men to a restaurant on Friedrichstraße, then arranged to have herself seated close enough to capture their luncheon conversation on a cell phone audio receiver. I'm watching her apartment building as we speak."

"Do we know who the men were?"

"Not yet, but I should hear from Col. Appleton soon...I've sent him a photo of the two men."

"Good to know, sir," said Hernandez just before Elliott broke the connection.

Appleton's call came through moments later.

"Elliott, sorry for the delay...I've been in a meeting and only got to examine the photo a few minutes ago, while walking back to the office. I have to say, you made a good guess...the two men in the photo, who by the way turned out to be key players at the Center, were both of captain rank...the one to the left in the photo is the military aide to the Planning Group member from Romania, while the one to the right is his counterpart from Poland."

"I'm guessing the spotter must have known who they were," Elliott mused. "Somehow, he was able to alert his boss in real time to the high value of the targets, who in turn alerted the female agent I encountered."

"Seems important that we learn how they're doing it," said Appleton.

"I agree, sir. I've got a man watching the spotter...I guess we could take him somewhere and interrogate him, but I'm inclined to wait on that until we've worked out the full extent of the intelligence gathering ring."

"It's your call, Elliott," said Appleton. "I suppose you don't want me alerting the two men about what happened today...that they'd come under surveillance by a hostile outfit?"

"I'd advise against it, sir. Word would get out to all Center personnel...they'd begin acting nervously—alerting whoever was targeting the Center that their presence had been detected. I think we can minimize the damage by taking down the network quickly...afterwords the Center's personnel could be informed."

"I understand...well, good luck, Elliott...and keep me informed." With that, Appleton ended the call.

As Elliott put down his phone, the waiter arrived with his coffee. The waiter, whom Elliott figured was probably in his sixties, ceremoniously placed the cup and saucer to Elliott's right, then carefully poured coffee into the cup from a shiny metal carafe, which he then placed on the table. Finally, he added a tiny pitcher with cream to the ensemble, along with a teaspoon and napkin. Elliott nodded his thanks, which the waiter acknowledged with a slight bow before walking back inside.

Elliott had barely begun sipping his coffee when he noticed another young woman approach the apartment building. Other than her hair being blond, she resembled the first one: long hair, slim build, of average height—and attractive. But she was dressed more formally in a tailored black pant suit and white blouse. Curious, Elliott rose from his chair, quickly removed his sport jacket and draped it over the back of the chair to signal to the waiter that he was not actually leaving, then stepped around the tubs of shrubbery and followed the young woman who had disappeared inside the building.

As he had earlier, he listened for the click of heels on stairs as the woman climbed. His count of the number of changes in her gait let him conclude that—as before—she had stopped on the third floor above street level, prompting him to give thought to the possibility the two women might be roommates.

He returned to his place under the awning, slipped his sport jacket back on, then resumed his watch.

* * *

At four o'clock sharp, Elliott texted his team to report in. Hernandez was the first to reply: "*Spotter followed to residence in Friedrichshain neighborhood near Holzmarktstraße. Will remain on site awaiting your orders.*"

Sgt. Leroy White was the next to text a reply: "*Within last hour eight operatives entered bookstore from alley entrance: seven men and one woman. Recognized one as your attacker,*

Vadim. Can now confirm he is associated with the bookstore operation."

Elliott was surprised by the number of operatives reported by Leroy as showing up at the bookstore. He surmised that some must be security personnel—like Vadim—and others might be couriers, since the transcriptions being deposited at the bookstore would somehow have to be taken to wherever they were ultimately destined, assuming the bookstore was not the actual headquarters but functioned merely as a cut-out. Still, Elliott suspected that the large number of operatives meant that something else was going on in the bookstore's back room.

As he mulled over that problem, Capt. Perez reported in: *"Hand-off agent just left residence. Sgt. Farrand is tailing. I'm about to attempt entry into subject's residence.*

That was quickly followed by a text from Farrand himself: *"Subject has left residence and has just now crossed Bruckenstraße, continuing north on Stralauerstraße."*

Elliott quickly texted Perez: *"Hold off on forced entry until Sgt. Hernandez makes it over to serve as lookout."* He then texted Hernandez: *"Break off surveillance on spotter. Rendezvous with Capt. Perez at hand-off operative's Holzmarktstraße residence."*

Perez texted back: *"Roger that."* As did Hernandez.

Elliott worried his men were being stretched to the point of fatigue, given the daylong assignments, but he didn't think he could afford to take them off duty until at least eight o'clock that evening, especially in the case of Sgt. White, and perhaps also for some of the others as well.

As he thought about these matters he continued to monitor the corner building where the two women were currently located. They hadn't reappeared and Elliott was beginning to wonder whether whoever was running the hostile surveillance team didn't view the transmission of the eavesdropped intel with the same level of urgency that he had supposed. But his doubts were quickly banished when he spotted an unkempt young man approach the main entrance to the building, hesitate momentarily, then open the door and step inside.

Elliott was sure it was same person he'd observed in the bookstore near his apartment early that very first evening, the one who had slipped an envelope under the inside flap of a book jacket, place the book back on the shelf, then walk out. Elliott noted that the young man was wearing the same dark gray sport jacket and brown slacks he'd had on when Elliott last saw him.

Elliott threw some money down on the table then hurried over to the building's entrance, hoping to confirm his impression that the man was intending to visit the apartment of the woman he'd tailed. He stepped inside the entrance hall and rushed over to the foot of the stairwell. He could hear the man's footsteps, but not soon enough to be able to use the sound to determine what floor he was on. A sharp knock on a door on one of the floor landings was followed by a door opening. Then he heard an exchange. A woman's voice, then a man's, but Elliott could not make out what was being said. Frustrated, he walked over to the entrance door leading to the street and stepped back outside, figuring he could at least tail the courier once he emerged from the building.

Chapter Seven

Capt. Perez gestured for Hernandez to give him a leg up so he could reach the window mechanism. They were concealed from the street by a line of tall evergreen shrubs. Perez had noted that one of the two windows facing the street had been left open a crack at the top and figured he could disassemble the locking mechanism that kept the window from swinging all the way down inside the apartment. Working quickly, he pulled the appropriate tool from his pants pocket and began to loosen the window-frame attachment of the metal bracket to his right. He repeated the process on the metal bracket to his left, but kept a tight grip on the window so that it didn't crash against the room's interior wall once the window was completely free to move.

"Okay, sergeant, I've freed it. If you can give me one more shove upwards I think I can slide in," said Perez.

With a final upward jerk, Hernandez bought Perez enough lift that he could rest most of the upper part of his body inside, balancing on the window sill at his waist. Still holding the window, Perez allowed it to gradually swing downward, finally allowing it to come to rest against the inside wall below the window. Then, with the window out of the way, Perez slid inside. As soon as his hands touched the floor he allowed them to take his weight then brought one leg after the other over the window sill and onto the floor.

"I'm in," said Perez, reappearing at the open window.

"Good work, sir," replied Hernandez, "I'll remain stationed out here."

Perez nodded, then turned his attention to the room he found himself in. He figured it to be the apartment's common room or parlor, with well-used 1950's vintage stuffed couches in a modernist style along with several pieces of utilitarian wood furniture. Minimal wall hangings and ersatz objet d'art completed the picture of what one would expect of a reasonably-priced flat rented fully furnished. Perez inspected the few personal objects in the room—mostly magazines and a few books—and learned from them that their target operative was most likely Romanian.

Perez then moved through the apartment systematically after first getting a feel for the layout of the place. It became immediately apparent to him that two men lived there. Each had his own bedroom, but shared a bath. The kitchen showed signs of fairly regular use, but by persons not fastidious about cleaning up after themselves.

In one bedroom Perez found photos of the man they'd been following. Papers in a drawer confirmed that he was Romanian, and that his name was "Daniel". The other bedroom was that of a man called "Mihai", who was also Romanian. There was a snapshot of him with his arm around the waist of a young woman. Perez snapped pictures of the photos in both rooms using his smartphone, figuring it was the best way to ensure he and the other members of the team could place a face with each name.

From the snapshot of "Mihai" Perez judged Daniel's apartment mate to also be in his early twenties. Both seemed too young to be seasoned operatives, Perez reasoned, leading him to speculate they'd probably been recruited on a cash basis from among the horde of transients flooding the cities of the West from countries in eastern Europe.

As Perez was finishing his search of Mihai's room he heard Hernandez shout "*Andalé!*" Mexican slang meaning "hurry up!" Perez rushed back to the room with the opened window and looked down at Hernandez, "*Que Pasa?*"

"A man just entered the building, sir. He looks like an eastern European...thought you'd better finish up in case he's headed for the apartment."

Perez nodded, wondering whether it was Daniel, the man he and Sgt. Farrand had originally followed to the apartment, but dismissed the thought, knowing Sgt. Farrand would have texted him a "head's up". Then he heard the front door of the apartment being unlocked and thrown open. "Christ!" he thought, it must be the roommate, Mihai. Perez signaled Hernandez he was coming out, then quickly climbed onto the window sill and jumped down. He gestured for Hernandez to follow him as he ran, crouched, along the side of the building, hugging it until he reached the corner, then making the turn.

They rested for a moment, safely concealed from Mihai if he should lean out the window and look for whoever might have broken into the apartment. "Damn!" uttered Perez under his breath, "I'd hoped to have enough time to somehow reposition the window so there'd be no obvious sign of a break-in."

"Maybe we should go back and take him out," whispered Sgt. Hernandez. Capt. Perez thought it over, but just as he was about to dismiss the idea with a shake of his head they both heard someone walking determinedly in their direction along the front side of the building. Perez motioned for Hernandez to stand back, then edged closer to the corner, his back tight against the building. The man came around the corner in a rush, holding a semiautomatic in a two-handed grip. Perez slashed down with his left hand, connecting with both of the man's forearms and momentarily depriving the man of the possibility of getting off any kind of shot. But the man didn't lose his grip on the weapon despite the blow, forcing Perez to direct a disabling punch to the man's sternum with his right fist before the man could recover his shooting stance.

Hernandez quickly came around and retrieved the man's weapon as Perez kicked his legs out from under him, causing him to fall face down onto the ground. "Let's tie him up," said Perez, reaching under the man's stomach to unbuckle his belt. While Perez held the man down, Hernandez used the belt to bind the man's wrists behind his back.

"Okay, let's drag him around to the front where he'll be fully concealed behind the shrubs," said Perez.

"He's going to yell wholly hell once he gets his wind back," advised Sgt. Hernandez.

"Tear up his shirt and gag him, sergeant," instructed Perez as he pulled out his smartphone and put a call through to Elliott, "Colonel, this is Capt. Perez. We've got a problem," he said once Elliott picked up.

After Perez explained their predicament, Elliott said, "I'll call Col. Appleton…I'm guessing he'll reach out to the Germans for assistance. In the meantime, get the man back into his apartment and stay with him until I can come with my car."

"Yes, sir," replied Perez, who then turned to Hernandez, "Col. Stone says to get this guy back into his apartment so let's walk him in." Perez and Hernandez pulled Mihai up then gripped him by his upper arms and forced-marched him towards the building entrance. They remained concealed behind the line of shrubbery until the very last minute, then—checking that no one was coming in or out—they hurried onto the the paved walkway and through the door. The entrance hall led to a central stairwell and a hallway that gave access to the apartments on the ground floor. The apartment of Daniel and Mihai was was the first one on the left. Perez reached into Mihai's pocket, retrieved the apartment key, and opened the door.

"You keep an eye on him, sergeant, while I fix the window… no need to let Daniel know we've been here."

"You think Col. Stone will want us to remove this guy?" asked Hernandez.

"That'd be my guess," replied Perez, "and assuming that's what's going to take place, I think we'd better get the guy a fresh shirt and a jacket."

* * *

Perez's call caught Elliott as he was about two blocks from the bookstore, tailing the unidentified courier. He abandoned the tail, pulled out his smart phone and activated the local ride service app, identifying Poststraße 16 as his destination. A vehicle came within minutes and Elliott jumped in. As the driver headed towards the Nikolai District, Elliott put a call through to Col. Appleton.

"Colonel, my men have taken into custody a Romanian national by the name of Mihai who we believe is one of a team of couriers linking the eavesdroppers with the bookstore," said Elliott once Appleton picked up.

"Damn! That's going to complicate your efforts at keeping the operation under wraps, Elliott."

"I know, sir, but I think we can keep our involvement below the radar if we can get the Germans to hold him incommunicado long enough for us to roll up this espionage outfit."

"You plan on interrogating him?"

"No, sir…it'll take too much time…and we don't think he's got much useful information…at least any information above and beyond what we're already compiling."

"Okay…let me get hold of my contact at the *Bundesnachrichtendienst*…see if they'll play ball."

"Very good, sir. In the meantime, we'll hold him at my apartment building...turns out back in the Communist era the place was a police station...the basement serving as a jail."

"Christ, who would have thought," said Appleton with a laugh. "I'll get back to you as soon as I can."

Elliott put away his smartphone and began thinking how he should break it to his wife's grandmother that he'd need to use the basement of the building to hold a prisoner. Before he'd thought it through his driver pulled up in front and came to a stop.

"Thanks," said Elliott who quickly climbed out. As the man drove away, Elliott jogged around to the rear of the building and used his remote to unlock his SUV. Slipping into the driver's seat, he started it up, then backed out of his space and drove hastily out the driveway that curved around to the front of the building and on to Poststraße.

* * *

"He's here!" shouted Hernandez, who'd been looking out the front window Perez had managed to reassemble. "It's Col. Stone's SUV!"

"Okay, give me a hand, sergeant," said Capt. Perez.

The two of them gripped the man they'd identified as Mihai and again forced-marched him—this time out of the apartment, then out the building and down the entrance walkway to the street where Elliott was holding open the rear door of the SUV. Mihai still had his hands bound behind his back, but the gag had been removed from his mouth. He was now wearing a fresh shirt, a suitable jacket, and despite being pressed tightly between his two captors looked all the world like a man suffering no obvious distress.

"All three of you climb into the back seat," ordered Elliott.

Once they were all in, Elliott carefully closed the door then walked around and slipped back into the driver's seat. Moments later, he pulled away from the curb and headed for their base of operations.

"What's the plan?" asked Capt. Perez.

"Col. Appleton is trying to get the German Federal Intelligence Service to take the man off our hands…in the meantime, we'll lock him up in the basement of my apartment building…there's a couple of jail-like rooms down there that originally were intended to serve as storage areas for food and wine," replied Elliott.

"You think they'll work?" asked Capt. Perez.

"I should think so," replied Elliott as he drove, "the Communists used them in that fashion when the building served as a police station."

"We going to post a guard?" asked Sgt. Hernandez.

"I believe we should," replied Elliott. "You up for that duty, sergeant?"

"Be happy to oblige, sir," replied Hernandez.

"I'm hoping it won't be for long," added Elliott.

Once they reached Poststraße 16 Elliott drove around to the back and parked in his assigned spot. "There's a door back here that leads directly to the basement," said Elliott. "Keep him in the vehicle while I go around and open the door from inside."

"Will do, sir," replied Capt. Perez.

All the time Mihai had been in their custody, Perez observed, he hadn't said a word. Perez was rethinking his original impression that Mihai was just some east European transient that the espionage team had recruited locally for what seemed like just a low level courier job. Both the man's evident training in the handling of a handgun and his self-control despite being treated roughly while being subdued, then later during his confinement, all pointed to a level of professionalism.

A few minutes later, Elliott emerged from a door immediately to the left of the SUV and waved them over. Perez climbed out, then lent Mihai a hand as he followed along. Hernandez, on the other hand, exited from the right side of the vehicle, then came around to assist Perez in walking Mihai over.

They followed Elliott inside. "Put him in there," he said, once they'd helped Mihai down the short flight of stairs. Elliott was pointing to a door directly in front of them. "It leads to two storage rooms. Choose whichever seems free of stored furniture," he added. Perez checked the two rooms out and chose the one closest. Both had stout wooden doors and exterior dead bolt assemblies as well as keyed door locks.

Hernandez untied Mihai's hands and pushed him into the room. "I'll be out here so don't get any ideas," said Hernandez as he closed the door and slid the deadbolt home.

"There's a wash-up room with sink, toilet and bath just on your right as you head for the interior access staircase," said Elliott, "but I wouldn't let him visit it...just have him use a bucket...there's several lying around."

Hernandez nodded, then looked around for a chair to sit on.

Elliot gave him an encouraging wave, then both he and Perez headed up the interior stairs on their way to Elliott's apartment. It was now close to five o'clock and Elliott needed to check in with his other team members. But first, he had to alert his wife's grandmother about his use of the basement. He knew he probably should do it in person, but knowing Alice he knew she'd invite him in for coffee and he didn't have time for that.

"Alice, it's Elliott, I need to tell you something," he said once she answered her phone.

"Yes, dear, what is it?"

"I've got something of a temporary problem...I've taken into custody a foreign operative, and until the German authorities show up I've locked him in the basement, with one of my men standing guard."

"My, how exciting...how can I help?"

"Well, if any of our fellow tenants get wind of it I'd be grateful if you would reassure them there's nothing to worry about."

"I don't see why any of them should learn of it, Elliott, but if they do I'll tell them it was my idea...that it's in the spirit of the place—you know, since having once served as a police station back before unification."

"Thanks, Alice...I'll fill you in as best I can once this whole operation is over."

"You do that...an old lady like me feeds on that kind of news," she replied with a self-deprecating laugh."

With that chore out of the way, Elliott began checking on the rest of his team.

"Sergeant, what's your current status?" asked Elliott once Sgt. Dan Farrand answered the phone.

"Can't talk now, sir" replied Farrand quietly. "The courier met up with strikingly attractive young woman who'd come out to meet him. He took possession of a document from her then walked off...probably on his way to the bookstore. I'm now heading for the entrance to her building in hopes of engaging her in conversation before she disappears inside."

"I understand, sergeant...before I sign off you should know the man you've been following is named "Daniel"...he's Romanian."

"Good to know, sir...it just might be the entrée I need to strike up a conversation."

Elliott ended the call with a shake of the head; he marveled at the cockiness of the guy from Newark, and hoped the sergeant's good looks and charm would turn the trick. He then called Sgt. Leroy White, whom he believed was still watching the rear entrance of the bookstore.

"Any new activity, sergeant?" asked Elliott once Leroy White took the call.

"None, sir," replied White. "What I'm thinking is that those inside have tasks that'll keep them on the premises until about closing time...you think I should break off surveillance until then?"

Elliott gave the idea some thought, then said, "I'd like to say yes, sergeant, but I think we need to confirm your suspicions.

We do know that at least two couriers will have made their way to the bookstore within the past hour, perhaps others as well. That would support your hunch. It also suggests that some of the people you saw entering are somehow tasked with processing the transcription documents being delivered by the couriers. In any case, I'm going to send Capt. Perez over to relieve you…at least for a short break. But I'll want both of you on station, ready to follow at least a couple of the operatives once they leave the bookstore."

"Yes, sir," replied Sgt. White.

Elliott pocketed his smartphone then walked into the kitchen where Capt. Perez was snacking on some leftover takeout.

"Once you've finished up in here, captain, I'd like you to join Sgt. White at the bookstore…Sgt. Hernandez and I will follow once we've turned over the man we've got locked up downstairs. Sgt. White thinks the eight operatives he observed entering the rear of the bookstore will begin leaving around the bookstore's eight o'clock closing time. We'll want to be in a position to follow as many of them as we can."

"I understand, sir," replied Perez as he got up to rinse out his dish.

Chapter Eight

"Excuse me, did I just see you talking with Daniel?" asked Sgt. Dan Farrand, as he held the door open for her.

The young woman stopped and turned to him, "I'm sorry, what did you say?"

"Daniel...I thought I saw you with Daniel...he's a neighbor of mine and from the way he talked I'd always thought he had few acquaintances in Berlin so I guess I was taken by surprise... I'm sorry if I startled you."

"You are a friend of Daniel?" she asked warily.

Farrand shrugged, "Not really...as I said, he's a neighbor. We talk sometimes...I have to say, I didn't expect to discover he's in a relationship with a woman as attractive as you."

"We are not in a relationship!" the woman replied, challengingly. "Daniel is a business associate."

"I see," Farrand replied apologetically, "Look, I didn't mean to pry...it's just that I'm also something of a newcomer to the city and thought maybe we had something in common."

The woman gave Farrand a puzzled look.

"I'm not saying this very well…listen…can I buy you a cup of coffee, or maybe a glass of wine? My name is Dan Farrand, by the way."

"You're an American," she said matter-of-factly.

Farrand nodded, "Yeah…out of New Jersey, but also ex-US Army…I've just separated from the military and now find myself spending a bit of time here in Berlin…up to now, I've been billeted on a base down near Stuttgart."

The woman looked up at Farrand with a new, more appraising glance. "Were you an officer?"

"A non-commissioned one…sergeant first class to be exact," replied Farrand with mock pride. "But…hey…how about that coffee…there's a place just down the street."

Farrand got the impression the woman seemed to be struggling with a reply—giving him brief glances as she worked through the problem. Finally she turned to him and said, "All right, Sgt. Farrand…I'll join you…my name is Galina, by the way."

"Great! And please call me Dan," he said as they turned and headed for the cafe.

Galina nodded, but didn't say anything.

"I get the impression you're also from somewhere else," observed Farrand as they walked.

Galina smiled, "I come from Latvia."

"Well, you're English is perfect…that I can tell you," said Farrand, returning her smile.

The cafe was located in a small storefront wedged in by a cleaners and a wine purveyor. They took a small table near the window. Farrand studied her as she glanced around the room. He figured her to be in her late twenties, and noted that she wore her light brown hair in a no-nonsense shoulder-length cut. She had on a dark brown suede jacket over a black T-shirt and black stretch pants. 'Stylish but economical', was his assessment.

"I thinks she's coming over," said Galina, referring to the young woman who had been talking with the man operating an espresso machine behind the standup counter.

"Guten Tag, Was hätten Sie gerne?" asked the server.

Farrand looked at Galina expectantly.

"Nur normaler Kaffe, bitte," replied Galina.

"The same," said Farrand.

"You don't speak German?" she asked once the server had left to give the order to the man behind the counter.

"No...you'd think I'd have picked it up after a year's posting to Stuttgart, but what with living on base and being regularly deployed primarily in one or another eastern European country for maneuvers it just didn't happen," replied Farrand with a shrug.

"So, you were in the infantry?"

"Kind of...but in a special forces unit."

Galina nodded.

"How about you...what brought you to Berlin?" asked Farrand, casually.

She shrugged, "I do clerical work for a local firm...Daniel picks up the work and delivers it."

"So you work at home?"

"Mostly, yes...so does my roommate, Taisija."

"I'm guessing your German is pretty good," said Farrand, impressed.

Galina smiled modestly.

At that moment, the server brought over their coffee, together with a small plate holding two Biscotti.

They quietly sipped their coffee and sampled the Biscotti. Finally, Farrand broke the silence, "I've been to Riga a couple of times…is that where you come from?"

Galina nodded, "Yes, I grew up and attended university there."

"A business degree, I suppose," said Farrand.

Galina smiled, "Yes…I come from a family of small time farmers…aspiring to professions like law or medicine was not something I gave much thought to. A practical curriculum like business seemed a much surer way to ensure employment."

"But you grew up in the city…surely that must have changed your family's point of view," protested Farrand.

"Ordinarily it would," agreed Galina, "but it is not so easy when one is of Russian ethnicity…even in Riga, which is home to many Latvian Russians."

"Is that why you're working in Berlin rather than Riga?" asked Farrand.

Galina shrugged, "Perhaps…but it's also because Berlin's an exciting place to be when one is young."

"I can see that…even after being in town only a short time," agreed Farrand, thoughtfully. Then, after a short pause, he added, "Listen, there's a really neat restaurant in the Nikolai District— on Poststraße—that I'd love to show you. I'm guessing you're through with work today, seeing how Daniel's already been here...so, what do you say...will you join me?"

Galina looked askance at him, taken aback by his sudden invitation. But held off from dismissing the offer out of hand, reasoning the American might turn out to be a useful informant. And instead countered with, "Can my roommate come also?"

"Sure...why not," replied Farrand, easily. "I'll come by to pick the two of you up at about seven this evening...that be all right?"

"I'll have to check with her, but I think she'll want to come," said Galina, thinking out loud.

"That's okay...either way...but I will need your apartment number so I'll know which door to knock on," said Farrand

Galina smiled, took out a small pad of paper from her purse, together with a pen, then wrote down her address, tore off the sheet and handed it to him.

"Are you looking to stay in Berlin now that you've separated from the Army?" asked Galina as she picked up her cup to take another sip.

Farrand nodded, "I'd like to...at least for a while. There's a NATO think tank that I've put feelers out to...I've been told they're looking for ex-noncoms with special operations training and experience."

"Why would a think tank want someone with your qualifications?" Galina asked, apparently genuinely puzzled.

"I don't know...maybe they're into military planning and don't want to rely only on the opinion of senior commissioned officers...that would be my take on it."

"So, you don't think it might be something else…maybe a covert operational headquarters?" speculated Galina.

"Hell, no!" said Farrand with a laugh. "If it was something like that they'd want real military personnel. Anyway, where'd you come up with such an idea?"

"Oh, I don't know…it's just that everyone seems so secretive in a city like this…and you did say you've spent a lot of time in eastern Europe performing military maneuvers of a kind that I imagine you can't talk about."

Farrand nodded, "Good point".

"Well, I should be getting back…I need to ask Taisja whether she'll want to join us," said Galina, getting up from her chair.

"Do encourage her," said Farrand, also rising.

"Thank you for the coffee," she said, shaking his hand.

"It's been my pleasure," said Farrand. "Until this evening, then," he added as she walked away.

Farrand returned to his seat, signaled for the check, then called his team leader, Lt. Col. Elliott Stone.

"Col. Stone, I've successfully made contact with one of the female surveillance agents," began Farrand once Elliott picked up.

"Excellent, sergeant. What can you tell us so far?"

"She and her roommate—I'm guessing another surveillance agent—are Latvian nationals, going by the names "Galina" and "Taisija". Galina is of Russian extraction and reports growing up in Riga. I've arranged to take them out for dinner tonight at that restaurant near your apartment…the one on Poststraße…I'm thinking it would give you or Capt. Perez a chance to look them over."

"What's the time frame?" asked Elliott.

"I'll be meeting them up at seven o'clock…should be at the restaurant by seven-thirty."

"Okay, I'll see what we can manage," said Elliott, who then added, "Try to get an opportunity to check out the apartment, sergeant…we need to know what the transcription setup is— whether it's just a desktop computer/printer station, or something more hi-tech."

"Will do, sir…and unless you've got something else you need me for I'd like to return to the apartment and freshen up for this evening's event."

"You do that, sergeant. As it turns out, I'm still at the apartment along with Sgt. Hernandez awaiting news the German Federal Service will take the prisoner off our hands."

"Good to know, sir…see you shortly."

Elliott had scarcely ended his conversation with Farrand when Appleton called. "Elliott, they've agreed…though I have to say they're not real happy about it. A team from the Berlin office of the Bundesnachrichtendienst should arrive momentarily. They'll keep the prisoner under wraps for a few days but in return want to be dealt in. They've assigned a Capt. Ernst Becker to serve as an observer. He'll simply shadow you. I've been assured he won't have any authority to challenge your decisions, or to supply his superiors with ongoing operational details. But he can be used as a conduit should you need the Service's assistance going forward."

"I understand, colonel," said Elliott resignedly. "Let's hope he's had some experience working with US Army personnel…I wouldn't want him getting all up tight about how we feel free to improvise."

"They didn't brief me on the man, Elliott, so I can't comment one way or the other, but the Service is a savvy bunch so I'm thinking they took that into account in making their selection."

"Understood, sir," replied Elliott before breaking off the call.

Elliott left the apartment and went outside to await the arrival of the Service team. He was somewhat surprised that Appleton had been so successful in limiting the involvement of the German intelligence agency. Ordinarily, they would have simply co-opted the operation—ordering Elliott's team back to its base in Stuttgart. As he thought more about it, he began to suspect the Service worried a strong pushback might persuade NATO they'd need to relocate the Planning Center to some country that would tolerate active involvement by counter-intelligence personnel of other NATO countries. Certainly, he reasoned, the Germans seemed to have been unaware of this specific espionage operation until Appleton's phone call, though they'd probably been given a head's up by the Berliner Polizei that something was going on after Appleton had alerted the police about the presence of an American armed counter-intelligence team operating in their city.

As Elliott continued to mull over these concerns, an unmarked white passenger van pulled up in front of the petit palais. The side windows of the vehicle had been darkened, making it hard for Elliott to tell how many persons were inside, but almost immediately the front passenger door opened and a man dressed in civilian clothes, who Elliott figured to be in his early thirties, climbed out and walked up the steps to where Elliott was standing.

"I take it you are Col. Stone…yes?" asked the man, using a somewhat butchered English version of a fairly common German expression.

"I am. And you are?" asked Elliott, calmly.

"Capt. Ernst Becker, reporting, sir."

"Yes, I've been informed you will be joining us…it's good to meet you, Capt. Becker," Elliott replied, shaking the man's hand.

"Now, if you will direct me to where the suspect is being held…"

"Have your men bring the van around to the rear of the building…the suspect is in the basement and can be transferred to your van through a door leading out to the rear."

"Very good, sir," said Becker, with a curt nod of the head.

As Becker turned and headed back to the van, Elliott called out, "While you arrange for the van to be repositioned I'll go down and unlock the basement's outside door."

Becker gave a wave of acknowledgement, then climbed into the van. Elliott watched as the van made a U-turn then turned left into the drive leading to the rear of the building. As the van disappeared from view, Elliott stepped back inside the building and hurried over to the door leading to the basement.

"Sgt. Hernandez!" he called out as he went down the stairs, "A German team has arrived to take Mihai into custody!"

"Yes, sir. I'll get the door to the outside open," said Hernandez.

By the time Elliott reached the bottom of the short staircase leading up to the door Hernandez had it open and Becker was coming down.

"Follow me," said Elliott, who then walked over to where the storage rooms were located. "Unlock it, sergeant," said Elliott, pointing to the one holding Mihai.

Hernandez complied, then stood aside as Becker stepped in. "You are the Romanian national named Mihai?" asked Becker in English, addressing the man he encountered in the locked room. Mihai nodded in the affirmative.

Becker motioned for the four men who had followed him down into the basement to take Mihai into custody.

Once the German team had removed Mihai from the premises, Becker turned to Elliott and said, "The Service has now complied with your request, Col. Stone, so I would appreciate receiving from you a more thorough review of what you believe is transpiring beyond what your Col. Appleton has related to my superiors."

"All in good time, captain," replied Elliott. "Sgt. Hernandez and I are due at a nearby bookstore where much of the espionage activity is believed to be taking place...we can talk as we walk over."

* * *

"The objective of the espionage operation appears to be NATO's plans for reinforcing its military posture along the Eastern Flank," began Elliott as he and Becker walked along

Grunerstraße towards the cobblestone street where the bookstore was located. Hernandez followed along behind, keeping an eye out for any sign of counter surveillance.

"Somehow, the espionage team learned of the presence of the new NATO Planning Center on Jagerstraße and has tasked at least four female operatives to eavesdrop on conversations in public settings involving personnel assigned to the Center. Their technique is fairly straightforward, one of the young women—tipped off by a spotter—tails a likely pair of staffers as they walk to a local restaurant intent on getting their midday meal, then manages to secure a table nearby. Once in place, the operative—using the advanced microphone capability found in current smartphones—records the conversation. She prepares a written transcription of the conversation back at her apartment, along with notes that might be helpful in further identifying the speakers, or in assessing the degree of seriousness the speakers display while engaged in any given segment of the conversation."

"What then?" asked Becker.

"A courier—so far we've identified three, one of whom is the man you now have in custody—visits the apartment of the female eavesdropper and collects the written transcription document, then takes it directly to the bookstore we are now approaching. There, the document is processed—how, and for what reason, we still don't know. All we do know is that a team of about eight operatives show up at the rear entrance of the bookstore at about the time the bookstore opens for business. One of them we've identified as a Belarusian by the name of Vadim who appears to be an enforcer."

Sgt. Becker nodded, taking it all in, then asked, "And what is it you and your men intend to do this evening?"

"This evening, you and I, together with Capt. Perez, and Sergeants Hernandez and White, will attempt to observe the operatives as they leave the bookstore, then follow several back to where they live, or to where they're likely to make contact with others involved in the overall operation."

Chapter Nine

Sgt. Dan Farrand was dressed in dark slacks, a white dress shirt and a dark brown houndstooth sport jacket as he climbed the stairs to the first floor of the building. Upon reaching the landing he glanced one final time at the address Galina had given him, then walked over to the door and knocked.

He heard the clicking of heels on a bare wooden floor, then stepped back as the door was pulled open. "He smiled, pointed to his wristwatch, then said, "Seven o'clock…right on schedule… you young ladies ready?"

Galina returned the smile and motioned for him to come in. "Taisija has agreed to join us…let me introduce her." She led Farrand through a narrow hallway and into a small parlor. Seated on a couch was a young woman with blond curly hair, wearing a short black skirt and a tan, light-weight all-weather jacket. "Taisija, this is Sgt. Dan Farrand."

"Very glad to meet you, Taisija," said Farrand, walking over and taking her hand. I'm pleased you'll be coming along…I think you'll both approve of the restaurant."

Taisija smiled, gently removing her hand from his grip. "Galina tells me you've only recently left the army."

Farrand nodded, "My enlistment was up and I'm hoping a job materializes here in the city since I'd kind of like to stay for a time."

"I'm told there are various private contracting jobs for ex-military who possess special skills," commented Taisija, "would that be something you'd qualify for?" she asked.

Farrand shrugged, "I believe so, but we'll have to see... as I told Galina, I've got my eye on a possible job working for NATO."

"Just let me get my coat," said Galina, hurrying out of the room.

"Galina tells me you and she do freelance clerical jobs... working right from here...but I have to say this room doesn't have the feel of an office," said Farrand as he looked around.

"We use the dining table over there," Taisija replied, pointing to a wooden table off in the corner. "Knowing you were coming, we put away our laptops and other equipment...usually the room is a mess," she added with a laugh.

"Are you also from Riga?" asked Farrand as they waited for Galina to return.

"Yes, but from a different neighborhood...as it happened we met at University," she added.

Farrand nodded.

"Okay, we can go," said Galina, who'd returned to the room, buttoning her coat.

"Let me order a car," said Farrand, pulling out his smartphone and activating the ride app. He busied himself entering both the building's address and their ultimate destination as he followed the two women out of the apartment and down the flight of stairs. Only minutes after they'd reached the street, a car pulled up. "You ladies slide into the back seat...I'll join the driver up front," he said, holding the door open for them.

The drive over didn't take long since the distance was less than a mile. Farrand hadn't uttered a word all during the drive, intent on listening to the quiet chatter between the two women seated in the back seat.

"Okay, we're here!" said Farrand, with mock bravado. "Careful of the cobble stones," he warned as he helped them out of the car. With each gripping an arm, he guided them over to the front entrance of the restaurant.

After passing through an old fashioned door of dark wood-framed panels of window glass, they entered a rectangular room furnished with a long bar and a series of diminutive tables for two. To the left was an opening to a much larger room filled with linen-covered tables and darkly upholstered banquettes. The walls of both rooms were covered with poster-style photos of 1930's and 1940's movie and theatre celebrities, along with framed prints of notable Expressionist art. Art Nouveau flourishes could be seen in the rich interior wood paneling.

"It's lovely," exclaimed Galina as she took off her coat.

A manager approached and after confirming it was the Farrand party led them to a banquette in the large room. Menus were handed out, then the manager left them to make their choices.

"I've only eaten here once before," began Farrand, "but on that occasion I was in the company of a couple of military buddies from Stuttgart. All of us were pleased with our selections so don't hesitate…choose whatever you wish."

"And wine?" teased Galina.

"Of course, wine, but I'll have to rely on the two of you to make the selection. Fancy dining is not something enlisted men in the US Army know much about…even if they're of senior rank."

"Well, we're probably not any better qualified," protested Galina. "It's not as if we get taken out to fancy restaurants all that often."

"I'm really surprised you'd say that," said Farrand, seemingly shocked, "I've got to believe men approach the two of you for dates all the time, given how young and attractive you both are."

"That's kind of you to say," replied Galina, "but the truth is our work schedule and the fact we work in our apartment doesn't leave much of an opportunity for us to mix in public. Anyway, our employer likes to know we're pretty much always available in case a special rush job comes up."

Just then, a server came over to take their order. The two women spoke with the server in German; only Farrand spoke in English.

"So tell me about your employer," said Farrand, breezily, once the the server had left with their order.

Taisija looked nervously over at Galina, who replied offhandedly, "It's a Moldovan start-up specializing in EU cross-border marketing."

Farrand nodded absently, then looked up, "But why here? Surely, they'd enjoy much lower overhead, and maybe some government support, if they'd remained in their own country."

Galina replied evenly, "What they've told me is that they've based themselves in Berlin to avoid the kind of discrimination they believe they'd surely encounter if they operated out of Transnistria, a tiny enclave in Moldova where the start-up's founders are from. They're convinced they'd be regarded as just a bunch of ambitious kids from a tiny landlocked country in a remote part of eastern Europe."

Farrand nodded thoughtfully, "Makes sense...but are we talking about a small company...you know...one with less than a dozen employees...or are the people you and Taisija work with just the front office staff...with a big back-office operation located back in Transnistria?"

Galina shrugged, "Could be...but all we know is that we get our pay from an office here in the city."

Taisija stared at Farrand, "Why all this interest in our employer?"

Farrand raised his hands in surrender, "Sorry...it's just that I'm a little preoccupied with finding a job...thought maybe there'd be something I could do for the start-up...you know, being an American and all."

"That's not going to happen," replied Galina dismissively. "They're only interested in European companies."

"You sure about that?" asked Farrand. "A hell of a lot of American firms have branches here in the EU...maybe you should let me talk with someone in management at the start-up…even my military background could prove helpful in approaching prospective American companies."

"Taisija looked worriedly over at Galina, who looked at Farrand with suspicion, "I think you should leave it alone."

Farrand shrugged, "Okay, just thought I'd try…anyway, here comes our food."

The server stepped away once the plates of food had been placed before them and their glasses replenished from the bottle of white Latvian wine the girls had discovered on the wine list.

Conversation during the meal was decidedly frosty despite Farrand's best efforts at charming the young women. Finally, after their plates had been cleared and coffee served Farrand tried once again, "Listen, I know you don't want to talk about your employer—though for the life of me I can't understand why—but can we at least talk about what it is you do for the start-up? I know you perform some kind of clerical task but that's a little vague."

Taisija seemed to soften a bit, saying, "We're given audio tapes of product feed-back sessions by small groups of likely consumers, which we transcribe."

"So guys like Daniel take your transcriptions and do the work of analyzing what's being said…is that it?" asked Farrand.

"No…Daniel is simply a courier," interjected Galina, "analysis is done by specialists back at the office."

"Do you ever get to see the product…you know…what the analysts have compiled in the way of useful data?" asked Farrand innocently.

Taisija shook her head, "No…it goes directly to the boss."

"I think we'd better be on our way, Taisija," said Galina angrily. "Sgt. Farrand seems more interested in our employer than in us."

"Hey, don't be upset, Galina," said Farrand, hoping to placate her, "I'm new to this game. Hell, up until a few weeks ago there was always someone up the chain of command who told me what to do and how to do it…you ladies are among the first I've encountered who've had the patience to give me some feedback on how to get along in real world."

"Well, you seem to be far more worldly than how you wish to be regarded, Sgt. Farrand," said Galina sternly. "So, if you don't mind, perhaps you'd order us a car."

Farrand shook his head, seemingly perplexed by Galina's intransigence, but dutifully made the call. "There'll be a car out front in just a few minutes," he said as he signaled the server to bring over the bill.

"Fine…we'll find our way out," said Galina formally, "and thank you for the dinner…I only wish we better understood your motives," she added as she put on her coat.

Farrand watched through the restaurant window as the two women climbed into the waiting car. After a brief exchange the driver nodded, then drove away. He lingered at the table, going over in his mind the evening's conversation. Despite the way it ended, he felt the evening had been productive. With a small sigh, he took a final sip of coffee, paid the bill, then got up from the table and made his way out to the street.

It was a little after eight o'clock in the evening and the irregular surfaces of the cobble stones of Postraße captured complicated facets of light from the overhead street lamps. Farrand, needing privacy, walked a short distance away from the restaurant entrance, pulled out his smartphone and made the call.

"Col. Stone, this is Sgt. Farrand reporting in," he said once Elliott picked up.

"I take it your dinner companions are no longer with you... how did it go?" asked Elliott.

"Somewhat of a mixed bag, sir. I think they suspect I'm not whom I portray myself to be...whether they believe me to be a counter-intelligence agent or just a nosy opportunist is not clear. What is clear is that they'll probably have nothing further to do with me and insisted on leaving the restaurant alone."

"Did you get any new intel despite that?" asked Elliott.

"I believe so, sir. I can now confirm the women do handle not only eavesdropping but also transcription, and that the couriers like Daniel take the documents to the bookstore for the purpose of content analysis. The final product is subsequently delivered elsewhere...to someone whom they refer to as the "boss". From the way they said it, I believe this person is most likely also located in the city. Most intriguing—at least to me—was their backstory regarding the company that employs them...they mentioned the company as having its origins in Transnistria— that politically marginal enclave of Moldava."

"Hmm...well worth thinking about," mused Elliott, who then added, "Good work, sergeant. One final question...did you get the impression the women were professional espionage agents or simply bit players hired locally on the basis of their evident suitability?"

"In the case of Taisija, I'd be comfortable judging her to be a bit player, but in Galina's case I'd have more difficulty making that call. She seemed more in control of what she was willing to reveal, and had a better grasp of the back story. It wouldn't surprise me to learn she recruited Taisija…only sharing with her what she needed to know to do her job."

"Good to know. Listen, sorry I wasn't able to get over to the restaurant to check out your dining companions, but things are probably about to begin over here."

"Understand, sir. Do you want me to head for the bookstore?"

"I believe that would be best, sergeant. Although the rest of the team is here we're anticipating the need to monitor eight or so operatives once they begin making their way out of the bookstore where they've been quartered over the past four hours. We could use your help in tailing the agents to their final destinations."

"Yes, sir…I'll quick-time it over…count on an ETA of twenty minutes or less."

"Roger that…if we've already left someone will text you the location of a meet-up point." With that, Elliott broke the connection and resumed his watch.

* * *

Elliott and Capt. Becker were positioned at the south end of the alley, while Capt. Perez, Hernandez and White took up positions at the north end. Shortly after Elliott got off the phone with Farrand the rear door to the bookstore opened and a woman and three men stepped out. With only the scattered light from three widely spaced lamp posts to illuminate the narrow street, getting a good look at four was problematic, but despite the poor visibility, Elliott felt sure he recognized one of the men as Vadim, the man who had attacked him that first night. Elliott texted Capt. Perez to have Sgt. White tail the foursome.

Becker leaned in to read the text, then looked at Elliott inquiringly.

"We believe Vadim is an enforcer," Elliott whispered. "Having him provide security for the four probably means all or most of them are likely to be going to the same destination. It's an assumption we have to make since we don't have the manpower to tail each of the persons Sgt. White observed entering the back room of the bookstore earlier in the day."

Becker nodded.

The four from the bookstore walked towards the north end of the alley, forcing Perez and his two men to step away and seek anonymity by taking seats at several different tables of the outdoor cafe closest to the alley. Mentally timing the appearance of the bookstore foursome at the mouth of the alley, Sgt. Leroy White casually got up from his chair and walked to the adjoining street, paused for a moment—allowing the foursome to commit to a direction—then began ambling along behind them.

Once the foursome were well away, Perez and Hernandez returned to the north end of the alley and awaited the appearance of others still in the bookstore.

Next to emerge were two men, each with a nondescript leather bag slung over the shoulder. They exchanged a few final words then took off in opposite directions—one heading towards the north end of the alley, the other to the south end.

Elliott quickly texted Perez, "*Each of you take one of these men. I'll cover whoever else comes out.*"

"*Roger that,*" texted Perez back.

Again, Becker leaned in to read the text exchange, "Who is it you are waiting for?" he asked.

"According to White, there were, altogether, eight persons that showed up around four o'clock. We've observed six, which leaves two besides the bookstore clerk. I'm thinking the initial foursome consisted of the text analyzers and their security—but their respective roles—except for Vadim—remains to be determined. The two guys with the sling-bags I make out to be couriers. Which leaves us with a big question mark: who's in charge? I don't think it's the clerk, and I don't believe an operation of this importance runs without a fairly robust chain of command. So, I'm guessing one of the two guys still in there is most likely the guy in charge of the bookstore operation."

Some minutes after that exchange Elliott spotted Farrand turning into the alley. He pointed him out to Becker, "That's Sgt. Dan Farrand, one of Capt. Perez's men." Elliott stepped under the nearby streetlight and gave a wave, then stepped back into the shadows. Farrand nodded, then advanced toward them.

Elliott quietly introduced the two men, then put up a hand, cautioning them to be watchful. "The door's opening," he whispered, nodding in the direction of the bookstore's rear entrance. All three stared at the exit as the door opened tentatively—almost as if whoever was opening it feared what he would encounter. Finally, a man stepped out. His right hand was positioned behind him—near the lower edge of his windbreaker, his left hand gripped on the door.

"The guy's nervous as hell," whispered Farrand. "He's primed to pull out the handgun I'm guessing he's got wedged behind his belt at the small of his back."

"The others weren't nervous…at least they didn't seem to be," observed Elliott. "I wonder what's spooked him?"

"Damn! You know what it could be?" said Farrand in a whisper. "It could be Galina, that operative I had dinner with this evening, really did suspect me of being a counter-intelligence agent and alerted the bookstore."

"Well, she must have called only minutes ago," whispered Elliott.

Just then, the guy with the gun pulled the door open all the way, letting a much older man pass through.

"He's got to be the local boss," whispered Elliott, "the nervous guy's probably his bodyguard."

"Yes…what you say makes sense," whispered Becker excitedly, getting into the spirit of Elliott's counter-intelligence operation.

Chapter Ten

Sgt. White stood at the far end of the U-bahn car, glancing surreptitiously at the foursome who had taken seats near the exit door. The woman and one of the male operatives were seated together, while the man known as Vadim was seated next to the other male. Hoping to appear bored, White idly looked around, taking in the other passengers, the advertisements above the seats, and finally the schematic of the U-bahn line located above the door. He learned they were heading in the direction of Potsdamer Platz, and wondered if that was the where they'd disembark.

Out of the corner of his eye, White caught a sudden movement by Vadim. He watched as Vadim scrunched up, then reach into the side pocket of his jacket. White could see Vadim had retrieved his cellphone. Not having heard any audible ring, White surmised that whoever was contacting Vadim had sent a text message or an email.

Whatever was in the message seemed to have a marked effect. Vadim stared at the screen, almost disbelievingly, then tapped his seat mate on the shoulder, prompting him to also read what was written. For a moment, they looked at each other, gauging each other's reaction, then the other man nodded in the direction of the pair of operatives seated nearby, but Vadim shook his head.

White wasn't sure what had just taken place, but it made him uneasy.

Minutes later, the foursome exited the U-bahn at the Potsdamer Platz station. White felt Vadim and his colleague seemed far more wary as they walked along the station platform—as if those around them might prove to be a threat. It was another sign—one White believed he shouldn't dismiss— that those he was following were now operating at a heightened level of suspicion. Certainly a level far higher than earlier, when the foursome had boarded the U-bahn in Mitte. Being cautious, White gauged his exit for the very last moment, hoping the foursome would begin climbing to street level before he was forced to emerge from the car. He wasn't totally successful; although most of the party were already heading up the stairs, Vadim turned and looked back just at the moment White stepped onto the station platform.

White immediately turned away, then began walking briskly towards the opposite end of the platform. When he thought enough time had elapsed for Vadim to reach street level he doubled back and raced up the stairs.

He spotted the foursome just exiting the Potsdamer Platz complex at its southwest corner—a point which led on to Stresemannstraße. The sidewalk was filled with pedestrians at this time of the evening and White believed himself well-concealed as he took up a position about fifty feet back from the foursome as they made their way south along Stresemannstraße.

But at the first intersection, White watched as the foursome turned east off Stresemannstraße onto a side street. Pedestrian traffic there was sparse and White wasn't sure how to proceed, so he held back, hugging the corner of a building, trying to monitor their movements as inconspicuously as possible.

About 500 meters ahead, he observed them turn right—into what looked to him to be an unfenced construction area. Thinking it was a shortcut, White hurried after them, anxious to spot where they'd ultimately end up. As he stepped off the street and entered the construction site he realized something was wrong. The site was not lighted, and in the darkness of night, he knew any attempt to cross it on foot would be hazardous, given the presence of scattered debris. Christ! he thought, it's an ambush!

Before he could react, a muffled shot knocked him to the ground. His training instantly kicked in and he crawled painfully towards a large stack of concrete blocks, anxious to get out of the glare of the street lights that had made him such a tempting target. Huddled up against the concrete block stack, he quickly drew his military issue Glock 17 semiautomatic, then reached into a side pocket and pulled out a suppressor, screwing it expertly onto the muzzle of the weapon. As he waited for his attackers to make their next move he focused on the need to determine the location and severity of the wound. The burning sensation emanating from his left thigh let him know where he'd most likely been hit, and the fact he'd been able to crawl, he figured, probably meant the femur hadn't been fractured, nor the femoral artery cut. He knew he'd soon have to improvise a tourniquet but figured that could wait. He suspected it had been Vadim who'd shot him, and believed the enforcer would hunt him down—if for no other reason than to learn his identity.

White listened intently, hoping to hear movement from deeper in the construction site. He suspected the reason he wasn't dead, only wounded, was due to the shooter having been forced to take a sudden, impulsive shot as he realized White was about to take evasive action. Either that or Vadim wanted him alive so that he could be interrogated.

After a minute or so, during which the only sounds White heard were those emanating from car traffic on Stresemannstraße, he crawled away from the stack of concrete blocks and over to the left rear tire of a truck parked further in—a position that would give him a better line of sight should Vadim or his fellow operative make a move. White tried to do it quietly, but his injured leg dragged a little as he elbowed his way forward.

Perhaps their decision to suddenly approach was prompted by the sound of his leg dragging, which gave them White's general location and confirmed the fact he'd been injured but not immobilized; all White knew was that the faint profile of two men in a crouch and heading in his direction was the first thing he saw once he was in position.

White knew his dark skin and dark clothes blended with the rubber of the truck tire, making him virtually invisible as long as he didn't move. So he waited patiently as the two men came closer and closer. When they were about thirty-five feet out he took careful aim at Vadim firing twice in rapid succession, aiming for the man's chest. Then, just as quickly, he fired one round at the other man, aiming low, hoping to wound, not to kill. With gritted teeth White scrambled forward as fast as he could, shredding the clothing at his elbows in the process, hoping to close with the wounded man before he managed to retrieve his handgun from wherever it had fallen. But as White got within ten feet of where the two men lay, the wounded man rolled onto his stomach and extended his right arm in White's direction. White quickly slapped his left hand against his right, creating a stable aiming grip on his Glock 17 semiautomatic and fired, but not before the wounded man got off a shot.

White felt the impact as the bullet smashed into the soft flesh above the bone of his left shoulder. He desperately fought to remain conscious despite the pain and shock. After a pause to assess the seriousness of his new wound, he resumed clawing his way forward, albeit with excruciating slowness—relying on his right elbow and uninjured leg to gain traction.

When he finally reached the two men he confirmed both were dead. White's final shot had hit the man squarely in the head, killing him instantly.

He took a moment to listen for any signs that the half-dozen muffled shots had caused anyone in the vicinity to raise an alarm. He heard no shouts or any distant sound of emergency sirens, but knew discovery of what had transpired would come soon—sooner than he'd like. Using his remaining good arm, he fished out his cell phone and put a call through to Col. Stone.

"Sir, Sgt. White here…I'm in need of urgent assistance," he said between gasps, finding talking painful.

"What is it, sergeant?" asked Elliott, who motioned for Capt. Becker to stand by.

"There's been a gunfight, sir. I've incurred two wounds… my two assailants are dead."

"Where are you, sergeant?"

"In a construction lot, five hundred meters east of Stresemannstraße, down the first side street south of the Potsdamer Platz complex," said Sgt. White.

"Are there other hostiles nearby?"

"Don't think so, sir. I believe the two others in the party left before the shooting began."

"Okay, sergeant…hang on…we'll be there shortly," said Elliott before breaking the connection.

While activating his car service app, he turned to his companions, "Sgt. White's been shot and there are two dead hostiles." Then added, "It'd be helpful, Capt. Becker, if you could arrange for a team from your security service to collect the bodies and put off any inquiries by the local police. Meanwhile, I'll alert Col. Appleton."

Becker nodded, then pulled out his cell phone and made the call, while Elliott put a call through to Appleton.

"Colonel, it's Col. Stone…sorry to interrupt your evening, sir, but we've got a situation that needs your immediate attention."

"I'm listening, Elliott."

"One of my Delta operatives has incurred two bullet wounds in a firefight near Potsdamer Platz. He'll need immediate medical attention, then air transport to the U.S. military clinic in Stuttgart."

"Give me the location…I'll have our embassy doctor come out with an ambulance and a couple of paramedics."

Elliott relayed Sgt. White's location.

"Okay…I'll get on it right away…is the soldier able to hold on for a while?"

"I'm not sure, sir…he didn't describe his condition other than to say he'd been shot twice, but from his voice I gathered he was in pretty serious shape."

"Understood!" said Appleton, who then abruptly signed off. Elliott stood nervously at the curb, willing the car service vehicle to appear. As he waited, he looked ahead, watching the two men he, Farrand and Becker had been following. "Sgt. Farrand, I'll need you to continue tailing our two targets, but keep sharp…it seems we were right to think they may be on to us."

"Yes, sir," replied Farrand with a nod then, without further comment he strode quickly away, anxious not to lose sight of the pair of men now some distance away.

* * *

"The recovery team's been dispatched," said Becker.

"Thanks, captain," said Elliott, who then waved as a black limo approached.

Becker and Elliott climbed in, with Elliott giving the driver their destination even before they were fully seated. "It's an emergency, driver," said Becker in German as he showed him his federal government I.D. "Make it fast!"

As they sped through the city, Elliott gave some thought to his impression the situation seemed to have changed rather drastically now that the espionage crew had resorted to attempted murder for a second time. He couldn't help thinking they'd become desperate, but why? As the question lingered in his mind, the only thing he could think of was that it must somehow be connected to the quality of the intel product they anticipated recovering, or had already recovered. With a barely audible grunt of frustration Elliott pulled out his smartphone again and prepared a text, sending it to both Capt. Perez and Sgt. Hernandez: *"Recover all intel documents in possession of the two couriers, preferably only after they've deposited the material at dead drops, but earlier if you deem it necessary."*

Elliott was worried he and his team had been put off track by the innocuous nature of the transcription he'd originally grabbed that first evening in the bookstore. It now seemed as if the espionage operation had already become far more consequential than he'd earlier imagined. But to confirm his suspicions he knew he'd need to examine the intel the couriers were carrying that evening. He just hoped he wasn't too late.

* * *

Elliott and Capt. Becker were the first to arrive. They scrambled out of the limo, with Elliott shouting "Sgt. White!". White—barely conscious—activated the flashlight app on his smartphone, guiding Elliott and Becker to his location.

"Hang on, sergeant," Elliott said quietly as he knelt beside him, "a medical team is on its way." White nodded feebly, then fell unconscious. Elliott patted him lightly on his good shoulder, then stood and walked over to the two bodies lying nearby. Pulling out his smartphone, he shined the flashlight on the faces of the two men. He confirmed that one of them was Vadim. Anxious to identify the other agent, Elliott searched the man's pockets, retrieving his wallet and passport. Scanning the documents quickly, Elliott learned he was named Arkady, and like Vadim held Belarusian citizenship. The stamp in his passport indicated he'd arrived in Germany a month earlier. Knowing Capt. Becker and his Federal Intelligence Service colleagues would insist on taking possession of the documents, Elliott slipped the items back in Arkady's pocket then stood up and walked over to Becker.

"The two men are Vadim and Arkady...both of Belarus. Arkady has a wallet and passport on him...Vadim's wallet is in my possession...I'll get it to you. As for his passport...it's probably in his apartment. I suspect both will prove to have cell phones on them. Should your people succeed in hacking into them I'm counting on you to pass on any actionable intel that might be found."

Capt. Becker nodded soberly, then pointed towards the street where an ambulance with flashing emergency lights had just pulled to the curb. Elliott motioned vigorously with his activated flashlight, signaling the medical team. While the paramedics went about the task of pulling a collapsible gurney from the ambulance's rear compartment a man in a white lab coat emerged from the vehicle and hurried over.

"I'm the embassy physician," he said between deep breaths. "Let's take a look," he added as he clicked on a powerful flashlight and bent down, playing the light over White's body in search of the locations of the two reported shots. "Okay, I see them." He then checked White's breathing. "Soldier, can you hear me?" he asked. Sgt. White nodded feebly but kept his eyes closed.

"You're Col. Stone…is that right?" asked the doctor, looking up at Elliott.

"Yes, sir…any way I can help?"

"Take this light and aim the beam onto his leg wound while I try to examine it. And you, sir—referring to Capt. Becker—I'll want you to put some pressure on the shoulder wound." Then, taking a pair of surgical scissors from the outer pocket of his lab coat he carefully cut away White's trousers in the area of the wound.

As he was in the process of examining the wound, the two paramedics arrived with the portable gurney. "Let's get him onto it," said the doctor as he stood up.

The paramedics placed the collapsed gurney on the ground next to White, then with in a well-rehearsed motion gripped White, lifting him slightly, then gently placing him face up on the gurney.

"We'll get him stabilized and bandaged up in the ambulance where we have some light," said the doctor, motioning for the paramedics to head for the vehicle. "Don't worry, colonel, I've done a couple of tours in Afghanistan as a surgeon in a MASH unit so I'm pretty familiar with situations like this," he added, hoping to reassure Elliott that White was in good hands.

"Good to know, doctor," said Elliott, resting a hand on Sgt. White's good shoulder, then giving it a gentle squeeze.

As Elliott stood and watched White's gurney being loaded in the back of the ambulance, Capt. Becker came up to him, "Sir, I've collected the firearms of Sgt. White and the other two, but I'm having difficulty locating the ejected brass given how dark it is out here."

"Don't worry, captain, once the bodies are removed there shouldn't be any reason for anyone to go looking for evidence of a firefight," replied Elliott absently.

"Yes, sir," said Becker, who now joined Elliott in monitoring the parked ambulance—anxious to see it drive away, knowing it meant White had been properly attended to and was now on his way to the airport.

Finally, the ambulance pulled away from the curb, its emergency lights flashing.

* * *

As the minutes ticked by, Elliott could see that Capt. Becker was growing impatient. The removal crew from the Federal Intelligence Agency was slow in coming. "I'm going out to the street," he said, abruptly, "maybe they need to be flagged down."

Elliott nodded sympathetically.

Shortly thereafter, Elliott watched Capt. Becker lean out into the street and wave his arm furiously. Then a white paneled truck—much like the one used to take Mihai into custody—rolled to a stop next to the German captain. Two men dressed in protective outer garments climbed out. Becker waited until they'd retrieved a litter and two body bags from the back of the truck, then guided them to where the bodies of the deceased agents were located.

With practiced efficiency, the removal team slipped the remains into body bags then, one after another, placed them on the litter and carried them to the panel truck. Becker seemed to have some last minute instructions to give to the men and walked over just as they were finishing up. Elliott watched, idly wondering whether Becker would ultimately decide to accompany the remains to wherever they were to be taken. Eventually, however, he stood back as the men climbed into the vehicle, then gave a brief wave as the driver executed a U-turn and headed back towards Stresemannstraße.

"A dirty business...yes?" commented Becker once Elliott joined him.

Elliott nodded absently, his mind preoccupied with the probable repercussions of what had taken place. Whatever organization was behind the espionage effort would now have surmised their operation was no longer secret. Not only that, but with three operatives missing, and two female operatives having reported being approached by a man they suspected of being a counter-intelligence agent, whoever was in charge would most likely now be planning to shut down those segments of the operation believed to be under attack by either German or NATO counter-intelligence agents. To Elliott's way of thinking, that meant the eavesdropping/courier teams would be recalled, and the backroom operation at the bookstore shut down. Elliott looked at his watch, it was approaching eleven o'clock. Despite the late hour, he figured he needed to arrange for his team to meet him at the bookstore, believing a clean-up crew would soon be ordered to sanitize the back room—something Elliott believed would take place that night.

Chapter Eleven

All but one of the cafes along the cobblestone street had closed for the night by the time Elliott and his team had assembled, and even that one had only a couple of customers—a middle aged pair, seemingly reluctant to return to their tiny apartment. A bored waiter leaned against the wooden frame of the cafe's entrance, subconsciously hoping the pair would finish up and leave. But when he saw a group of five men approaching he stepped away from the doorway and quickly emerged from beneath the overhanging canvas awning—almost at the curb— where he would be visible to prospective customers and from where he could urge them to select a table.

Elliott acknowledged the waiter's welcome and chose a table closest to the street where they'd have a modicum of privacy as they talked. The table seated four comfortably, but an extra chair was pulled over.

When do you close?" Elliott asked the waiter.

"Please don't trouble yourself, sir," replied the waiter, "we don't officially close until midnight."

Elliott nodded, then turned to the others and said, "Well... please give the gentleman your order...just coffee will be fine for me." The others also ordered coffee, knowing they'd need to be alert for another couple of hours, though several also ordered sandwiches.

After their food had been served and Elliott was confident the waiter was no longer interested in them—having resumed his idle posture up against the entrance to the cafe's interior seating area—he turned to the assembled team and briefly summarized the events that had resulted in Sgt. White's injuries and the conclusions he had drawn from that incident. He concluded by saying, "I'm guessing they'll send in a team shortly after midnight to go over the back room, removing anything that would hint at what it had been used for, knowing that's when the last place of business on this street closes for the night. I figure that gives us maybe a half-hour for debriefing before we take up positions inside the bookstore. Capt. Perez, why don't you lead off?"

"Yes, sir," he replied, then reached into the outer pocket of his jacket and pulled out a thick envelope. "The courier I'd been tailing serviced a dead drop located near the corner of Zimmerstraße and Friedrichstraße—a restroom in an eating establishment. After the courier made the drop I recovered the packet containing the intel and have it here with me. As you'll note, sir," continued Perez, handing the packet to Elliott, "the intelligence summary refers to earlier intel regarding a purported plan of NATO to accede to the requests by Poland and Lithuania to station large ground forces permanently on their soil...something I've always believed was ruled out despite Russia's annexation of Crimea. That's followed by what is characterized as a partial listing of military units scheduled to be deployed, and the countries tasked to furnish them."

Elliott put the thick envelope aside, "No way such a listing could have been assembled by merely eavesdropping on someone's luncheon conversation," he said disgustedly.

"That was my feeling as well, colonel," said Capt. Perez. "I think we need to consider the possibility they've succeeded in turning someone who's employed there."

"Which, of course, shines a whole new light on the eavesdropping operation…it might not be principally a conduit for scraps of intelligence but a rather clever blackmailing scheme," said Elliott worriedly.

"Does the intel in the packet identify the source?" asked Capt. Becker.

Everyone looked at Perez, who shook his head, "The only thing that might possibly refer to the source is a cryptic label at the beginning of the document that reads: "Doc-2/PC-2". What that actually means I couldn't say".

"A worst case interpretation," said Elliott grimly, "would be to imagine it meant: "The second document provided by Planning Center Informant Number Two".

"Let's say you're right, colonel," said Sgt. Farrand, quickly following up, "that would mean there are at least two compromised staffers at the Planning Center, and that at least one of them has already been forced to supply an initial trove of intel…intel that's probably now in the pipeline to whatever organization is behind the operation."

"Can you supply any light on the matter, Sgt. Hernandez?" asked Elliott.

"I'm not sure, sir," replied Hernandez. "The courier I was tailing gave me the slip near the campus of Humboldt University where I suspect the dead drop was located. I waited around and eventually spotted him, though by that time he'd already made the drop."

"I gather he knew I was following him since he began to run when he saw me. I ran after him...eventually catching and subduing him. We scuffled a bit, but he didn't really put up much of a fight. Despite my threatening him with bodily harm he refused to take me to the dead drop, arguing it wouldn't do me any good to retrieve the packet he'd left there since the other courier—the one you were tailing, Capt. Perez—would be dropping off a duplicate collection of intel. Knowing you'd most likely been more successful, I didn't press the matter. In hindsight, I probably shouldn't have let him off so easily."

"Did you learn who he was?" asked Capt. Becker.

"I did better than that, captain, I confiscated both his wallet and his passport," replied Hernandez as he pulled the items from an inside pocket of his jacket. "His name is "Petro" and he was carrying this Ukrainian passport," he said as he handed Capt. Becker the two items.

"So you let him go," said Elliott.

"I did, sir...didn't see any benefit in placing him in custody since we now know who he is, what he looks like, and what his role has been in the espionage operation."

"What about you, Sgt. Farrand...any success in tailing the last two men to leave the bookstore?" asked Elliott.

Farrand put down the sandwich he'd been eating, took a quick sip of coffee, then turned to Elliott, "I believe so, sir. As in the case of the four persons Sgt. White was following, my pair took the U-bahn to Potsdamer Platz then walked south to Stresemannstraße, but unlike the first group that kept to the eastern side of the street the two men I was following crossed it, heading west. The pair ended up in a neighborhood undergoing renovation, where a number of pre-war buildings could still be found. Their destination was a travel agency located on the ground level of one of the pre-war multi-story apartment buildings to be found in that neighborhood."

"Did the agency have a name?" asked Elliott.

"No, sir...the sign just said "Reisebüro", and on the door it said "By Appointment Only" in German."

"So, they went to an office, not to a residence," mused Elliott. "Did you hang around, sergeant?"

"I did, sir, and things began to happen. First off, one of the two men I'd been following—the younger one—almost immediately stepped back outside and took up a position in front of the office entrance. It pretty much confirmed my suspicion that he was some sort of bodyguard or security professional. The older guy he'd been with remained in the travel office."

"Then what?" asked Elliott.

"Well, about ten minutes later two men with slender shoulder bags made of some sort of black technical fabric stepped out of the office and glanced inquiringly at the security guy, who gave an affirmative nod—as if to say the two men were not under surveillance as they set out. I watched as they walked towards Stresemannstraße."

"I'm guessing they were headed for the dead drops," said Capt. Perez. "The shoulder bags were the giveaway."

"Which would mean we've probably located the Berlin headquarters of the operation," said Elliott. "Did anyone else come out of the travel office, sergeant?"

"Not while I was there, sir," replied Farrand.

"Okay, that'll be our next target...but now let's make our way into the bookstore," said Elliott as he got up from the table. The waiter, realizing his customers were on their way out, rushed over with the check. Elliott, without a glance, paid it in cash then began walking towards the main entrance of the bookstore; his team followed.

The five men stood idly in a loose group engaged in quiet conversation, waiting for the waiter and those working on the inside to finally close the cafe. It took what Elliott felt was an exasperatingly long fifteen minutes before the the sidewalk tables were securely cabled, the chairs brought in, and the front door locked. Then, after a further interval, the interior lights of the cafe were shut off. The entire block-long cobblestone street was now largely cloaked in darkness, with only the lights from the nearby bordering streets penetrating any distance.

"They'll leave from the alley," said Capt. Becker, knowingly, referring to the waiter and the others who'd been working in the cafe.

Elliott nodded, then signaled for Capt. Perez to force the lock on the front door of the bookstore.

Perez pulled out a set of tension picks and approached the door. Sgt. Hernandez assisted, using his smartphone flashlight to illuminate the key hole. The lock yielded to Perez's skill with the picks in less than two minutes.

"You'll probably have to also use the picks on the door leading to the back room," said Elliott to Perez as they entered the front retail space of the bookstore.

"Yes, sir," replied Perez, "just lead the way."

Elliott led Perez and Hernandez down the far left bookshelf aisle which ended directly in front of the backroom door. As Hernandez shined a light on the door, Perez turned the handle, checking to see whether the door was locked; it was. Then, after a cursory examination of the locking fixture, he said in a relieved voice, "Not too challenging," then retrieved the tension picks from his jacket pocket and went to work.

"Okay, we're in," said Perez, stepping aside.

Elliott was the first to enter. What he found was a large unfinished space that held several desks, each with a laptop computer, pads of lined paper and a scatter of ballpoint pens. There was also a conference table that could seat a half-dozen people located near a wall-mounted wet bar. A small microwave and pocket refrigerator were on a shelf above the wet bar. The only other piece of furniture of interest was a wooden side table that held an office-grade laser printer, several reams of printer paper, and a network wi-fi router.

"There seems to be an active local wi-fi network," said Hernandez, looking at the screen of his cell phone, "but there's no evidence it's linked to the internet."

"Check the router," said Perez as he examined the contents of one of the desk's drawers.

Hernandez walked over to the device sitting on the side table, "Router's internet link doesn't appear to have been switched on."

"They could have easily used a cellular link from their smart phones," said Capt. Becker dismissively.

Hernandez shrugged, "Yeah, but cellular transmissions can be just as vulnerable as wi-fi to electronic surveillance and these guys seem anxious to avoid such risks, which is why they seem to depend mostly on old fashioned spy craft."

"Look at this," said Elliott, drawing the attention of the others to a large blow-up of a detailed street map of central Berlin tacked to the far wall. "See anything curious about it?"

Capt. Becker shrugged, "It doesn't seem to have been marked up."

"Exactly," said Elliott. "Wouldn't we expect to see certain locations circled that were of special interest to the analysts working here...you know, like restaurants favored by personnel affiliated with NATO's Planning Center, or maybe the locations of dead drops?"

"What are you implying, sir?" asked Capt. Perez.

"That it's likely digital facsimile maps of Berlin with all such markings are to be found in the stored files of these laptops. This wall map was probably used primarily for last minute briefings."

"So we'll need to gain access to those and any other files," said Capt. Becker. "And since it's likely the files on the laptops are encrypted we'll need to have encryption specialists at the *Bundesnachrichtendienst* take a stab at breaking into the computers."

"Can you arrange to have your Service give priority to the effort?" asked Elliott.

Capt. Becker shrugged, "I can try," he said as he pulled out his cell phone and prepared to make the call.

Just then, Capt. Perez gave a vigorous hand gesture meant to instill quiet, then whispered, "There appear to be some people coming down the alley...I can hear them talking."

"Okay, douse the lights," said Elliott quietly. "Becker, you and Sgt. Farrand stand next to the alley entrance door...Capt. Perez, you and Sgt. Hernandez step back into the front retail area just in case somebody comes in through the street entrance... leave the door open a crack...meanwhile, I'll try to draw their attention to me as they enter," he added as he attached the suppressor onto his Beretta M9 then held the weapon at his back—out of sight.

"I'll bet they're coming to retrieve the laptops," whispered Perez to himself as he threw the switch for the lights, then followed Hernandez into the bookstore, partially closing the door behind him.

They all remained quiet as the espionage team approached the alley entrance. A key was noisily inserted into the lock, then the door was pulled open. Someone reached an arm inside and switched on the lights, then they all doggedly made their way into the room, tired and sleepy from a long day, and not happy about having to come back so late at night, realizing it meant something had seriously gone wrong.

Almost by way of habit, all five headed mechanically towards their work areas, not giving much attention to the room as a whole. Suddenly, as the bookstore clerk made his way towards the door leading to the retail area, he shouted, "You!" having just spotted Elliott standing quietly at one end of the conference table.

The other four instantly began reaching for their handguns, but before they managed to work them free from where they were concealed Capt. Becker and Sgt. Farrand shouted, "Freeze!"

Then the door to the front retail area was thrown open and Capt. Perez and Sgt. Hernandez burst in, their suppressed Glock 17's held in a two-handed grip, ready to fire.

"On the floor...face down!" shouted Elliott as he pointed his Beretta M9.

As four members of the espionage team began to comply, one suddenly raised his weapon, pointing it at Elliott. Elliott, Capt. Perez and Sgt. Hernandez all fired at once, killing the man instantly.

"He's the bodyguard," said Sgt. Farrand, looking down at the body, as Perez and Hernandez stripped the four surviving men of their weapons, passports and wallets. Farrand then kneeled down and performed the same task on the dead man. "His name is Fedor, and it appears he's a Latvian Russian," said Farrand as he handed the documents to Capt. Becker.

"And this one's the courier I tailed to the dead drop," said Capt. Perez pointing to one of the men lying on the floor…he's a Ukrainian named Andriy according to his documents."

"Do you see the courier you followed, Sgt. Hernandez?" asked Elliott.

"Yeah, it's Petro all right," replied Hernandez as he pointed to one of the other men lying on the floor.

"I can personally identify the bookstore clerk," said Elliott, pointing to the formally dressed middle-aged man resting uncomfortably on the floor. "What'd his documents say he is?"

"He's Moldovan," replied Capt. Becker who'd been collecting all the documents.

"So…there's only one who's role continues to be a mystery," said Elliott, pointing to the oldest of the four men lying prone on the floor. Heavy-set, with thinning gray hair and a countenance that Elliott figured placed him somewhere in his fifties, the man remained impassive, seemingly reluctant to speak.

"His documents give his nationality as Moldovan," interjected Becker, "and his name appears to be "Florin"."

"Okay, Florin, stand up…you others…remain where you are!" ordered Elliott.

Florin grudgingly stood and faced Elliott, an expression of bitter contempt on his face.

"Capt. Perez…take this man to the front retail area…confine him there…with the door shut."

Perez nodded, then took plastic handcuffs from an outer pocket of his jacket and cuffed Florin's hands behind his back. With a shove, he propelled the cuffed man—stumbling—towards the doorway. Then, grabbing a fist-full of bunched material at the back of Florin's jacket, he pushed him through the doorway, letting the door slam shut once both of them were through.

"Okay, you...the clerk...get up!" shouted Elliott.

The bookstore clerk rose tentatively, unsure of his legs after being forced to lie prone on such an unforgiving surface.

"What's your name!" asked Elliott.

"Cristian, sir," replied the man unhesitatingly.

"Well, Cristian, you and the others will be turned over to the German authorities and prosecuted for the crime of espionage. Clearly, the severity of your punishment will be affected by the role you played in the operation. Am I to believe you're the ringleader of this operation...or should we imagine it's one of the two couriers lying there on the floor...or could it perhaps be the man identified as Florin...now securely confined and unable to hear whatever it is you wish to tell us?"

Cristian looked down at his two compatriots, then said, "It is Florin...these men will attest to the truth of what I say."

"Is he right?" asked Elliott, addressing the two couriers.

They both nodded their heads.

"Good...we're getting some place. Now...tell me...who does Florin report to...and where might we find that person?"

Cristian shook his head, "I've not been told...only Florin knows."

"Not even these couriers? Surely they must know."

"We deliver the product to dead drops, sir. We know nothing about what happens to it once it's picked up," said the courier named Andriy from his prone position.

Elliott nodded, satisfied it was likely what they reported was true. "So tell me, then, Cristian, what was it you and the others hoped to accomplish by returning to the bookstore at this late hour?"

"We were to collect the laptops, check that no traces of work product could be found on any of the pads of paper, or in the waste receptacles, or that none of us had left any personal belongings that might make it possible for the authorities to identify us," said Cristian, anxious to please.

"And to wipe down all surfaces so that our fingerprints could not be retrieved," added the courier Andriy.

"Final question," said Elliott soothingly, "Can any of you give us the password and encryption override for each of these laptops?"

They all shook their heads, "Only Florin and the two compilers had that information...they were the only persons based here at the bookstore that had any reason to use the devices," said Cristian plaintively.

Elliott looked over at Capt. Becker, who nodded his concurrence. "Well, we'll leave it at that. Capt. Becker, these three men, along with Florin, are now in your care...please arrange for them to be placed in custody. And have the Agency send over a CSI team as well as a removal team."

"Do you want to interrogate Florin, sir?" asked Capt. Becker as he waited for someone to pick up the call he had just placed.

"No, captain," replied Elliott, "I suspect getting him to cooperate will take more time than we have available. Anyway, we know where we need to go next."

Chapter Twelve

Elliott arrived at the U.S. Embassy at ten o'clock the following morning. Col. Appleton met him in the reception area and escorted him up to his office on the third floor of the consular wing. As they rode the elevator Appleton asked, "Have your men finally gotten some sleep, Elliott?"

"They have, sir…last night, but this morning's duty remains light…it'll give them time to attend to their personal gear."

Appleton nodded, then let further talk slide as they reached their floor.

"Grab a seat and I'll pour us some coffee," said Appleton as they entered his office. Elliott settled into a comfortable armchair and watched as Appleton busied with the carafe and cups and saucers. Finally, he brought the refreshment tray over, resting it on a low coffee table within easy reach of both Elliott and himself. "So, give me a rundown on where we stand," said Appleton as he poured the coffee.

"Well, sir, we've successfully rolled up both the field surveillance operation and the intel analysis section located at the bookstore," said Elliott. "Let me break it down for you. Four females—two identified as having Latvian-Russian nationality—were the ones tasked to eavesdrop and record conversations. They would take their audio recordings back to their apartments where they'd transcribe the conversation, adding commentary about any visual cues, such as gestures, facial expressions, or suggestive postures they might have observed."

"Hand-off agents would then visit the women's apartments, collect the transcriptions and take them to the bookstore where they'd be placed surreptitiously behind the inner dustcover flap of designated books. There appears to have been only two hand-off agents, one of whom is now in custody; both have been identified as holding Romanian passports. The bookstore clerk, a Moldovan, would immediately visit the shelf of books where the item was concealed, retrieve the envelope containing the transcription, and bring it to the rear operations room where the intel would undergo further processing."

"As to how the personnel of the NATO Planning Center were targeted, all we know at present is that the solitary spotter we've so far observed seems to be the one making the call. After the choice is made he appears to text a female surveillance agent waiting nearby who then picks up the pair, following them into an eating establishment. What criteria he uses in picking the target pair still remains to be worked out."

"Do you have the spotter in custody?" asked Appleton.

"No, sir…but as in some of the other cases we've been able to follow him back to his residence."

"So tell me what you think was going on at the bookstore," said Appleton as he put down his cup.

"Well, sir...based upon the document retrieved from the dead drop at the corner of Zimmerstraße and Friedrichstraße, two intelligence gathering functions appear to be going on at the same time. Ostensibly, the eavesdropping transcriptions are carefully studied by analysts in the back room for the purpose of collecting actionable intel from inadvertent security slips during a luncheon conversation. But the eavesdropping appears to have a more serious objective...blackmail. Some inadvertent slips are so compromising that the person becomes vulnerable to a threat of exposure unless he or she agrees to cooperate with the surveillance agents—supplying them with detailed intelligence. Apparently, agents at the bookstore make that call, then task one of the female operatives to approach the victim and issue the threat. From what we've learned so far, two persons affiliated with the Planning Center have already been turned."

"Christ! Elliott...are you sure?" asked Appleton.

"Not entirely, sir...in the sense that we've been able to get those apprehended to testify to it, but the document found at the dead drop was titled: "Doc-2/PC-2", which I take to mean: "The Second Document provided by Planning Center Informant Number Two". And in that document are references to earlier intel about NATO's intention to permanently station substantial numbers of ground forces in Poland and Lithuania, followed by a partial list of NATO military units expected to be called upon for that purpose."

Appleton shook his head, "This business is looking worse and worse the more you and your men delve into it."

"Yes…I believe that's a fair assessment, sir," agreed Elliott sympathetically.

"What do we know about the personnel at the bookstore?" asked Appleton.

"Well…we believe the actual analysis was being undertaken by two operatives working in the backroom of the bookstore—a man and a woman—who we've yet to identify. They apparently got away during the firefight where Sgt. White was wounded. However, we've placed in custody the presumed leader of the bookstore operation…a Moldovan named Florin. In addition, we've identified three security agents, all of whom are now dead—killed in firefights with my team. Two couriers—both Ukrainian—tasked with making the dead drops are also in custody…as is the bookstore clerk—the Moldovan named Cristian."

"Those dead drops you mentioned……do we know who's collecting the intel placed there?" asked Appleton.

"We might have a lead on that, sir. Sgt. Farrand followed the last two persons exiting the bookstore yesterday evening… one of the men he figured to be a bodyguard for the other—a guess that turned out to be correct when the man returned to the bookstore late last night, along with the others, and tried to shoot it out with my team. In any case, Sgt. Farrand tailed the two men to a travel agency south of Potsdamer Platz and west of Stresemannstraße. While remaining on station, Sgt. Farrand later observed two men leave the travel agency who are believed to have been couriers. It's likely they were on their way to the dead drops when Sgt. Farrand observed their departure."

"First a bookstore, now a travel agency...can you make any sense of it?" asked Appleton in evident frustration.

"I believe we can, sir," replied Elliott. "The role of the travel agency began to become clearer when we identified the man who the bodyguard had accompanied to the travel agency as being the leader of the intel analysis team at the bookstore. His abrupt departure for the travel agency seems to have been precipitated by a message from one of the female espionage agents Sgt. Farrand had invited out to dinner—the two women had become spooked by Sgt. Farrand's persistent questioning and had left the restaurant full of suspicion. I figure the leader—the man called Florin—needed to inform his superiors about a possible breach of their covert status, and the travel agency was where his superiors were based—in short, the travel agency appears to be Berlin headquarters for whatever outfit is running the espionage operation."

"But you haven't had a chance, yet, to confirm your suspicions...is that correct?"

"Yes, sir," replied Elliott.

Appleton nodded sympathetically, then asked, "I know it's early in the game, but have you given any thought as to who might be behind this operation?"

"I have, sir...my best guess is that it's some sort of multi-national syndicate whose leadership is either Moldovan, or is headquartered in Moldova. I base this on the fact that we've got agents of five different nationalities involved, and the two key operatives identified so far—the bookstore operations leader and the bookstore clerk—are both Moldovan."

"So...what's your next step?"

"Well, as I see it, sir, we've got three targets—the travel agency, the two people supplying intel from the NATO Planning Center, and the Moldovan connection," explained Elliott. "We've temporarily shut down the link between the espionage team and the blackmailed informants so we probably can safely take a bit of time figuring out the identity of the two compromised persons. And since we don't yet have enough intel to pursue those in ultimate command of the operation—wherever they may be based—it seems best to focus most of our resources on the travel agency."

"Shouldn't you have hit that target earlier this morning?" asked Appleton, clearly concerned. "Hell, they might have already abandoned that location for somewhere else."

"You're right, of course, sir, but the men needed some down time, and the way I figure it the headquarters staff at the travel agency would have had no way of knowing Florin's return to the bookstore was a bust...at least not right away. Obviously, by now they would have begun to suspect something had gone wrong—having not heard from Florin. I think we still have time."

"So, when did you figure on undertaking that operation?" asked Appleton, clearly frustrated.

"The operation is about to get underway as we speak, sir... led by Capt. Perez. He has orders to take into custody whoever they find at the travel agency, and to collect whatever intel might still be on the premises."

"You've cut it pretty close, Elliott," said Appleton sternly, "let's hope your assessment of how soon they'd react wasn't fatally off the mark. When do you expect an action report?"

"The fact I've heard no news yet, sir, indicates Capt. Perez felt no need to stand down...the headquarters team—or some fraction of them—appear still to be on the premises."

Appleton nodded, evidently relieved. "And in the meantime... how can I help?" asked Appleton.

"Were you able to get an up-to-date account of personnel at the Center? If so, perhaps we could spend some time this morning going over it and seeing if we can't narrow it down a bit."

"I'll get it," said Appleton as he got up from his chair and went over to his desk. "As I mentioned when we first talked about it, the list is long—some forty-four persons including myself. Why don't we work over here...the desk'll give us a surface on which to markup various staffing lists," he added, gesturing for Elliott to join him.

Elliott got up and moved to a chair across the desk from Appleton.

"How do you want to start?" asked Appleton as he spread out sheets containing staffing manifests.

"Well, sir, I imagine it might be helpful to begin by eliminating certain categories of personnel...for example, those with the greatest responsibility for ensuring the success of any covert or future-oriented actions designed to strengthen our Eastern Flank," said Elliott.

"You're referring to military personnel, I presume…like senior officers and their military aides?"

"Yes…they'd be the most adversely affected by indiscretions of that sort, I imagine, so it stands to reason they'd tend to be far more circumspect than civilians—all things being equal," argued Elliott.

"It's a good point, Elliott, and one that's strengthened, I think, by keeping in mind the likelihood any officer working at the Center would most likely be loath to unnecessarily divulge privileged country-specific information, even to his NATO colleagues—especially out in public," offered Appleton.

"That jives with the evidence supplied by the detailed intel contained in the document retrieved from the dead drop," added Elliott, "You'll remember it touched upon classified information affecting multiple NATO countries—not the kind of thing one would expect military personnel from a given country to supply."

"So where does it put us?" asked Appleton.

"In my way of thinking, sir, it suggests we give higher priority in our search to those at the Center who are there in a civilian status…like the military planning specialists and those in the secretarial pool," replied Elliott.

"That would allow us to cut our list by more than half," observed Appleton as he set aside manifests dealing with senior military staff and their aides.

"And here, I'd probably want us to focus our attention on the secretarial pool," argued Elliott. "I say this because planning specialists are professionals, with years of experience handling classified information. It's not reasonable to assume they'd make a greenhorn error like talking loosely of confidential matters while in a public space."

Appleton put down the document he was holding, and leaned back in his chair, "You're making a lot of questionable assumptions, Elliott…you and I know all too well that even generals can screw up when it comes to classified intel."

"I know, sir, but we've got to narrow the list someway, and I figure we can always come back and reassess our priorities if our initial investigation doesn't produce a couple of suspects."

Appleton nodded, "Okay, Elliott…we'll do it your way…how do you want to begin?"

"I've got to believe you've got video surveillance at the entrance to the building…is that right?"

"Yeah…there's a record of all traffic in and out of the Center."

"Can you get your IT staff to give us a remote feed…onto your computer screen?"

"I don't know…I'll call over and see," replied Appleton as he picked up the phone.

"Sam, can you put Harry on the line?" Then, in a low voice he said to Elliott, "Harry's the embassy's top IT man…if anyone can make it happen he can."

"Harry…you got a minute?" asked Appleton once the man he was trying to contact picked up. "Listen, I've got a potential security problem over at the Center and need to review stored video of all traffic in and out of the Center during daily lunch breaks for…let's say two weeks…and I'd like to do it here in the office. Can you hook me up a remote feed?"

"Shouldn't be problem, colonel...we archive that footage here in the embassy. Give me a few minutes to set up the time parameters on the video stock, then get the links up and running," replied the embassy's IT man.

"Thanks, Harry," said Appleton before breaking the connection. "Okay, Elliott, we should have our video stream momentarily...what should we be looking for?"

Elliott gave the question some thought, then said, "Sir, how familiar are you with the people that work at the Center...can you identify them by name...or at least by what it is they do?"

Appleton shrugged, "Some I'd be able to name...others I'd more than likely be able to tell you whether they're military or civilian. Gender might play a role in differentiating military planners from members of the secretarial pool, given that the planners tend to be male."

Elliott nodded, "Okay...that's not ideal, but I think we can make it work. What I'd like us to do is to freeze the images of paired civilians leaving or entering the building, then create a time-stamped digital file of the images where the individuals can be identified by name and occupation."

Appleton nodded, "I think I see where you're going with this, but assuming I can manage to make the identifications using personnel files, how are we to zero down on persons who might warrant being regarded as suspects?"

"I'm counting on pattern disruption," replied Elliott. "Over the two-week period archived, we'll try to determine any regularity in midday departures and arrivals, then look for evidence that one or both persons in any of the original pairing deviates from it. The working hypothesis would be that any recent alteration in a pattern that couldn't otherwise be accounted for—say, for example, a doctor's visit—might be a sign that the individual or individuals in question wish to avoid routines that had originally made them targets of blackmail, and might now bring them to the attention of authorities."

"But Elliott, if a person has been blackmailed his or her handler would insist that person be sufficiently accessible to the handler that an opportunity could arise for a hand-over of the classified information...and what better a ruse than holding tight to a routine. No, Elliott, I don't think your pattern disruption approach holds much water."

Elliott laughed, "You may be right, sir, but you've overlooked the psychological needs of the person being blackmailed. There would be guilt and fear of discovery...not to mention how such discovery might expose the person to unpalatable consequences— like loss of one's career, or even criminal prosecution. The victim—and don't mistake it, the person being blackmailed is a victim—will feel a need to take some sort of protective action, and the most direct sort would be to cease the kind of behavior that brought the person into that situation in the first place."

"Give me an example," challenged Appleton.

"Let's say our victim is a middle aged woman who regularly has lunch with an office mate at a restaurant on Friedrichstraße. Over lunch, she confides details of what she's working on at the moment with an office mate who shares a comparable level of clearance, thereby reassuring her she doesn't have to worry the information will leak to outsiders. Unbeknownst to her, one of the female operatives we've identified records her remarks and ultimately confronts her. Now she's forced to comply with the demands of the espionage group or risk everything. The one thing she knows she must do is to avoid detection. Knowing that her previous habits got her into this fix the least she can do is to cease what it was she was doing—hence pattern disruption. It may take the form of dining at noon with someone not affiliated with the Center, or dining alone—perhaps even going so far as bringing lunch from home."

"So how—in this hypothetical scenario—does the espionage team get your middle aged woman to pass on the requested intel if she's so panicked by fear of discovery?" asked Appleton.

Elliott sighed, "I wish I knew, sir. That's one of the reasons I'm hoping Capt. Becker and his colleagues at the German Federal Intelligence Service have some luck getting one of those we've detained to open up."

"But you think they'd have had to take into account the psychological needs of those they'd turned?"

"I do, sir...even if it posed something of an inconvenience, or exposed them to possible detection."

Appleton nodded, giving Elliott's arguments further thought. "Okay, Elliott, I'll run with it. Once Harry comes through, I'll review the footage with your ideas in mind. In the meantime, why don't you get over to the *Bundesnachrichtendienst* and see what success—if any—Capt. Becker is having with the interrogations."

"Yes, sir," said Elliott, getting up from his chair. "I'll also check on Capt. Perez and his team. They should have something to report by now."

Chapter Thirteen

An hour earlier, Capt. Perez was staring at the windows of the travel agency, trying to ascertain the level of activity going on inside. He was accompanied by Sgt. Farrand and Sgt. Hernandez. Capt. Becker was not present—having been called to the Federal Intelligence Agency to supervise interrogation of those held in custody.

Perez could see movement, but the partially draped windows and low interior lighting complicated the effort at getting a clear picture of who was in there and what they were doing. "I'm going to guess there's somewhere between three and five," he said under his breath.

Perez and his team were hunkered down in the shadows of a recessed entrance to the building across the street. They'd been watching the front of the agency for about a half hour. The only people to have entered through the street entrance during that time were the two couriers Sgt. Farrand had seen leaving the agency the previous evening.

"If there's now only three of them inside," reasoned Farrand, "then it's not likely they've got any security personnel with them."

"Given the amount of movement, I'm figuring they're packing up…ready to relocate," said Hernandez.

"How do you want us to handle it, sir?" asked Farrand of Perez.

"It's complicated," mused Perez. "The fact that at least one operative—and perhaps as many as three—have a residence in the building, above the agency, suggests they're just as likely moving documents out of the office and upstairs to the apartment as they are packing everything up to take to another location."

"So, why don't we split up…post one man out front to watch the street entrance, then have the other two enter the building from the side entrance where they might be able to identify which apartment is linked to the agency," suggested Hernandez.

Perez nodded, "Let's do it…Sgt. Farrand, you take the front…Sgt. Hernandez and I will head inside."

Perez hesitated for a moment—long enough to reassure himself that nobody inside the travel agency was monitoring the street—then, with a "follow-me" gesture meant for Hernandez, he took off in a run, crossing the street and continuing into the narrow, tree-lined pathway along the building's right side. The two of them kept close to the trees as they worked their way towards the building's entrance.

"You stay here…I'm going to see whether the entrance door is locked," said Perez. After getting a nod from Hernandez, Perez crossed over to the double door, checking through the narrow side windows whether anyone was in the front hall, then—seeing no one—he gripped the handle of one of the doors and turned it. The door move effortlessly as he pulled it towards him. With a shake of his head, Perez signaled for Hernandez to join him.

They both stepped inside and allowed the door to close behind them. Perez and Hernandez looked around. They found themselves in a reception area about twenty-five meters square, with a tiled floor, a staircase leading to the upper floors, a serviceable chandelier, and three interior doors.

"The one on the left has got to be the rear entrance to the travel agency," whispered Perez. "The one on the right most likely leads to a ground floor apartment, and the door adjacent to the staircase probably allows access to the building's basement."

Hernandez nodded.

"Should we check the names on the mailboxes?" asked Hernandez, pointing to the brass wall fixture containing ten locked mailboxes.

Perez shook his head, "We don't know the names of any of the operatives based at the travel agency so it won't do us any good. But we can use the mailboxes as a pretext for being in the entrance hall...we'll stand next to the mailbox panel and if anyone challenges us we can say we're trying to figure out which apartment our friend lives in."

"And if someone asks who it is we're looking for?" questioned Hernandez.

"We'll just give the person a fictitious name...maybe "Herr Shultz". That way we won't be caught using one of the names on the boxes—someone the questioner might know well, or who turns out to be the person we're presumably looking for.

The worse that can happen is that we're told we must be in the wrong building."

Perez and Hernandez had just finished familiarizing themselves with the names on the mailboxes when they heard a door on the first floor above street level open. "It's the apartment facing the street," whispered Hernandez.

Perez nodded.

"Are these the last of the boxes, Olek" asked a man in German, as two men could be heard stepping out onto the upstairs landing. "Ja, Marius," came the reply.

Perez and Hernandez kept quiet and watched as two men— one middle-aged, the other much younger—appeared at the top of the staircase. Each was carrying a cardboard box large enough to require both hands.

The older of the two put down his carton, pulled out a key and unlocked the rear door of the travel agency. "Hey, Dmytro... come help!" he shouted.

"Marius, look!" said Olek, glancing back at Perez and Hernandez who were unselfconsciously staring at the operatives from across the entrance hall.

Marius turned and looked, then shouted through the open door, "Dmytro, get Bogdan and Miroslav!"

"What you want!" shouted Marius at Perez and Hernandez.

"We're trying to figure out which apartment Herr Schultz lives in," said Perez calmly, in American-accented German. "His name doesn't appear on the mailboxes and we were wondering whether you two might know him."

"Nonsense!" shouted Marius dismissively just as three men stepped through the door, two holding handguns. "You are trespassing!" he added, "so leave!"

"Really, sir, we mean no harm," said Perez in a pleading voice as he began to walk towards the operatives, his right hand extended—as if to shake the other man's hand—while his left hand was held behind his back, with his Glock 17 in its grip.

"Schnell!" shouted Marius to the one called Dmytro, pointing to the cardboard carton on the tile floor. Dmytro quickly picked up the carton and hurried inside, followed by the man called Olek who was still holding a carton. "Make them leave!" shouted Marius to the two men holding guns, then rushed after the pair who had disappeared inside.

"Come no further!" shouted the armed man closest to Perez, pointing his gun menacingly.

"Okay…okay," said Perez as he backed away, his right hand gesturing for the two armed men to cool it.

Hernandez stepped over to the entrance door and opened it. "See, we're leaving," said Perez.

As Perez followed Hernandez out the door, the two security men backed into the travel agency, closing the door behind them.

Once outside, Perez texted Farrand, *"Confirmed five men in agency, two as security personnel. They've made us…or at least they're suspicious. Believe they'll make a run for it out the front door."*

"Roger that!" came Farrand's response.

"Okay, sergeant, I want you to guard this exit…don't let anyone leave the agency office through the back door. You don't need to shoot them, just fire warning shots if the door begins to open…hopefully that should be enough to persuade them their only egress is out the front door," said Perez to Sgt. Hernandez.

Hernandez nodded, positioning himself up beside the tall, narrow window to the left of the building's entrance, where he could watch for any activity inside the front hall.

Capt. Perez gave Hernandez a lazy salute, then advanced towards the front of the building, taking up a position at the building's corner, where he'd be clearly visible to Sgt. Farrand, hidden across the street, and from where Perez would be able to maintain intermittent surveillance of the agency's front entrance.

A half-hour went by, then things began to happen. A tall van of German manufacture, painted black and without any commercial markings, pulled up in front of the travel agency. The driver and another man climbed out. The one emerging from the passenger side had on a bullet-proof vest and was carrying a Heckler & Koch MP7 submachine gun. He took up a position at the rear of the vehicle where he could watch the street. Meanwhile, the driver of the van walked over to the agency's front entrance and knocked on the door. The door opened, words were exchanged, then the driver headed to the rear of the van and unlocked the double doors, swinging them wide open.

First to emerge from the agency's office were the two security men who had threatened Perez and Hernandez in the building's front hall. Their guns were concealed, but their attitude of tense alertness made clear they were prepared for opposition if it should appear.

Then came two younger men each carrying a cardboard box. As they loaded them inside the rear compartment of the van, Sgt. Farrand texted Capt. Perez, *"Those two loading the van are the one's we've tentatively identified as couriers."*

"Roger that," replied Perez, *"They're called Olek and Dmytro, and the head guy, who's still inside is called Marius."*

"Should we attempt to interdict the removal operation?" texted Farrand.

Capt. Perez gave the matter some thought, then replied, *"They appear ready for a fight, and I don't think Col. Stone or Col. Appleton wants us starting a major firefight on a quiet Berlin street—so no, we'll let them redeploy...we know their names, the license plate of the vehicle and whatever office lease data is on record at the office of the Berlin Polizei."*

Just as Perez was returning his cell phone to his pocket, a shout rang out from one of the security guards who, having walked to the front of the van, had caught sight of Perez. Before the operative could free his semiautomatic from beneath his jacket, Perez reacted—firing once with the suppressor attached and hitting the operative in his side, the side where Perez believed the man's gun was concealed. The security operative was knocked to the ground by the bullet's impact and began to painfully crawl into the street, seeking the protection of the vehicle's right front wheel and fender.

Meanwhile, the other security man and the guard from the van began hurriedly to reposition themselves behind the street-side of the van, intending to repulse any further attack from that corner of the building. But Perez had already retreated down the walkway—to where Hernandez had taken up a defensive stance behind one of the trees.

"Schnell!" shouted Marius from the travel agency's doorway, urging the two couriers on as they ran back to the office to retrieve what turned out to be the third and final carton containing files that had been hurriedly assembled and boxed. They emerged moments later—one carrying the box, the other at his side, urging him on.

"Help me up!" groaned the wounded security agent, pointing to his fellow office security guard, now crouched down less than two meters away. The security operative looked at the guard from the van, who nodded his assent, then holstered his semiautomatic and made his way forward.

All of this was in the full view of Sgt. Farrand, hunkered down directly across the street. Farrand held his fire, letting the scene play out.

The wounded agent was placed in the back seat of the van. Then the two couriers, having signaled they'd completed the loading of the cartons, were given an affirmative nod from Marius to climb into the van's third row of seats, behind the wounded operative. The driver shut the double doors at the rear of the van then hurried forward. Once he'd climbed behind the wheel and had started the engine, Marius left the protection of the office doorway and rushed to the open rear passenger door on the left side and climbed in. Only then, did the second security operative slide in on the opposite side, next to his wounded associate. The guard with the submachine gun was the last to jump into the van.

"*Abfahren!*" shouted Marius.

The driver nodded, then burned rubber as he pulled away from the curb and sped off down the street.

"*We're clear!*" texted Farrand, before getting up from his crouched position and walking across the street.

Capt. Perez and Sgt. Hernandez came warily out from the side walkway, meeting up with Farrand in front of the travel agency office.

"They didn't bother to close or lock the door," observed Farrand as he pulled the door wide open. "Should we check the place out?"

Perez nodded.

"Christ, the place is a shambles," observed Farrand as the three of them moved about the two-room office complex. A stack of unfolded cardboard cartons and a roll of packaging tape lay on one desk. Desk drawers stood open. Travel posters hung askew on the walls.

"Doesn't look like they left anything behind that we'd be interested in," said Hernandez.

"Not so fast...I think we may have something," called out Perez from the inner office.

"What'd you find?" asked Farrand as he walked in.

"This filing cabinet," replied Perez, pointing to the four-drawer steel cabinet located to the far left of the desk. "It contains client accounts...damn! these guys seem to have actually run a travel agency."

Farrand joined Perez in rifling through the files, "Just like the bookstore in Mitte, the operatives based here were clearly serious about keeping to their cover," observed Farrand, shaking his head.

"Hey captain!" shouted Sgt. Hernandez from the front office.

"What've you got?" asked Perez as he continued to rifle through the files.

"I've been looking at the various travel brochures scattered around the outer office," called out Hernandez. "They're mostly about package tours to Romania, Poland, and other countries of Eastern Europe...you think that's significant?"

"That jives with what we're seeing in these files, captain," said Farrand. "I'd estimate that almost three-quarters of their clientele were people heading to one or another of the Eastern Flank countries."

Perez nodded, then after taking some moments to consider the findings of his two teammates, said, "You're both probably right, but I don't think it takes us anywhere...chances are these files would not have been left behind if they contained information that would compromise their operation."

"I don't know, sir," countered Farrand politely, "What caught my eye was the number of clients making travel arrangements to various parts of Moldova."

"Yeah...I noticed that too," commented Perez, who then shouted, "Sgt. Hernandez, do the travel brochures highlighting the Republic of Moldova focus on any specific towns or regions?"

"Let me check," Hernandez shouted back.

"Sgt. Farrand, why don't you do the same...here, I'll pull all the files with a Moldova link and hand them to you," said Perez.

A quarter of an hour later, the three Delta Force soldiers—temporarily tasked with a NATO counter-intelligence mission in Berlin—pulled up chairs around the desk in the inner office of the travel agency and began to review their findings.

"Well, if they chose to fly their only option seems to have been Chisinau, the capital," said Farrand, looking at his notes. "Those planning on going further...like to Tiraspol...tend to be booked on buses or maxicabs for the final leg," he added.

"Isn't Tiraspol the capital of that Moldovan breakaway enclave of Transnistria?" asked Sgt. Hernandez.

"Yeah, sergeant," replied Capt. Perez as he leaned over and studied the notes Farrand had made. "It's a real flashpoint along the Eastern Flank...even more so than the Republic of Moldova itself...why do you ask?"

"Well, sir, Tiraspol seems to feature prominently in the brochures...almost as much as Chisinau, the capital."

Capt. Perez shrugged, "Hell, why not...it is the second largest town in Moldova...even if it's somewhat cut off from the rest of the country."

"So, you don't figure it means anything, sir?" asked Farrand.

"I didn't say that, sergeant...we'll bring it to Col. Stone's attention...let him assess its significance...if any."

"Okay, are we ready to check out the apartment upstairs?" asked Farrand.

"Why don't you and Sgt. Hernandez take a look...I'll phone in a report to Col. Stone," said Capt. Perez as he pulled out his cell phone.

Farrand nodded, then—with a "come along" gesture to Hernandez—he got up from his chair and headed out of the room.

Chapter Fourteen

Elliott was on his way to the Berlin office of the Federal Intelligence Service when he got Capt. Perez's call.

"Everybody okay?" asked Elliott after Perez identified himself.

"Roger that, sir…though I inflicted a body wound on one of the security men attached to the travel agency staff."

"Start from the beginning, captain."

"We observed activity by members of the agency's staff that we believed involved packing up documents. Our assessment turned out to be confirmed during an encounter with several members of the staff. During that encounter we were able to ascertain that those involved in preparations for a vehicle egress from the neighborhood were five in number. Their roles and given names are as follows: "Marius", person in charge; "Olek" courier #1; "Dmytro", courier #2; "Bogdan", security operative #1; "Miroslav", security operative #2."

"And the injury you report…was it committed during a firefight?" asked Elliott.

"Yes, sir…though it only involved a single shot on my part… taken to counter a lethal threat by security operative #1, Bogdan.

The other travel agency operatives chose not to engage further, and we undertook to disengage."

"What happened next?"

"A late model van with no markings drove up. The driver opened the rear doors to the van and prompted those inside the travel agency to quickly load up all the packed cardboard boxes. A heavily armed guard riding shotgun on the van maintained watch, along with security operative #2. The wounded man was placed inside the van…and shortly afterwards the rest of the travel agency personnel climbed in."

"Colonel, we made no attempt to interdict the van, figuring a firefight involving perhaps a half-dozen or more shooters was not something that could be justified since we were not in danger and we believed any such shooting would make your job more difficult."

"Good thinking, captain," said Elliott. "I take it you got the license plate of the van."

"Roger that, sir. We also took the opportunity to search the premises of the travel agency, and of an apartment located above the office where we believe one or more of the operatives had been living."

"Anything of interest?"

"We're not sure, sir…the agency seems to have been a real one—actually booking travel for various customers. The operatives left behind client files…which we examined."

"The only thing that aroused our attention had to do with client destinations. In general, the agency seems to have specialized in travel to countries we've identified as constituting

NATO's "Eastern Flank". And in particular, there seemed to be a special emphasis on travel to Moldova."

"Hmm…might suggest the agency served a wider espionage function…facilitating the movement of intelligence agents into and out of Berlin that were regarded as friendly with Russia or with other ostensible adversaries of NATO," mused Elliott.

"Couldn't say, sir," replied Perez. "Do you want us to pack up these files and bring them to your residence?"

"Probably not necessary, captain," replied Elliott, "but in any case I'll notify Capt. Becker and let him know the files exist… he may want his men to collect them during their inspection of the premises."

"What about the apartment upstairs…anything come of your search up there?" asked Elliott.

"No, sir. They seemed to have taken extra care to sanitize that location…probably meant they knew it could yield leads to the identification of specific individuals associated with the operation."

"Understand…well…why don't you and your men return to my place and await further instructions," said Elliott. "I'll try to get through Capt. Becker's briefing quickly on what, if anything, his colleagues have learned during interrogation of those in custody, then join you."

"Very good, sir." replied Perez.

Just as Elliott put away his cell phone his ride service driver pulled up in front of the large *Bundesnachrichtendienst* building in central Berlin. He thanked his driver, climbed out, and headed for the building's main entrance.

"Please contact Capt. Ernst Becker and let him know I've arrived," said Elliott to a member of the security staff tasked with screening all visitors. Despite Elliott's NATO counter-intelligence credentials he didn't have clearance to walk into the German foreign intelligence facility unaccompanied. He'd have to hope they could locate Becker then have him come down. Elliott took a seat near the entrance and waited—spending the time reflecting on what Perez had told him while idly studying the various persons who made their way in from the street.

"Glad you could make it, colonel," said Capt. Becker as he approached Elliott. "I'm sorry I wasn't down here when you arrived," he added as they shook hands.

"Not a problem, captain...it gave me a little time to process Capt. Perez's report on what transpired at the Berlin headquarters of the espionage outfit we've been following."

"Good news, I hope," said Becker.

"Well...they've managed to confirm the location has been shut down, but no one was placed in custody and all indications are they'll simply set up shop somewhere else in the city. I'll give you the details later."

"Sorry to hear that, sir...but I might have a line on where they'll show up," said Becker, "but I'm getting ahead of myself... come, let's go up to my office."

Capt. Becker's office was on the fourth floor of the northwest wing, with windows looking out onto an interior courtyard. It was a small, fairly spartan room meant for someone of modest rank. Becker seemed a bit awkward about the fact his guest outranked him.

"So...how's the interrogation going?" asked Elliott in an offhand way...hoping to relax his host.

"Well, sir, we've gotten hardly anything from the Moldovans—Florin and Cristian—and it turns out our two Ukrainians—the couriers, Petro and Andriy—are ethnically Moldovan as well. It seems they've all been well trained to withstand hostile interrogation."

"So...they're professionals...is that what what you're saying?"

"No doubt about it, sir...but we'll keep at it. We did, however, make some progress with the Romanian hand-off agent, Mihai. He pleaded that his role was simply that of a messenger boy...a nobody who was never given covert operational skills or training. And to support his argument he insisted the only thing he'd ever been told—of a confidential nature—was where he should go if for any reason the bookstore's backroom operation had to be moved."

"A safe house of some sort?" asked Elliott.

"That's our impression," replied Becker. "I imagine he felt revealing the location was of no consequence since those intent on using it had now fled or were either in custody or dead."

"I take it you're of a mind that the safe house served a more general purpose...a place to be used by any of the operative units of the espionage group...a place kept available but intended to be used only until more permanent arrangements could be made," said Elliott.

"Mihai wouldn't have known that, surely, but assuming it to be true, there's a chance it's where the headquarters team intends to set up temporary shop."

"We should definitely check it out, captain," said Elliott. "How did he describe it...is it another sort of commercial space?"

"Yes, apparently it is...Mihai said it's an independent insurance brokerage. He says it's located in an older apartment building that's situated on a quiet street northwest of the Alexanderplatz Bahnhoff...here, I'll write down the address for you."

"According to Mihai, the office is in a storefront...to the right of the entrance to the building," Becker added as he handed Elliott the piece of paper with the address.

"So, we've got to assume the insurance broker is in some way connected to the espionage group...though it may be something wholly innocuous...like having received a generous retainer to accommodate the group if and when it becomes necessary," mused Elliott.

"We can have the Berlin Polizie pull the rental agreement... see if there's anything about the lease holder that might link him to these people," said Becker as he picked up the receiver of his desk phone.

"While you're handling the dispatch of a crew to the travel agency and talking with the property registration people, I'll head over to the brokerage," said Elliott, getting up from the chair. "Join us as soon as you can," he added.

"Will you have your team there?" asked Becker as he waited for someone at the police agency to pick up.

"Yeah…I'll alert Capt. Perez and his men," said Elliott. "We'll move against the target just as soon as we can confirm your suspicions, captain."

Becker nodded, then gave a wave as Elliott left his office.

* * *

Elliott awaited the arrival of Capt. Perez and his two sergeants at the south end of the block on which the brokerage office was located. He knew they'd taken a car service from their temporary base on Poststraße and he figured it would be another ten minutes or so before they'd show up. It was the middle of the day and residential streets were largely free of pedestrians given that most people were in their apartments having their midday meal, or simply resting. Elliott wanted to capitalize on that, hoping to avoid bystanders from complicating the assault he was planning.

"*ETA in two minutes,*" texted Perez, prompting Elliott to step away from the corner of the building where he'd been standing, hoping to make himself more visible.

Almost to the minute, a full-sized black sedan pulled up—its car service's logo pasted on the inside corner of the windshield. Capt. Perez opened the front passenger door and climbed out; Sgt. Hernandez and Sgt. Farrand weren't far behind—emerging from the vehicle's back seat through hastily-opened doors. All three had Army-issue Glock 17 semiautomatics holstered beneath loose nondescript windbreakers. Awkward bulges visible in the side pockets of each windbreaker suggested each was carrying extra clips together with an easily attachable noise suppressor. Elliott nodded approvingly.

Once Elliott had finished shaking their hands in greeting, he studied them for a moment, quietly appraising their readiness, then said, "Let's do it."

The four of them—with Elliott in the lead—headed down the side street, towards the building where they hoped to find the Berlin leader, Marius, and his staff.

"Colonel, that looks like the vehicle used in this morning's headquarters removal," said Capt. Perez, pointing to a tall van parked at the curb further down the street.

"I think there's someone standing next to it," said Farrand.

"Yeah, I see him," added Hernandez. "If it's the guy riding shotgun he won't be able to make us, but if it's that security guy Miroslav he'll recognize me and the captain."

"How do you want to handle it, colonel?" asked Perez.

Elliott took out his Beretta and screwed on the suppressor. "I'll approach alone...Sgt. Farrand, you cross to the other side of the street and stay parallel—giving me cover. Captain...you and Sgt. Hernandez prepare to double-time it to the office once I've disarmed or neutralized whatever threat the guy next to the van poses."

"Sir, if it's the same van, there's a good chance the driver is also there...probably sitting behind the wheel," warned Hernandez.

"Good point, sergeant," replied Elliott. "Perhaps Sgt. Farrand you should advance ahead of me. From a vantage point across the street from the van you'll be able to spot the driver—assuming he's there—before I reach the guy standing next to the vehicle. If warranted, you could make a move on the driver just before I came abreast of my target."

"Makes sense, sir!" said Farrand with a nod.

"Okay…let's get underway," said Elliott, quickening his pace.

* * *

As Elliott drew nearer to where the van was parked he intently scrutinized the man standing beside the van, trying to get a sense of who he was. The first thing that struck him was the man's size; he wasn't tall or short—maybe five foot, ten inches—but he had a broad, heavily-muscled torso, and on top of that Elliott suspected he was wearing a bullet-proof vest. The whole effect was one of intimidation, and Elliott concluded the man must be the one Hernandez referred to as the bodyguard who rode shotgun on the van. An incoming text message from Sgt. Farrand, walking ahead of where Elliott was, and consequently noticeably closer to the vehicle, caught his attention: *"License plate confirms it's the van used earlier…the man you are approaching is the bodyguard!"*

Elliott signaled Farrand "message received" with a slight but noticeable nod as he kept walking. When he reached a point no more than a hundred feet from the van he watched as the front door to the brokerage was flung open and two men emerged from inside. The older of the two men, briefcase in hand, headed directly for the van, with the bodyguard on the street hurrying over to open the door for him. The younger of the two men hesitated, turning his attention towards Elliott, and the two men walking briskly behind him. He seemed to squint as he narrowed his focus on to Perez and Hernandez, then with a sharp cry of recognition he pulled out a semiautomatic equipped with a suppressor and began to take aim.

Elliott dove behind a parked car. The man fired two rounds at Perez and Hernandez as they made a mad dash for the closest building entryway. Both shots missed their targets but now the man advanced towards them, his gun clasped in a two-handed shooting grip, hoping to score a hit before either Perez or Hernandez could reach the protection of the entryway, still some distance away. The shooter seemed to have ignored Elliott's presence, probably thinking he was an innocent bystander, and kept his focus on the two men he'd recognized from their encounter earlier that day—an encounter that had led to the wounding of the man's partner.

As the man came close to where Elliott had hunkered down behind the parked car Elliott stood up, and in one fluid motion raised his Beretta, aimed, then shot the man, putting one round in the man's head and two in his upper body.

"Watch out, colonel!" shouted Capt. Perez from where he and Hernandez had sought protection, pointing back towards the parked van.

Elliott turned in time to see the bodyguard reach through the open window of the front passenger door and pull out a Heckler & Koch MP7 submachine gun. As the bodyguard twisted back towards Elliott, racking a round into the chamber in the process, he seemed intent on quickly laying down a burst of automatic fire in Elliott's direction. Then, out of the corner of his eye Elliott saw Sgt. Farrand sprinting across the street, closing on the attacker, his Glock 17 firmly aimed in a two-hand grip. A rapid series of shots were unleashed and Elliott caught a glimpse of the bodyguard going down as he himself desperately sought protection by throwing himself flat on the hard concrete surface of the sidewalk.

As Elliott warily began to stand up, his Beretta at the ready, he heard Farrand resume firing. He immediately began to crouch down, thinking the bodyguard had somehow survived, or someone else in the espionage group had taken up the fight, but when he glanced over at Farrand he saw he was firing at the van, which had pulled away from the curb and was rapidly accelerating in an attempt to escape.

Farrand shook his head in frustration as he lowered his gun, "It's an armored model," he shouted over at Elliott, "I couldn't make a dent in it."

Elliott nodded, then stood up.

"You okay, sir?" asked Capt. Perez as he and Hernandez joined Elliott.

"Yeah, I am…thanks to Sgt. Farrand…you two go on ahead… you'll need to secure the office before someone inside gets any further ideas. I'll check out the two shooters, then join you."

"Yes, sir," said Perez, who signaled Hernandez to accompany him, then broke into a run.

Elliott kneeled next to the body of the first shooter. A search of his pockets confirmed it was the second security man from the travel agency—a guy named Miroslav who happened to be Belarusian. When he reached the inert body of the large man who had been riding shotgun on the van he found Farrand already standing over him.

"The guy's bullet-proof vest deflected two of my rounds, and a couple of them hit him in the legs...it was the round that caught him on the side of the head that finished him off," observed Farrand quietly as Elliott studied the body.

"Let's check his pockets," said Elliott, kneeling down. After some moments searching he found the man's identification. "It says here that he's a Ukrainian named Taras," said Elliott, glancing at the man's passport. "But I wouldn't be surprised if he turns out to be ethnically Moldovan...just like Petro and Andriy...the two couriers we've got in custody," he added knowingly.

"What do you make of the speedy departure of the van?" asked Farrand.

Elliott shrugged, "I caught a glimpse of an older man with a briefcase climbing into the back seat just before the shooter, Miroslav, began firing. If I had to guess, I'd figure it was the espionage group's top man in Berlin...the one called Marius," replied Elliott.

"Sorry I couldn't stop his escape, sir," said Farrand quietly.

"It's okay, sergeant," said Elliott. "Actually, it might turn out to be something of a blessing in disguise. We'll know better once we've interrogated whoever Capt. Perez and Sgt. Hernandez have been able to round up inside, but I'm guessing Marius—if that's who was in the vehicle—is intent on making a beeline to wherever his masters are based. I can't believe he's intent on sticking around in the hopes he can reestablish anytime soon the surveillance and blackmailing operations he'd been running."

Chapter Fifteen

"Capt. Becker, we've got another situation where we'll need one of your collection teams dispatched," said Elliott once he was put through to the man's office.

"Can you give me the particulars, sir," said Becker, scrambling to retrieve a pad and something to write with.

"The bodies of two deceased espionage operatives are lying on the sidewalk close to the entrance to the insurance brokerage. Both were armed and were attempting to fire at my men or myself when taken out by return fire."

"Anything known about their identity?" asked Becker.

"One's Belarusian, the other Ukrainian, captain," replied Elliott. "Both were familiar to us—one being the second security operative attached to Marius' Berlin headquarters; the other was the bodyguard riding shotgun on the van."

"Okay...I'll have a team over there momentarily," said Becker, "but in the meantime are you able to keep bystanders away?"

"I'll keep Sgt. Farrand out front...he'll make sure things don't get out of hand. Right now, though, there's no one on the street except ourselves."

"Good...I'll be right over, colonel. I take it no one in your team was injured...is that right?"

"That's correct, captain...though I haven't yet checked on what's been going on inside the brokerage office—Capt. Perez and Sgt. Hernandez entered the premises some minutes ago."

"Well, I won't keep you...best of luck, colonel," said Becker before breaking the connection.

"Capt. Becker and a couple of units from the Federal Intelligence Services should be here shortly, sergeant...keep an eye on things out here until they arrive," said Elliott as he headed for the entrance to the storefront where the insurance brokerage had its offices.

"Yes, sir," said Farrand.

Elliott entered the front office warily, unsure what he would encounter. The front office, facing out onto the street, was unoccupied and didn't appear to have been disturbed: chairs and desks and other furnishings were still arranged in an orderly manner, and office computers were still on-line, streaming breaking news from around the world. But through the open door to the inner office Elliott could see a bunch of people and paper files strewn across the floor.

"Capt. Perez...please report!" shouted Elliott.

Perez stepped out of the back office and approached Elliott, "Sir, we seem to have interrupted what appears to have been a desperate effort on the part of the people in there to shred all the documents taken from the travel agency."

"How far did they get?" asked Elliott, studying the disorder visible in that part of the back room he could see from where he was standing.

"They appear to have been successful in destroying all the files in two of the cartons...files that contained eavesdropping transcripts that I suspect would have revealed the identities of those being targeted...and in addition, files containing summaries of the intel derived from those transcripts, including probably the names of Planning Center staff vulnerable to blackmail."

"How do you know...did they admit it?" asked Elliott.

"The cartons are labeled, sir...in German."

"What about the other cartons...what do they purport to contain?" asked Elliott.

"There were two other cartons, sir...and based on their labeling one of them—like the first two—contained documents that had originally come from the bookstore. It appears there was an ongoing effort to keep to a minimum the presence of compromising documents in the bookstore's backroom... probably because it was felt the bookstore was more likely to be raided by the authorities than their headquarters in the travel agency."

"So, what does it contain?" asked Elliott impatiently.

"As best I can determine, sir, the box contains miscellaneous scratch pads with notes taken during content analysis of the transcriptions. I suspect there's good intel mixed in with other jottings but it'll probably take analysts some time to ferret it out."

"And the final carton?" asked Elliott.

"That's the one I'm counting on to yield immediately actionable intel, sir," replied Capt. Perez. The label simply says "communications" and from the few sheets I've had a chance to glance at the carton promises to contain an archive of messaging between various organizational units—the bookstore, the Berlin headquarters, individual operatives, and maybe even documents giving us some idea about the espionage group's central headquarters."

"You're saying the contents of this fourth carton, unlike the others, were taken from filing cabinets at the travel agency?"

"I believe so, sir...but there's a problem...when Sgt. Hernandez and I busted in the people in the back room were busily shredding files from the fourth carton, so we don't have its full contents; what's survived may be the less critical papers."

"I understand, captain," said Elliott wearily, "let's go in and take a look."

But as Elliott was about to head for the door, two shots rang out, followed by screams. Both men pulled out their weapons and approached the open door to the back room cautiously. Bunched up against the far wall to the left of the doorway were two women and one man; directly across and to the right of the door another two men were crouched down; and in the middle of the room stood Sgt. Hernandez, bleeding, his gun pointing down at a wounded man lying on the floor, writhing in pain.

"What the hell happened?" shouted Elliott once he and Perez had assured themselves the others in the room were no threat.

"This guy pulled a gun on me," explained Sgt. Hernandez. "He got off one shot before I returned fire."

"You okay?" asked Capt. Perez as he approached his teammate.

"Yeah...it's just a flesh wound," replied Hernandez dismissively.

"Who is he?" asked Elliott.

"The guy's name is Daniel," replied Hernandez. "He's the woman's assistant here at the brokerage."

Elliott looked down at the man. It appeared he'd been hit in the abdomen; blood could be seen seeping through the trousers of his suit. He pulled out his cell phone and put a call through to Capt. Becker.

"Captain...what's your ETA?" he asked once Becker was on the line.

"We've just pulled up, sir."

"Good to know...now we've got another problem...one of the safe house operatives—a young man named Daniel—has incurred a serious abdominal wound...he'll need immediate medical attention."

"I think we've got it covered, sir...the collection team from Federal Intelligence Services includes a paramedic. They report they'll be here momentarily."

"Fine...why don't you join us inside...and tell Sgt. Farrand to come in as well. I imagine you've got a couple of men who can secure the street until the removal van pulls up."

"Will do, sir…just as soon as I have a word with the arriving team's paramedic. He'll want to call in an ambulance and get some more medical help."

"Good…tell him there's also another injured party—one of my men—who'll need patching up."

"Yes, sir," Becker replied before terminating the call.

Elliott put his phone away and began studying the people Hernandez and Perez were now guarding. Sgt. Farrand, who'd made his way into the back office, sidled up beside him and said, "I recognize those two," he said, pointing to two of the men crouching against the opposite wall. "They're the two couriers from the travel agency."

"Yeah, I recognized them also," said Perez. "One's named Olek, the other, Dmytro…they were in the tall van when it left the outfit's headquarters."

"Who are the others?" asked Farrand.

"The older woman," volunteered Capt. Perez, "identifies herself as the proprietress of this establishment…the wounded man, Daniel, is her assistant." Elliott glanced over at the woman—elegantly and expensively dressed in a dark-colored light wool skirt, together with a matching jacket worn over a creme-colored silk blouse.

"And the others?" asked Elliott.

"I'm not sure, sir," replied Capt. Perez, "but if I had to guess I'd say they're probably the two analysts from the bookstore… the ones who escaped when Sgt. White was wounded."

"Well, we'll let Capt. Becker's men figure it all out," said Elliott. "In the meantime, we'll need to examine the papers from carton number four that were saved from shredding...see if they'll lead us further up the food chain."

* * *

An hour passed with Elliott growing increasingly impatient as Capt. Becker's men busied themselves taking notes for a report they'd need to prepare on the events that had taken place both out on the sidewalk and in the rear office. The dead bodies of the two security operatives had been removed, along with any lingering signs of the firefight. And the young brokerage assistant, Daniel, had been rushed to the Intelligence Service's medical clinic for treatment. Sgt. Hernandez insisted on simply being patched up by the paramedics, arguing that he'd have time later to have the flesh wound looked at during a followup visit once he got back to his base outside of Stuttgart.

All that remained before Elliott could begin searching through the contents of the fourth carton was to get Becker to give up any attempt on his part to have the five operatives now in custody to be interrogated on the premises. Finally, after ardent reassurance, Becker got the message that Elliott was content to leave all questioning to Becker's German colleagues, and he promptly began to have his men place the operatives in a van parked outside for transfer to Federal Intelligence Service facilities.

Once they were all gone, Elliott leaned back in his chair and watched Farrand and Perez gather up the various documents strewn across the floor while reflecting on his sense of the growing urgency attached to identifying the outfit involved in sponsoring the eavesdropping operation. Sgt. Hernandez, nursing his injured arm, had taken up sentry duty in the front office of the safe house, ensuring they wouldn't be surprised by the unexpected arrival of any of the various operatives still believed to be on the loose.

"Although the individual files are in disarray, colonel, I think one way to organize them is to sort them along the lines of some of the major folder headings," said Capt. Perez.

"Like what, captain," asked Elliott.

"Well...I think a good number of the documents were originally organized by where they originated...you know... like a communication from the bookstore to Berlin headquarters would be filed with other such messages in a filing cabinet drawer labeled "Bookstore"," replied Perez. "Then, it seems such documents were further sub-divided into groups based upon the destination of the message...like "messages from bookstore to operative X, or to Berlin Headquarters," added Perez.

"Is there some kind of notation that would make it possible to sort them that way?" asked Elliott.

Perez sighed, "Unfortunately, not, sir...at least not that I can see. I think we'll just have to briefly scan the contents of each document then make a judgement call."

"Christ, that'll take forever!" said Elliott, clearly exasperated.

"Sir, what about sorting by language?" asked Sgt. Farrand.

"How do you mean, sergeant?" asked Elliott.

"Well, most of the documents appear to be in either English or German—certainly readable enough—though some look as if they're in Ukrainian or Russian…and a few are in a language I'm not familiar with…here, take a look," said Farrand.

Elliott reached for the document Farrand was holding. Fluent in Ukrainian and familiar with Russian, Elliott could see the document wasn't in one of those languages or in any closely related language. Then it hit him, "I think it's Romanian," he said. "I can spot words that resemble Italian."

"That's what I mean, colonel," continued Farrand, "if only a modest number of documents are in Romanian, we could search for them and ignore the rest."

"You're suggesting that since Moldovans speak and write the Romanian language dispatches in that language might more likely be ones between key members of the outfit's leadership since they tend to be ethnic Moldovans…is that right?" asked Elliott.

"To the exclusion of the rest…yes, sir," replied Farrand. "Only the top man at the bookstore and the store's front clerk have been identified as Moldovan…the others associated with the bookstore operation were either Polish, Latvian, Ukrainian or Romanian. And at Berlin headquarters—in the travel agency— only Marius, the top man, is suspected of being Moldovan…the others we know were either Belarusian or Ukrainian."

"What do you think, captain?" asked Elliott.

Capt. Perez shrugged, "It might work, colonel…the language is easily recognized as a Romance language, which sets it apart from the Germanic and Slavic languages that most of the documents we've got to sort through are written in. And from what we observed regarding itineraries and brochures at the travel agency all indications are that whoever is behind this espionage outfit is likely either based in Moldova or has some sort of close association with Moldovans."

"Okay, let's go with it," said Elliott, getting up from his chair. "I'll leave the three of you here to get on with the job while I head for the embassy to brief Colonel Appleton."

"Sir, it may be helpful if I have Sgt. Farrand relieve Sgt. Hernandez…Hernandez is fluent in Spanish—as I am—making it easier for the two of us to spot documents written in Romanian, given the close resemblance between the languages."

Elliott nodded, "Do that, captain…and while the two of you are at it try reading what's being written. Even if you can only catch a few words in each sentence it may be enough to get a sense of what the communication is about."

"Will do, sir," said Capt. Perez.

* * *

Elliott climbed into the rear seat of the car service vehicle and settled back for the twenty-minute ride to the American embassy. He began to review in his mind what he needed to summarize to ensure Appleton was brought up to speed on the events of the last few hours. A lot had happened since he'd talked with Appleton over coffee at the embassy—there'd been the travel agency operation by Capt. Perez and his team; Capt. Becker's news regarding the existence of a safe house operation at the brokerage; the brokerage encounter itself; and now the search of the files by Perez and Hernandez.

Fortunately, he thought, none of it so far had resulted in police interference, nor had any of it been leaked to the press. But he knew it was only a matter of time before word got out about the unprecedented role of NATO operatives—in the form of US Army special forces—in leading a counter-intelligence operation aimed at combating an international espionage ring working in the heart of Berlin. He also knew it would be up to Appleton to calm the media and to confront the political storm such revelations would invariably bring about. And Elliott knew that for Appleton to be effective he'd have to give the man as upbeat an account of those events as he could honestly muster.

As the vehicle came within sight of the embassy, Elliott began thinking about the fact Appleton, himself, had most likely been engaged for a good part of the day in viewing video surveillance footage taken at the NATO Planning Center. Elliott couldn't help wondering whether the exercise undertaken by Appleton had been useful in identifying which of the Center's staff might have been compromised through the eavesdropping operation.

Elliott shook his head in frustration as he exited the vehicle, cognizant of the narrowing time frame within which he and his team had to work.

Chapter Sixteen

Elliott checked his watch as he entered the US Embassy, noting the time to be about three o'clock in the afternoon. He passed easily through security and made his way to the elevator bank that would take him to the third floor wing where Appleton's office was located. He presented himself to the receptionist charged with screening visitors to the offices of the Defense Attaché, saying, "Lt. Col. Stone to see Col. Appleton...I believe he's expecting me."

"Yes, colonel...let me call and let him know you've arrived," she replied, reaching for the receiver of her desk phone.

Moments later, Appleton stepped out from his office and walked briskly towards Elliott, "Elliott, your timing couldn't have been better," he said as they shook hands. "I believe we might be close to wrapping up the blackmail part of this whole affair."

"What do you mean, colonel?" asked Elliott as he followed Appleton back to his office.

"I'll get into that a bit later...right now, bring me up to date on what's been happening outside...here...take a seat."

Appleton returned to the chair behind his desk as Elliott sat down facing him. "Okay...give me what you've got," said Appleton impatiently.

"Well, sir, events have been moving rather fast...I'll pick up where I left off at the end of this morning's meeting," said Elliott. "As you know, when I left your office I was heading over to the Federal Security Service complex east of the Spree River where I was scheduled to meet up with Capt. Becker."

"Yes, I remember," said Appleton, leaning forward, his elbows on the desk.

"While in transit, I received a report from Capt. Perez that he and his team had observed personnel at the local headquarters of the espionage outfit—a travel agency—preparing to shut the place down. They wisely chose not to engage, but one of the security men spotted Capt. Perez and was about to fire when Perez shot and wounded him. That prompted an immediate rush on their part to be gone, so they completed the transfer of documents and personnel to a waiting van and took off. My men made no effort to stop them. Perez and his team then undertook a search of the premises which proved fruitful in confirming the agency actually handled travel requests...most often for persons heading into eastern Europe."

"Anywhere in particular?" asked Appleton.

"Apparently, based upon the quantity of travel brochures, Moldova seemed to be a destination of particular importance to the agency...and possibly also to its clients," replied Elliott.

"Moldova? That's an odd choice," commented Appleton.

"I agree...it is, sir, but I've a theory that's gaining in credibility about the possible importance of Moldova in our investigation."

"I'll be interested in having you make that case at some point, Elliott, but right now why don't you go on with your brief."

"Yes, sir...when I arrived at Becker's office he informed me they'd managed to get one of the hand-off operatives from the bookstore—a Romanian—to cooperate. He revealed the existence of a safe house north of Alexanderplatz that operated under the guise of being an insurance broker's office. When my team and I arrived, we found the escape vehicle from the travel agency parked outside. As we approached on foot, two security men—recognizing Perez and Hernandez—opened fire. We returned fire, killing both of them."

"Then, the man we believe to be the leader of the Berlin operation—a man called Marius—suddenly slid the van door shut and had the driver take off. Again...we made no effort to stop the vehicle."

"Who'd he leave behind?" asked Appleton.

"Actually, quite a sizable group: the proprietor of the brokerage, her assistant, two couriers from the travel agency, and two others...a young woman and a man—both Polish—who we think might be the transcript analysts from the bookstore. You'll recall two persons—possibly the analysts—escaped during the firefight when Sgt. White was wounded."

"Any of them willing to talk?" asked Appleton.

Elliott shrugged, "Perhaps, sir, but they've been turned over to Capt. Becker and his men for interrogation. Based upon the difficulty Becker encountered getting those placed in custody at the bookstore to talk, I've concluded we'll make better use of our time focusing upon the documents retrieved from the brokerage…they're the papers that had been hurriedly removed from the travel agency."

Appleton nodded.

"There was also another shooting incident at the brokerage, sir…it happened inside the back office of the brokerage. The young man who was employed as assistant to the broker pulled out a gun and shot Sgt. Hernandez. Hernandez returned fire and wounded the man rather seriously. Hernandez, himself, suffered only a superficial flesh wound. Becker called in paramedics from the National Security Service who patched Hernandez up and took the wounded assistant to one of their medical clinics."

"Sorry to hear about Hernandez…is he out of commission?"

"No, sir…he's still on duty…both he and Capt. Perez are sorting through all documents from the travel agency's files written in Romanian, which is close enough to Spanish for them to get some idea of what's being said in the documents."

"Why only Romanian?" asked Appleton, clearly perplexed. "Is it because that's the language easiest for them to get a handle on?"

"No, colonel…though it's true they'd be unable to make any sense of the other eastern European languages used in documents found at the office. And it's also true that some of the material is in German…even English; languages they'd have no difficulty sorting through. No, the reason we've chosen to focus on documents written in Romanian is because it's the language used in Moldova, and it's my feeling that leadership at all levels of the espionage outfit will turn out to be Moldovan, or consist of persons with strong connections to Moldova."

Appleton nodded, "You're thinking it's those documents—above all others—which have the potential of leading you further up the chain of command."

"Yes, sir…that, and the fact they constitute a manageable fraction of the total number of documents still available to us once we were able to shut down their shredding operation. I've got to say, colonel, I believe the principal reason the Berlin chief, Marius, had his people head to the brokerage after closing down the travel agency was to make use of the large shredding machine located there."

"So, this fellow, Marius, must have believed the documents in the files held the potential to unravel the entire operation," said Appleton, "but what makes you assume they wouldn't have shredded the most sensitive documents first?"

"I think they did just that, colonel, but what they seemed to be most concerned about was eliminating any clues as to what kind of intel they'd been successful in capturing. In that sense, they've been quite successful…we're now forced to rely primarily on whatever testimony those who've supplied the intel can give us, which brings us back to the importance of successfully identifying the staffers believed to have been blackmailed into disclosing the intel."

"Well, in that department I believe we've made some progress, Elliott," said Appleton as he pulled out a file from the center drawer of his desk.

"I had my people screen the video footage for the preceding two weeks, focusing on repeated staff pairings—people exiting the building at midday together. Out of the forty-three members of the NATO Planning Center Group about a dozen persons paired up on a more or less regular basis. Towards the end of the two-week period video footage caught a break in that pattern among four of the pairings—two among the civilian military planning specialists, and two among members of the secretarial pool. The four planning specialists quickly reestablished new pairings, as did two of those in the secretarial pool, suggesting in their cases there wasn't really a pattern disruption after all since all that happened was a substitution of one luncheon partner with another...or with several others."

"So you chose to discount them, I take it," said Elliott.

"It wasn't an easy call...especially in the case of the military planners since they were persons most likely to have had access to a broad range of proposed measures to strengthen NATO's military posture along the Eastern Flank," replied Appleton.

"But then who were you left with?" asked Elliott, intrigued.

Appleton referred to one of the pages in the report, "A Latvian woman in her early thirties named Nastashia was one of them. She was hired locally but grew up in Riga. She'd been lunching on a regular basis with an American member of the secretarial pool named Henry Johnson. After that arrangement stopped, Johnson linked up with one of the other male secretaries and continued as before. Nastashia, on the other hand, wasn't observed going out for lunch for a couple of days—probably bringing her lunch with her when she reported for work. Then, when she resumed dining out she was observed leaving the building alone."

"Any other indicators she might be one of the people being blackmailed?" asked Elliott.

"Two things," replied Appleton, "first, her employment dossier indicates she is of Russian extraction, which in itself isn't incriminating, but perhaps makes her more vulnerable to being threatened with disclosure. Second, she served for a short time as a temporary assistant to several senior members of the military staff, giving her greater access to confidential materials than usual for a member of the secretarial pool."

"And the other?" asked Elliott.

"The other one is a Polish woman named Hanna. She'd been lunching regularly with a Romanian woman named Alina who we've no reason to suspect since she quickly joined two other women during the lunch hour once she and Hanna stopped leaving together. Hanna, on the other hand, displayed nervousness in the video footage taken after the breakup, and invariably left the building alone."

"Any corroborating evidence that she might be one of them beyond that of her behavior in the videos?" asked Elliott.

Appleton shrugged, "Not really, Elliott. She had only routine access to classified materials, and had been brought to the Center from Warsaw by the senior Polish military officer serving in the

Planning Group. Presumably, she'd been vetted there before arriving in Berlin to take up her duties."

"I know it's probably out-of-line to suggest it, sir, but might there be more to the relationship between Hanna and the officer who sponsored her than what otherwise appears to have simply been a routine administrative tie-in?"

Appleton leaned back in his chair and nodded reflectively, "You're suggesting she might have had access to classified papers he'd taken home…access during trysts in his apartment."

"It's a possibility, sir," said Elliott.

"Well, if it's true, that certainly would explain her nervousness…knowing that if she were to be found out it would not only jeopardize her future but that of her lover," said Appleton.

"So, how would you suggest we proceed?" asked Elliott.

Appleton sighed, "No way we're going to get around the fact we'll need some sort of proof our suspicions aren't simply a lot of hot air."

"Why don't we press them…get each of them in a room and confront them with our suspicions…see how they react," said Elliott.

Appleton nodded, "It might work…if they complain we're harassing them we can blame the whole questioning thing on it being one of the Center's periodic need to do a security check of the staff…yeah…I like it…let me call over and set it up," he added as he picked up the phone.

* * *

It was half past four by the time Col. Appleton and Elliott were ready for their first suspect to appear. They'd been given use of a committee room on the ground floor of the NATO Planning Center's headquarters on Jagerstraße.

"We'll talk with Nastashia first," said Appleton, opening up the young woman's personnel file.

There was a gentle knock on the door of the committee room, then the door was opened and a woman stepped through who Elliott figured was probably in her late twenties. She had long blond hair which she wore piled high on her head and pinned. Her outfit was youthful and simple, and accompanied by minimal jewelry. She took the seat offered by Col. Appleton then stared nervously at the two men seated across from her.

"Let me begin, Nastashia, by advising you that we understand the intense pressure our adversaries place upon all of us in their pursuit of classified intelligence, especially intelligence relating to military issues. What is critical is not whether we inadvertently or under duress divulge information we shouldn't have, but in learning what intel they've been successful in acquiring…however they've managed it. Do you understand what I'm saying?" asked Appleton.

"Yes, sir," she replied quietly.

"Good…now it's come to our attention that through some sort of lapse on your part during a lunch break you were overheard by a hostile espionage agent divulging classified information to your luncheon partner. This may have occurred more than once…though that's not important. What is important is that you apparently revealed enough to make yourself vulnerable to being blackmailed. What we're here to learn is what you eventually turned over to these people in exchange for not having yourself publicly implicated."

Nastashia became rigid, then tears began to stream down her face, "I'm so sorry, sir...I didn't think I was doing anything wrong talking with Henry since he seemed to be familiar with such things himself...I guess I thought we were just talking shop. It didn't occur to me that anyone could overhear what I was saying."

"We understand how this might have happened, Nastashia, and I'm sure you've learned your lesson, but what we need to know now is something of the circumstances surrounding their approach at the time you were threatened with blackmail," said Appleton in a kindly manner.

Nastashia took a handkerchief from a pants pocket and wiped the tears from her face, then taking another minute to compose herself she began, "A woman I'd never seen before came up to me in the U-bahn station and asked me in fluent Latvian to listen to something on her smart phone. I thought she needed me to translate something...you, know...something in Russian or Latvian maybe that needed to be translated into English. What I heard was my own voice talking with Henry...saying things which in that context sounded ominously inappropriate. When she sensed I understood the severity of my indiscretion she became all business-like, threatening to inform my employer if I didn't cooperate with those she worked for."

"Did she identify the person or organization with whom she worked?" asked Elliott.

"No, sir…and I didn't ask. I was so scared."

"Then what?" coached Appleton.

"Then she ordered me to assemble information on the plans being prepared in the Center, and assured me that if the quality of the information was sufficiently high there would be no further contact required and I would be left alone."

"So what did you manage to give her, and how did you deliver it?" asked Appleton.

"Even though I knew it was a risk, I decided that initially I'd try to avoid giving her any information on actual plans being prepared by the Center, hoping she would be satisfied simply knowing what the Planning Center intended to focus on," said Nastashia.

"Can you be more specific?" asked Appleton.

"I went through files I had access to and copied topical headings highlighted as agenda issues. I can't remember all of them but the report I prepared for her included references to a NATO Black Sea fleet, also the Center's interest in addressing chain-of-command issues such as the authority of the Supreme Allied Commander in Europe, whether to subordinate NATO forces to a single chain of command, how best to adjust operational level commands…things like that."

"What else?" asked Elliott, resuming his questioning.

"Well, I mentioned infrastructure topics like questions of road transport and railway upgrades needed in connection with the movement of NATO forces along the Eastern Flank, and the upgrading of military bases. The only other things I remember including were an interest in updating contingency plans regarding the Eastern Flank and the need to adjust NATO's nuclear policy on tactical weapons in the light of new realities."

"How was this intel received by your contact and her superiors…did your information satisfy them?" asked Appleton.

Nastashia looked downcast—almost as if she was reliving her conversation with the woman, "No…she said what I'd given them was insufficient…that they wanted me, in particular, to supply them with details on changes to NATO's nuclear policy on tactical weapons."

"Where did this follow-up conversation take place?" asked Elliott.

"In the U-bahn station on Leipzigerstraße, near Friedrichstraße. She knew I used that station on the way home from work. That was also the place where she first confronted me."

"Did you comply with her demand?" asked Appleton, clearly worried.

"No, sir…I only received her instructions a few days ago… she told me she'd give me a week to get the information…we're to meet in the U-bahn station at the end of the week…anyway, I didn't believe I'd be able to access such information even if I'd wanted to. I told her that, but she told me to find a way."

Both Appleton and Elliott were visibly relieved.

"You needn't worry any further about this female agent, Nastashia," said Appleton gently, "she's either in federal custody or in hiding. The espionage operation she's a part of has largely been dismantled. But you must understand, what you've done constitutes a criminal offense under German law. However, since your involvement began naively and proceeded under duress I'm of the opinion a reprimand placed in your file should be sufficient—assuming, of course, that you can assure Col. Stone and myself that you're not about to make such a mistake again."

"Oh, no, sir! I'll never utter a word outside the building about what goes on there...ever!"

"Very well, Nashtashia, you're free to return to your work... this interview is now over," said Appleton as he closed the woman's dossier and pushed it away.

"Thank you, sir," she said as she stood up, hesitated awkwardly, not sure she was actually being dismissed, then— prompted by a nod from Appleton—hurried towards the door and let herself out.

"What do you make of it, Elliott?" asked Appleton once she was gone.

"Frankly, I think they were probably delighted to get what amounted to our operational agenda at the Center," said Elliott. "It meant they could fine tune their demands, designating specific victims to secure specific classified information...very much in the way they pressed Nastashia to get intel on tactical nuclear weapons deployment."

"What you're saying is that they now have a valuable overview of what this Center is all about," said Appleton.

"Indeed, they have, sir, but it looks like we've shut their operation down early enough to avoid having our secrets pass to them...that is, unless our other possible suspect turns out to have been under their control over a longer period," commented Elliott, worriedly.

"You think that may have been the case?" asked Appleton.

"I do, sir…and the reason I'm worried is having watched as Marius, the Berlin chief of operations, rushed out of the brokerage and into an escape vehicle parked at the curb just as our presence was detected. What was worrisome about it was the fact he was holding a briefcase in a grip so tight that it seemed to be of special importance. In contrast, he didn't seem a bit concerned about what would happen to all those members of his staff left behind in the brokerage."

"I see your point, Elliott…and should we suppose Nastashia to be "PC-1", or Planning Center informant No. 1, in the code used by the espionage team, then the information she supplied would probably have been designated "DOC-1", or Document No. 1. And that would suggest this Polish woman, Hanna—if she turns out to be implicated—is probably "PC-2", or Planning Center informant No. 2.

"I'd go along with that, colonel," said Elliott, "and we know something about what PC-2 has already given to the espionage outfit thanks to Capt. Perez' intercept of the packet he picked up at the dead drop in the restroom of the restaurant after following the courier from the bookstore."

"I think we can use that to our advantage in questioning this second suspect," said Appleton, getting up from his chair. "Let's call her in."

Chapter Seventeen

"Vera, could you let Hanna know we're ready for her," said Appleton once the German woman in charge of the secretarial pool came on line.

"I'm sorry, sir, but Hanna doesn't seem to be in the office... perhaps she's already on her way," replied Vera.

"Well, could you have someone try to locate her on the off chance she's not heading our way?"

"Of course, sir...I'll send Nastashia...she knows Hanna was scheduled to be up next for an interview."

"Thank you, Vera...let me know once you find her," said Appleton who then broke off the call.

Appleton shook his head, "It seems Hanna is temporarily unavailable...we'll give her five minutes or so, but if she doesn't show up we'll have to reschedule."

"You think that's wise, sir? She's likely to be a key part of our investigation...I'd recommend we make an effort to find her before putting off the interview," said Elliott.

Appleton nodded quietly as he thought about Elliott's suggestion, then reached for his cell phone and called over to the secretarial pool, "Vera, Colonel Stone and I are anxious to get our interview with Hanna done today…any chance you can expedite the search?"

"Sir, things are in a state of confusion…Col. Nowak's military aide, Capt. Kowalski, has just raised the alarm; he says Col. Nowak is dead…apparently stabbed to death in his office!" said Vera excitedly.

"What? When did he discover the body?"

"Apparently, only moments ago…he's asking for you."

"Tell Capt. Kowalski I'm coming right up…have him meet me in Col. Nowak's office…immediately!"

"Yes, sir…should I continue to have someone look for Hanna?"

"Yes…and inform the Landespolizei officers at the entrance to prevent anyone from leaving!"

"Yes, sir…I'll get right on it!" said Vera, who then sighed heavily, "To think we have a murderer in our midst…it's scarcely believable."

"What the hell is going on?" asked Elliott once Appleton put down his phone.

"Somebody has killed Col. Nowak…stabbed him apparently…let's get up there!"

The two men gathered up their notes and rushed out of the ground floor interview room. Senior military staff at the Center had their offices on the second floor of the building. Appleton and Elliott chose not to head for the elevators but hurried instead over to the staircase where, taking two stairs at a time, they quickly reached the upstairs hallway and spotted Capt. Kowalski standing next to the door to Col. Nowak's office.

Other staffers were also out in the hallway, having been alerted to what had happened.

"Show me!" ordered Appleton as he motioned for Capt. Kowalski to lead the way.

Col. Nowak's body was lying on the carpet in the area just inside his office, not far from the doorway. The body was lying at an awkward angle, the hilt of a popular brand of tactical assault knife clearly visible protruding from just below the ribs.

"The knife is Col. Nowak's," said Capt. Kowalski, quietly. "I recognize it as the one he kept on his desk to open letters with. He said it was the one he always had with him when on tactical manuevers."

"Have you notified the Landespolizei?" asked Appleton after kneeling down to check for a pulse.

"No, sir…I was waiting for you to make that determination," replied the captain.

"Well, go ahead and notify them, captain…this isn't something we can handle on our own," said Appleton.

"Yes, sir," replied Kowalski who immediately took out his cell phone to make the call.

While Kowalski was informing the Berlin Landespolizei, Elliott pulled Appleton off to the side and whispered, "Colonel, I wonder whether Nowak somehow learned of our possible interest in Hanna in connection with the espionage operation we've been trying to shut down…maybe Hanna mentioned something to him about her forthcoming interview…or maybe just idle office gossip caused him to worry…in any case, I think we shouldn't discount her involvement in this matter."

"What are you saying, Elliott, that he might have confronted her?"

Elliott shrugged, "It's a possibility, sir. I think we need to inquire whether anybody—particularly Hanna—was seen going into or out of Nowak's office sometime this afternoon... especially in the interim between when Nowak was last seen alive and when Kowalski discovered the body."

Appleton nodded, "We'll ask Kowalski...he'll probably know."

Ten minutes passed before Kowalski was able to get off the phone to the police. He pocketed his cell phone and turned to Appleton, "They're sending homicide detectives, a coroner, and a criminal investigation unit, sir...they say they'll be here shortly. Shall I task someone to meet them at the entrance?"

"Yes, have one of your colleagues go down," replied Appleton, pointing to a group of captains huddled together a short distance away.

Appleton watched as Kowalski went over and talked with the men, then he turned back toward Appleton and nodded. Moments later, the military aide from Germany broke free from the group and hastened towards the staircase. Kowalski walked back to where Appleton and Elliott were standing, "Capt. Kruger has volunteered to serve as escort to the police, sir."

"Good," replied Appleton absently, "I'll need you to remain here to secure the area."

"Very well, sir," replied Kowalski.

"Before I leave, captain, I need to ask when was the last time you saw Col. Nowak alive?"

Kowalski shrugged, "He and I had been in a meeting together earlier this afternoon…so I'd say he probably headed back to his office around three o'clock…about an hour or so ago."

"I take it you didn't have an occasion to monitor who might have visited him after that time…am I right?" asked Appleton.

"That's correct, sir, my office is too far down the hall… however, you might have better luck asking that clerical assistant who often works with him, the one named Hanna. She frequently comes to his office…you know, to bring him reports or to receive instructions."

"Think back, captain, did you happen to see Hanna here in the hallway at the time you and the colonel were heading back to your offices?" asked Appleton.

Kowalski shook his head, "No, sir…I'm quite sure she wasn't out here waiting for him when we returned."

Appleton nodded, "Thank you, captain…we'll leave you to manage things…text me if I'm needed."

"Can I ask where you'll be, sir?"

"Col. Stone and I have some inquiries to make downstairs, but I imagine we'll shortly be making our way to my office, captain."

"That is most helpful, sir…thank you,"

Appleton and Elliott took the stairs down to the ground floor and walked over to where the secretarial pool had its offices. They spotted Vera talking animately with several of the other secretaries as soon as they entered.

"Vera, could we have a minute?" asked Appleton.

Vera glanced in their direction, then broke free of the others and rushed over, "Col. Appleton, sir, I've just learned that Hanna received a call from Col. Nowak shortly after three o'clock demanding that she come up to his office!"

"How do you know?" asked Appleton.

"The call was taken by one of the other girls and the colonel's message given to Hanna when she returned to the office after delivering some documents," replied Vera. "Then about half past three she returned briefly…nobody has seen her since," added Vera, worriedly.

"I suspect she's left the building," commented Elliott.

"We'll check," replied Appleton, then, turning to the secretarial pool supervisor, he said, "Thank you, Vera…you've been most helpful. I know it'll be difficult, but I'm counting on you to keep the others as calm as possible during the lockdown. I'm afraid the police investigation may take some time."

"Do you think Hanna had something to do with this horrible crime?" asked Vera in a tone that betrayed her growing sense of shock.

"We simply don't know," replied Col. Appleton soothingly, "and on the off chance Hanna shows up please call me immediately…will you do that?"

"Yes, sir!" replied Vera emphatically, then watched as Appleton and Stone left the secretarial pool area, heading in the direction of the building's main entrance.

"Let's hope the two officers of the Landespolizei who are stationed outside are among those regularly assigned this duty and prove to be familiar enough with the staff that they can recall who've already left the building," said Appleton as he and Elliott passed through the entrance doors and approached the two men.

"Excuse me, officers, do you have a minute?" asked Appleton.

The two officers came to attention and the one in charge said, "Yes, Herr Appleton, what is it you wish?"

"I know you've been instructed to prevent anyone from leaving the building and we're certainly not interested in countermanding that order...no, what we'd like to know is whether a tall woman in her mid-thirties, with long blond hair, might have left the building sometime within the last hour?"

The two police officers conferred with one another briefly, then the senior officer said, "It is possible...yes...I didn't notice such a person, but my partner is sure he did."

"Did you get to know some of the people who work here?" asked Elliott.

The senior officer shrugged, "Not usually, sir. People are in a hurry and don't take notice of us...though a few will wish us a good day."

"And are there some that for one reason or another stick clearly in your mind?" pressed Elliott.

Again the senior officer shrugged, "Yes...some do...Col. Appleton, of course, and some of the Germans."

"And some of the women...the pretty ones," said the junior officer with a knowing smile.

"Is that why you believe you've seen the woman I've described?" asked Appleton.

The junior officer nodded, "She is very striking to look at, sir...and she smiles at us as she passes."

"Did she smile at you today?" asked Appleton.

The junior officer shook his head, "That is perhaps why I remember her, sir...she seemed not herself...preoccupied...not at all the way she usually is."

"But you don't remember her...is that correct?" Appleton asked the senior officer.

"No...I don't recall her having left the building, but I might have been distracted by something or someone...in any case, I trust my colleague's recollection in the matter...he is very observant...especially when it comes to pretty women."

"Well, thank you, officers...you've been a big help," said Appleton, shaking their hands. "Somebody will let you know when it's okay to allow those in the building to leave."

As Elliott followed Appleton back into the building he said, "You really think it's necessary to keep everybody from leaving, colonel...it's becoming fairly clear that Hanna is our primary suspect."

"I don't disagree with you, Elliott, but I don't think we've reached a point where we'd feel comfortable voicing our suspicions...let's go up to my office and talk it through...see if we can make sense of her possible involvement in the killing."

Just as Elliott and Appleton reached the second floor landing, one of the civilian military planning specialists intent on rushing downstairs stood aside impatiently to let them pass, saying, "The police have arrived!"

Appleton nodded in acknowledgement but said nothing. He and Elliott then walked calmly down the hall, past the staffers bunched together near the door to Col. Nowak's office. Appleton unlocked the door to his office and the two men entered. Appleton headed for his desk chair while Elliott sat down in one of the two chairs facing Appleton's desk.

"Okay, Elliott, take a stab at making sense of this crime," said Appleton once he got comfortable in his chair.

Elliott gave himself a moment or two to organize his thoughts, then said, "If we're to assume Hanna is the one who killed Col. Nowak then we've also got to assume she's more than just an innocent victim of blackmail like Nastashia."

"You're suggesting she's some sort of professional operative?" asked Appleton.

"It would make sense, colonel…she was sponsored by an all too credulous Col. Nowak while the two of them were still in Warsaw. If we assume Hanna managed to seduce the colonel, then persuades him she'd be available to him sexually throughout his posting to Berlin if he could manage to get her into the Planning Center's clerical pool, she'd be in a position to perform two functions benefitting the espionage outfit she worked for: single out the most likely persons working at the Planning Center who would serve as good subjects for eavesdropping, then get that information to the spotter positioned outside; and second, during evening trysts at Nowak's apartment she'd be in a good position to secure access to any top secret documents Col. Nowak foolishly might have brought back home to work on in the evening."

"But how could it have gone all wrong…so wrong that it ended up with her killing him?" asked Appleton.

"Remember our earlier conversation about Nowak possibly learning of our scheduled interview, then being informed he'd called Hanna to his office shortly after three o'clock this afternoon. I think Col. Nowak was feeling guilty. Perhaps he'd regularly been taking classified documents back to his apartment, and only after he'd learned of Hanna's possible involvement in disclosing privileged information did he put two and two together and suspect she'd surreptitiously gained access to his papers while he was asleep. I imagine he called her to his office to confront her with his suspicions and threatened to inform on her."

"I don't know, Elliott," began Appleton skeptically, "she could easily have simply denied it…to our knowledge there wasn't any hard evidence to support his suspicions. Hell, we hadn't even met with her, much less discovered anything incriminating in her answers."

Elliott shrugged, "It's a good point, sir…the only way I can get around it is to suppose she knew a targeted investigation by NATO counter-intelligence would almost certainly have revealed a history of association with questionable persons, thereby making her denials no more than a temporary fix. Fearing being placed immediately in custody she lashed out at Nowak, hoping to give herself time to escape."

"Yeah, but I have to believe she'd already been investigated by NATO counter-intelligence…even before being recommended by Col. Nowak," argued Appleton.

"I suspect you're right, colonel, but the level of due diligence for a routine appointment to the secretarial pool might not have been sufficient to penetrate the protective back story she and her superiors may have conjured up. No…she must have figured Nowak's accusations would trigger a full-blown investigation… one she didn't expect to survive, metaphorically speaking."

"Okay…let's assume you're on to something, Elliott," said Appleton, "there's still the matter of the killing…not too many people are able to react with such cool-headedness, and at the same time possess the kind of knowledge of killing that would make them confident they'd succeed with the weapon at hand."

"Sir, if you turn the argument around you'd see that the killing is itself evidence of the involvement of an operative who's been professionally trained…someone taught how to react in times of danger. Such an operative would have had no compunction about ending Col. Nowak's life given her fear that to do otherwise would end her usefulness and result in her incarceration. And it goes without saying that her training would have included mastery of weapons used in personal defense, and how to improvise when circumstances demanded it."

Appleton leaned back in his chair and nodded, then said, "I've one last question, Elliott…why today…why not wait until after we'd had a chance to question her before confronting Hanna with his suspicions? What drove him to push the panic button?"

Elliott got up from his chair and began to pace, "Two things keep coming to mind that seem linked to a possible answer to your question, colonel. One is the vivid image I carry with me of Marius rushing out to his escape vehicle at the brokerage earlier today, griping his briefcase as if his life depended on it. And the other is the bookstore courier—the Ukrainian named Petro—who was followed by Sgt. Hernandez as he serviced a dead drop at Humbolt University just before we shut down the bookstore operation."

"Go ahead," said Appleton.

"You'll recall that by the time Hernandez caught and subdued the courier he'd already made the document drop. When Hernandez threatened him with bodily harm if he didn't divulge the location of the dead drop the courier persuaded Hernandez not to bother since what was deposited was a duplicate of what was deposited at the other dead drop—the one Capt. Perez had visited. Hernandez bought that story and didn't insist on being taken to the Humbolt University dead drop. I now think that was a critical mistake."

"In what way?" asked Appleton.

"This is where the behavior of Col. Nowak begins to make sense," replied Elliott. "Let's assume that the night before last he took home an unusually important document...one that laid out the complete preliminary plan for strengthening NATO's Eastern Flank, with hard numbers for NATO's Response Force, for its Very High Readiness Joint Task Force, for the Follow-on Forces Group, as well as for the maritime and air component elements tasked in supporting roles. And let's assume that it also happened to be a night Hanna stayed over."

"I don't know, Elliott, he'd be taking a big risk...that document only came into existence less than four days ago," argued Appleton.

"I understand your objection, colonel, but hear me out," replied Elliott.

"In this hypothetical scenario Hanna slips out of bed well after Nowak falls asleep, quietly steps out of the bedroom and over to where Nowak has left his briefcase. Having on earlier occasions watched surreptitiously as Nowak entered the simple code unlocking the case, she uses that knowledge to gain access to its contents. She quickly photographs the document, page by page, using her smart phone, then returns the document to the case and re-locks it."

"The following morning both she and Col. Nowak return to the NATO Planning Center together. As a member of the clerical pool she has access to document preparation equipment and uses it to scan and print out the full report she had copied the night before. Once that's done, she deletes the document from her smart phone so there would be no evidence of her involvement in the document's dissemination, should it ever come to light."

"Then, after leaving the building at the end of the work day, yesterday evening, Hanna goes directly to the bookstore we've been watching and makes the handoff. Assuming she made the handoff sometime close to five o'clock, only Sgt. White would have been on surveillance duty, and he would have been stationed in the alley, not at the front entrance."

"I think I follow you," said Appleton, allowing his chair to spring forward as he eagerly took up Elliott's scenario. "You think it was that report which the courier heading for Humbolt University deposited at the dead drop later yesterday evening… the one that was successfully collected by the Headquarters' courier who had been observed leaving the travel agency shortly afterwards."

"Yes, I do," replied Elliott, "and I believe it was that report that made it so critical for Marius to move to the brokerage safe house this morning once he became aware of our surveillance. But it was his desperate attempt at escape from the brokerage safe house this afternoon that really became fixed in my mind; it was a foolhardy sprint on Marius' part—from the brokerage's front office to the escape vehicle. He could easily have been shot as we engaged in a firefight with his security personnel."

"So, you think this guy Marius appreciated the high value of Hanna's document and was bound and determined to get it to his superiors," said Appleton.

"Yes, and that's where Col. Nowak comes back into the picture," said Elliott. "The office scuttlebutt that you, sir, had launched a counter-intelligence operation probably got him thinking about whether his personal conduct could in any way have contributed to what he must have imagined was some kind of institutional vulnerability. That, in turn, might have led him to rethink the practice of taking top secret documents home…especially documents as critical as the one he'd taken home the night before last. Then this afternoon, out of the blue, he learns his lover—Hanna—has been scheduled to undergo interrogation in less than an hour in connection with the counter-intelligence operation. He orders her to immediately come to his office, confronts her with his suspicions and, unsatisfied with her response, informs her she's to be detained."

"And that's when she kills him," said Appleton, nodding. "I see how it all hangs together, Elliott...so, what's out next move?"

"If we're to go forward with this line of reasoning, colonel, we'll need to get some sort of corroboration for whatever parts of the scenario are capable of being checked out. First off, I think we need to ascertain whether Hanna can be located here in Berlin, and if so, whether she has an explanation for her abrupt departure from the building. If she's not to be found, then I believe we can proceed under the assumption she's fled... probably back to Poland. Clearly, the Landespolizei will have to examine her residence...see whether there's any incriminating evidence such as blood-stained clothes, though I doubt she'd be so careless."

"Well...I see I have my work cut out," said Appleton wearily. Then, after a further moment of reflection, he slowly came to his feet and stretched. "I'll inform the Landespolizei teams down the hall of our suspicions, then instruct senior staffers to inform everybody they're free to leave the building. What's your next step, Elliott?"

Elliott shook his head, "That's a good question, colonel. I guess I'll keep with the scenario we've put together and assume Hanna and Marius have taken flight. After checking with my team, and with Capt. Becker of the German Federal Intelligence

Agency I'll try to figure out a way to follow the trail of the espionage operatives and hope in doing so to intercept that document before it gets to whoever is its intended recipient."

"Good…I'd hoped you'd say that," said Appleton as he shook Elliott's hand. "Keep me informed…let me know how I can help."

Chapter Eighteen

Elliott sank into a comfortable leather chair in the room his wife had designated as his writing study, then punched in Capt. Ernst Becker's cell phone number. Elliot had gone directly home after leaving the NATO Planning Center, confident that Appleton and his subordinates could handle the police inquiry now underway. He sighed as he waited for Becker to pick up. It had been a long day, and although he knew he should get some rest, he felt he couldn't stand down until he got hold of some kind of intel that would point him in the direction of the two Polish agents who had made good their escape. He hoped Becker would have something for him.

Captain, it's Col. Stone," said Elliott once Becker came on the line.

"Yes, colonel...I suppose you're calling to inform me of the homicide at the Planning Center...a dreadful development! I got word of it through a contact with the Berlin Landespolizei...any way I can help?"

"Actually, captain, I'm hoping you can. What your contact probably didn't tell you, since we've kept it a bit under wraps, is that our primary suspect for the killing is a member of the

Center's secretarial pool…a Polish woman named Hanna. We believe she's a professional operative connected to the espionage group we've been tracking. To give you a little of the back history, she apparently worked her way into the affections of Col. Nowak a few weeks before he was posted from Warsaw to the Center, persuading him to have her assigned to the secretarial pool so that their illicit relationship could continue. We believe she somehow managed to access top secret documents he'd brought back to his apartment in his briefcase. Fear of disclosure by Nowack apparently prompted her to kill the man, then take steps to avoid being detained…at least that's the scenario we're working with right now."

"Jesus! You're saying you think there's been some kind of major security leak?"

"That's our belief, captain. So what I'm hoping you can do is to lean on the two Polish nationals you've got in your custody…Magda and Wiktor…and get them to tell whether or not there's some sort of headquarters or safe house in Warsaw, or elsewhere in Poland, that agents use when returning from field operations. I'm not that conversant with German criminal law, captain, but if it's true that the seriousness of the theft of state or NATO secrets matters in how the courts determine the severity and length of incarceration, you might wish to reveal Hanna's alleged intelligence coup and how it could very well affect the two of them."

"I understand, colonel," said Becker soberly. "We've spent very little time on those two, believing them to have simply been analysts…not active espionage agents. I'll get our interrogators on it immediately."

"Thanks, captain…let me know as soon as you have something…I'm back at my apartment waiting for my team to show up."

"Very well, sir," replied Becker before breaking off the call.

Elliott put his cell phone down, then looked at his watch; Capt. Perez's text message had him and his men arriving at the apartment within the hour. He decided to use the intervening time to shower, put on some fresh clothes then order in something for the four of them to eat.

* * *

Elliott was in the kitchen unwrapping the take-out food that had just been delivered when Capt. Perez and his men stepped into the apartment.

"I'm in here!" shouted Elliott, beckoning them to join him in the kitchen. As they took seats around the kitchen table Elliott glanced at them, noting the haggard expressions on their faces. "Looks like you're all about as tired as I am…hope the Romanian transcripts produced intel of some value."

"We think we found something we can use, colonel," said Capt. Perez wearily. "You want us to lay it out for you now?"

"No…let's eat first…and while you're eating I'll bring the three of you up to date on what's been happening over at the NATO Planning Center," replied Elliott.

Elliott had ordered freshly prepared pasta with a meat sauce, a vegetable salad and bottled beer from a nearby Italian restaurant. Perez, Hernandez and Farrand ate quietly and listened while Elliott—setting aside his own attention to the food in front of him—gave his men a detailed account of the killing and what he believed led up to it.

"So, you figure both Marius and this Hanna woman are on the run...and most likely heading for Poland...is that right, sir?" asked Perez, once he and his men had finished eating.

Elliott nodded, "It makes the most sense, captain...they both had access to vehicles—we know Marius escaped in the tall van with a driver, and Hanna is reported to own a private automobile. If they were heading to Poland they could have crossed the international border into Poland in just an hour and a half after leaving Berlin, assuming they took the A12 highway and used the Oder River crossing. And after another three and a half hours they could already be in Warsaw."

Perez took a moment to think about the time frame Elliott had laid out, then said, "Given when we observed Marius heading away from the brokerage safe house, it's likely he's already made it to Warsaw if that was his destination. And assuming the woman agent left the Center at about three-thirty, went to her apartment to pack and to retrieve her car, she'd probably been able to get underway by about four or four-thirty. Given what time it is now, it's likely she's somewhere about midpoint between the Polish border with Germany and Warsaw, with an ETA in Warsaw of about an hour and a half from now."

Elliott nodded, "That's what I figure."

"Any intel on the likelihood they're actually heading for Warsaw?" Asked Sgt. Farrand.

Elliott shrugged, "I've got Capt. Becker working on it… there are two Polish operatives in his custody…we're hoping he can get them to give us some sense of what resources—like safe houses or headquarters—the espionage outfit maintains in Poland…if any."

"We may be of some help in that department, colonel," said Perez. "The transcripts we went through at the brokerage…the ones in Romanian…included a handful that make reference to Warsaw. No other locations in Poland are referenced in the documents we looked at."

"Could you work out the context?" asked Elliott.

Perez shrugged, "Usually it's something about a house owned by a guy named Alexandru."

"What else do we know about this guy?" asked Elliott.

"That's the funny thing, colonel, the guy's name also pops up in connection with references to the Transnistria region of Moldova," replied Capt. Perez.

"Yeah, and Tiraspol, the capital of Transnistria is where a number of the communications we looked at seem to originate," said Sgt. Hernandez.

"What do you make of it?" Elliott asked Capt. Perez.

"Well, sir, it strengthens the theory we'd been developing ever since we searched the travel agency…you'll recall that the client files left behind at the agency gave us the impression that one of the more popular destinations of its clients were to locations in Moldova. And a cursory look through the piles of travel brochures lying around in the agency made it clear that travel to Moldova was being pushed far more energetically than to other eastern Europe countries. What I'm trying to say, colonel, is that Moldova...especially the capital city of Tiraspol in Transnistria...should be high on our list of possible places where the espionage outfit's main headquarters might be located," said Perez.

"I hear what you're saying, captain, and I think it makes sense," said Elliott. "But our first priority is—if at all possible—to intercept the documents Marius is carrying in his briefcase. It may turn out that both of the agents we're tracking merely plan on using Warsaw as a place to catch a plane to somewhere else...maybe even to Moldova. But considering how out-of-the-way that country is, especially the Transnistria region, I've got to believe the espionage outfit we're trying to fold up has got some sort of base of operation in a more central place...a place like Warsaw...even if it's only a way station."

"You thinking maybe we should plan on heading into Poland or Moldova, colonel?" asked Sgt. Farrand in his typical laconic fashion.

"Only if we get some hard evidence there's a specific location we can zero in on, sergeant," replied Elliott. "But one thing's for certain, we all need some rest. Let's give ourselves tonight to get refreshed, then revisit the question of whether or not we should head into eastern Europe first thing tomorrow morning...that sound like a plan?"

"Hooah!" shouted Elliott's team, then all three of them got up from the kitchen table and headed for their temporary digs in the first of the three large rooms that formed the principal floorplan of the apartment.

Elliott remained behind to clear away the take-out dinner and tidy up the kitchen. He was almost finished with the task when his cell phone rang.

"Col. Stone here!" said Elliott briskly, identifying himself to the caller.

"Colonel, it's Capt. Becker...I'm using a desk phone here in the Agency's lock up...there's no cellular connectivity down here."

"Yes, captain...you have something for me?"

"I believe I do, sir. You were right about those bookstore analysts, Magda and Wiktor. Once they heard about Hanna's successful acquisition of high value intel, and how that could impact their own situation, they readily agreed to avoid a heavier prison sentence by cooperating."

"Did they shed any light on what Hanna's next steps might be?" asked Elliott.

"Only to the extent that they laid out how they would have acted in such a situation."

"I'm listening," said Elliott impatiently.

"Well, they admitted it's likely Hanna, being Polish like themselves, left Berlin by private auto since despite the omnipresence of Europol, the international police agency, crossing an international border gives someone intent on escape a way to interrupt any police pursuit. They pointed out that this would have been particularly true in her case since the Polish border was conveniently nearby, and in crossing it she gained sanctuary owing to her citizenship."

"Having crossed the border, where do they believe she would most likely have been heading...to Warsaw?" asked Elliott.

"That's right, colonel," replied Becker. "They said there's a two-story house in the Praga Poludnie district, east of the Vistula River and north of the Lazienkowski bridge, where agents, once recruited, would receive their training. According to the analysts in our custody, the house also serves as a transient way station, with sleeping quarters. Although not explicitly spelled out, agents of Polish nationality working for the outfit all understand they should also regard the facility as a safe house when circumstances warranted it."

"Did they give you the address of this house?" asked Elliott.

"They did, sir, together with a map, since the streets in that district can be difficult to navigate. I'll scan the map and attach it to an email containing the address, then send it to your smart phone."

"Excellent!" said Elliott excitedly. "Captain, I can't thank you enough...you've probably made it possible for us to stay on course in our pursuit of both Hanna and the leader, Marius."

"That mean you'll be heading for Poland, colonel?" asked Becker.

"Absolutely! We'll leave first thing tomorrow."

Once Elliott got off the phone to Becker he put a call through to Col. Appleton. "Sorry to disturb you at home, sir, but I thought you'd like to know we've got fresh intel on the likely destination of the principal suspect in the killing of Col. Nowak."

"That'll be welcome news to the Berlin Landespolizei, Elliott, since they've chosen to be the lead investigators in the case...but am I right in feeling you've decided to run with it yourself...you and your team?" observed Appleton, knowingly.

"That's our plan, colonel...unless you countermand it. Ordinarily, I'd defer to Europol, but the new lead might also give us a chance to interdict the sensitive NATO report which we believe Marius is carrying."

"Spell that out for me, Elliott," said Appleton.

"Well, colonel, what we've learned...through what I must say was some impressive work by the interrogation staff at the Federal Intelligence Agency facility here in Berlin...is that there's a fairly important node in the espionage outfit's network that's located in Warsaw. My hope is that even those agents ultimately posted back to wherever the main headquarters is will transit through Warsaw. We've learned the facility has sleeping quarters for transients. So, assuming Marius was heading to Warsaw...which seems likely for a number of reasons...and reached the city earlier today...it's possible he'll spend the night there, then make the final leg of his trip sometime tomorrow."

"You think you can reach Warsaw early enough to catch this Marius fellow...providing, of course, that your take on what's going on holds up?" asked Appleton.

Elliott sighed, "That's a good question, sir...all of us are pretty tired...I guess the best we can do is catch a few hours of sleep then head out by car around midnight. That should put us in Warsaw a little before six o'clock in the morning. If we take turns we might be able to ensure whoever's driving doesn't fall asleep and run off the road."

"I hear you," laughed Appleton. "But seriously, have you given any thought to letting me order up a Blackhawk chopper from one of the U.S. military outfits based around Stuttgart?"

"I've considered it, colonel, but I think we'll need wheels as we head further east...if that's where the trail leads. And, anyway, a military flight would have the effect of alerting the Polish authorities...and at this point I don't relish the thought of having them underfoot as we attempt the interdiction."

"I understand," said Appleton, "well...good luck. And by the way, if you are successful in catching this Hanna woman, turn her over to the Polish security services...let them deal with the whole extradition matter. But let me know...I'll alert the Berlin authorities to the fact she's been arrested...it'll give me a chance to talk up the effective work of NATO counter-intelligence personnel, which in turn will help the NATO Planning Center build good relations with those government agencies responsible for the Center's security here in Berlin."

"Will do, sir," said Elliott. "I'll keep you informed as things develop," he added before breaking the connection.

Elliott checked his watch as he left the kitchen and headed down the hall to the room fitted out as the sleeping quarters of his men. It was approaching eight o'clock. Perez, Hernandez and Farrand were in their beds but not yet asleep.

"Okay...listen up," said Elliott as he stepped into the room. "Capt. Becker's delivered precise intel on the probable destination of both operatives…Hanna and Marius. At twenty-four hundred hours we'll head out in my vehicle en route to Warsaw. That'll give you all no more than about four hours of shuteye, so make it count."

"Hooah!" shouted all three, pleased there was the likelihood of action early the following morning.

Chapter Nineteen

"You seem to be favoring your left arm, sergeant," said Elliott as he watched Hernandez awkwardly butter his toast. The four of them were seated at the kitchen table hastily downing a quick breakfast. It was just a few minutes after midnight and they'd all just finished dressing and gearing up for the five and a half hour drive to Warsaw.

"My right arm is stiffening up...can't seem to work it loose, sir," said Hernandez as he attempted to extend, then contract, the wounded limb. The pain it caused was evident in his expression.

Elliott watched with concern, then said, "I think you need more medical attention, sergeant...and it probably wouldn't hurt for you to see a physical therapist. I want you to catch an early flight back to Stuttgart, then check in at the Patch Barracks Army Health Clinic...let them attend to you."

"But, sir!"

"Yeah, I know...you want to stay with the team, sergeant, but with your right arm screwed up you're likely to be more of a liability than an asset. Anyway, it'll boost Sgt. White's morale seeing you...and you can fill him in on where we stand in our counter-intelligence operation," said Elliott sympathetically.

Hernandez was about to protest further, but Capt. Perez looked over at him and shook his head, "The colonel's right, Hernandez. We'll need to move fast if we expect to have any chance at intercepting the two agents, and it's likely we'll encounter resistance, assuming they've got security personnel at the Warsaw safe house. You'd be putting us at a disadvantage since one of us would have to cover you if a firefight broke out, leaving our ability to press ahead with our mission impaired."

Hernandez took a minute to reflect on what Perez had said, then nodded.

"Good!" Said Elliott, seeing the matter was settled. "Sgt. Hernandez, I'll ask you to clear our breakfast dishes before you take off so the rest of us can head out...you okay with that?"

"Yes, sir," said Hernandez, nodding.

"Okay, men, let's mount up," said Elliott. "I'll drive the first couple of hours then Sgt. Farrand can take over...with you, Capt. Perez, pulling driving duty as we approach Warsaw.

Hernandez remained seated as Elliott, Perez and Farrand got up from their chairs, grabbed their day packs and headed out to where Elliott's SUV was parked.

Each day pack contained extra clips for their handgun of choice—Glock 17s for Perez and Farrand, the Beretta M9 for Elliott—plus a Heckler and Koch 416 assault rifle, broken down to fit inside the pack, together with several 20-round detachable magazines. Farrand's pack also contained a couple of flashbang grenades.

Despite the fact they each were equipped with formidable fire power, Elliott had nixed the use of a protective vest for himself and his men, believing their ability to operate annonymously in an urban context, and avoid triggering unnecessary alarm on the part of citizens, mandated they dress unencumbered in casual street attire.

* * *

When Elliott finally saw the lights of the bridge he checked his watch; it was two o'clock in the morning. Minutes later, he crossed over the Oder River into Poland. Signage changed; the river was now known as the "Odra River", and the highway was no longer the A-12, but the E-30. He wearily blinked his eyes, trying to refocus. His night vision had been affected by the the bright lights on the bridge and on the adjacent border control facility. He glanced over at Capt. Perez who was seated next to him, nodding approvingly to himself as he noted the man's sleep had not been disturbed during the bridge crossing. Sgt. Farrand was sprawled across the back seat, also sound asleep. Elliott was always impressed by the way special forces operators like himself and his men were able to will themselves asleep whenever a break in the action allowed for it. It had something to do with the way they were trained, at least that was how it was explained, though Elliott figured it had more to do with the need to escape from the heightened levels of fatigue and stress that were associated with the kind of action their missions entailed. He checked his watch again: he had another half hour to go.

* * *

Elliott brought the SUV to a gentle stop on the shoulder of the highway, hoping not to disturb Capt. Perez' sleep, then reached back and tugged at Sgt. Farrand's shoulder to wake him.

Farrand came awake easily and without making a noise. He nodded to Elliott then opened the rear door on the driver's side and slipped out. He stood for a moment, inhaling the cool, crisp night air, then stepped back to allow room for Elliott to climb out. Elliott had deliberately left the engine idling so Farrand wouldn't have to crank up the starter motor and risk waking Perez.

Farrand, who was about the same height as Elliott, didn't have to adjust the seat once he was behind the wheel. He waited calmly for Elliott to climb into the rear seat, then reached over and closed his door—firmly but without slamming—before pulling off the shoulder onto the highway, then quickly gaining speed.

Elliott tried to make himself comfortable, but knew he'd fall asleep in any case, seeing how tired he was after two hours of night driving—that on top of less than four hours of sleep. So in the interim he occupied himself with thoughts of what they'd likely encounter once they reached Warsaw.

* * *

Elliott woke with a start as Farrand drove into a brightly lit, all-night petrol station just off the interchange leading north to the nearby town of Konin. Perez was already awake.

"Sorry, colonel," said Farrand as he maneuvered through the trucks and parked cars, intent on reaching a fuel island, "thought we should gas up now...not wait until we reach Warsaw."

Elliott checked his watch; it was four-thirty in the morning and still well before sunrise. "Let's also grab some food...we may not have a chance later," said Elliott as he sat up straight and began to stretch, hoping to work out the kinks in his back and neck.

Shelves of packaged food lined the interior of the cashier's office. While Elliott paid for the gas, Perez and Farrand filled a basket with breakfast pastries, power bars, nuts, eatable sausage, and juice. "Add three coffees to all of this," said Elliott, showing the attendant the items his team had selected.

Once back in the SUV, they drank their coffee and juice, and snacked on the packaged items. Finally, after a visit to the restroom, they mounted up—Perez in the driver's seat, Farrand riding shotgun, and Elliott in the rear seat.

"I'm going to need you to get on your smart phone, sergeant, and use the mapping app to familiarize yourself with the streets of Warsaw," said Capt. Perez as he pulled out of the station and headed towards the E-30 cloverleaf. "As I see it, we'll probably hit the outskirts of the city in about an hour and a half, and once we're there I'll need you to serve as my navigator...it's for damn sure I'll be too busy with the traffic to help out much."

"I've got it covered, captain," said Farrand in a reassuring tone of voice. "Colonel, you want to text me the map Capt. Becker received from the agents during interrogation?"

Elliott reached into the breast pocket of his sport jacket and retrieved his cell phone, then texted the map to Farrand. "The trick's going to be helping the captain, here, navigate across the city to the neighborhood sketched out in the map," said Elliott.

"I understand, sir," said Farrand as he brought up the transmitted sketch map on his smart phone. "I'll also run a search on the specific address then plot a course to it from the west side of the city."

"Sounds like a plan, sergeant," said Elliott quietly as he closed his eyes and worked his body into a comfortable sleeping position.

* * *

"Okay, here we go," said Capt. Perez as he drove onto the Lazienkowski Bridge that spanned the Vistula River. Farrand had alerted them they'd be in the neighborhood of Saska Kepa, where the house was located, as soon as they took the turnoff at the cloverleaf immediately past the bridge. Perez offered no comment as Farrand, reading the sketch map, fed him directions. Elliott shifted mentally into tactical mode while the two men in the front seat worked together to bring the vehicle into proximity with the target location.

"That's it!" shouted Farrand, pointing to an imposing French-style two-story house in tan stucco that featured a distinctive mansard roof. The street was quiet; only the idling engine of Elliott's SUV broke the stillness of early morning.

"How do you want to work this?" asked Capt. Perez.

"Pull over and park, captain," replied Elliott calmly, "let's watch the place for a while...see if anyone comes out."

"Sir, that balcony above the front door...I think I could get up there using the drainpipe running alongside it from the roof," said Perez. "It looks sturdy enough, and once up there I could do a forced entry through the French doors into that room... flush out whoever's up there...make them move downstairs... maybe even outside."

Elliott thought about it, then said, "I can see the merit of that tactic, captain, but for it to work Sgt. Farrand and I would have to simultaneously force an entry through the front door otherwise there'd be a risk they'd box you in."

"Looks like we'll need to rethink that, colonel," said Sgt. Farrand in his slow, even voice. "Take a look," he added, pointing to the large man who'd just stepped through the front entrance.

"I'd make him to be a security man taking up his early morning post," said Capt. Perez, eyeing the way the man stood at ease, but attentive, just to the right of the front door.

"Yeah, and he's definitely carrying," said Farrand. "See the bulge under his jacket on the upper left side?"

Elliott nodded, "Actually, it's good news...it means we're likely to be at the right place, and now there's reason to believe there's someone inside that ranks high enough in the organization to warrant some protection."

"You think it might be Marius?" asked Perez.

Elliott shrugged, "Possibly, but for that to be true we'd need a hell of a lot of luck!"

"Well, I still think we need to get inside that house," said Capt. Perez, "and the faster the better."

"Okay," said Elliott, "here's how we'll do it...sergeant, take your silenced H&K 416 and conceal yourself behind the plantings bordering the front fence...but close enough that you'll have a good field of fire targeting the front stoop. Once you're in position I'll approach the entrance gate as if I intend to walk in...that'll draw the attention of the guard. Captain, you prepare to vault the fence with the objective of mounting the drainage pipe...are we clear?"

"Yes, sir!" said Perez and Farrand in unison.

The SUV was parallel-parked on the same side of the street as the house, but not directly in front. Elliott knew the guard's view of the vehicle would be impaired by the densely overgrown plantings along the fence—plantings that reached a height of over six feet. Still, he motioned for Farrand to move carefully. Farrand nodded, then slipped out of the vehicle, armed with his H&K 416 assault rifle and his Glock 17 sidearm. Both weapons were fixed with noise suppressors.

A hand signal from Farrand prompted Elliott to climb out from the back seat and walk casually towards the front gate of the house. He held his assault rifle at his side—the side away from where the guard was looking.

The guard turned aggressively toward Elliott, about to challenge him, when a silenced bullet penetrated his head, then continued onward, splintering the wooden frame of the front door with an audible smack.

Elliott stepped aside as Perez, his H&K 416 strapped to his back, made a running approach at the fence, vaulting it with ease then continued on to the drain pipe at the corner of the building.

He was halfway up the pipe when the front door opened and another large guy looked out. Before he could process what had happened to his partner, Farrand fired two bullets into his chest.

At that point, Elliott, who'd checked and found the gate to be locked, also vaulted the fence and ran for the open entrance, his H&K 416 at the ready.

"Go!" shouted Elliott as he heard Perez clamber over the balcony's balustrade and come down hard. He hesitated a moment, waiting until he heard Perez kick open the French doors, he then stepped inside, keeping tight against one wall, the muzzle of his assault rifle aimed forward as he carefully swept the room. "Clear!" he shouted. He then advanced towards the rooms at the rear of the building. But just as he was about to check the next room—one that appeared to be used for formal dining—his peripheral vision caught some movement. Elliott quickly glanced back—in time to see Sgt. Farrand slip inside. Farrand signaled with a nod his intention to provide cover as Elliott checked and cleared the rest of the rooms on the ground floor.

"Looks like the two security guys were quartered back here," said Sgt. Farrand as he pointed to the two rooms fitted out with a bed and personal belongings. As they headed back towards the front of the building, Farrand added, "I figure the mess in the kitchen means they'd probably just finished breakfast and were about to begin their morning duties when we showed up."

"You all right, captain?" shouted Elliott up the wide staircase leading to the upper floor where he could hear two people talking.

"Roger that, sir!" shouted Perez. "I'm on my way down!"

Elliott and Farrand stood at the bottom of the staircase and watched as Perez led a blond haired woman, her hands bound with plasticuffs, towards them. "Caught this one about to leave," said Perez.

Elliott recognized her immediately, "It's Hanna," he said. "Take her into the living room."

As Perez led the woman into the large room at the front of the house, Elliott said, "I'll need to talk to her…while I'm doing that, captain, you and Sgt. Farrand should probably drag the bodies of the two guards into the front hallway and shut the door."

"I don't know, colonel," objected Capt. Perez, "the bodies are pretty well concealed from the street…and if, as I expect, you plan on giving the Polish security service a head's up…they'll probably expect us to leave the crime scene intact."

Elliott gave the captain's objection some thought, then said, "It's a question of what's better, captain, an intact crime scene or possible public disclosure of the sort of event the security service would rather keep under wraps. My guess is they'll prefer to avoid disclosure even if it means disturbing the crime scene. So, please proceed with some haste, captain…someone walking by might see the bodies at any moment."

"As you wish, sir," said Perez resignedly. "I guess while we're out there we might as well check to see if the noise made during entry brought out any curious neighbors," said Perez.

"Good thinking, captain…oh…and while you're at it, see if one of the guards has the key to the lock on the gate…we'll eventually want to egress with a little less of a spectacle than the way we arrived," said Elliott soberly.

Chapter Twenty

Elliott waited until Perez and Farrand had left the room, then took a seat across from the couch where Hanna sat staring defiantly at her captor—anger and frustration apparent in her expression.

"Capt. Perez says you were preparing to leave when he encountered you upstairs...you mind telling me where you were heading?" asked Elliott evenly.

She shrugged, "back to Berlin, of course...why wouldn't I be...I have done nothing wrong."

"And your brief visit to Warsaw...to this particular house... how am I to understand it?" asked Elliott, innocently.

She shrugged again, this time in a more exaggerated way, then said, "Why should I care what you think, colonel? What I do with in my own time is of no concern to the Center."

"Ordinarily, you would be correct in making that assumption, Hanna, but circumstances are such that in this instance the Center happens to be particularly interested," said Elliott.

"And why would that be so?" asked Hanna dismissively.

It was Elliott's turn to shrug, "It appears you are the key suspect in the murder of your countryman, Col. Nowak."

"That's absurd!" Hanna said forcefully, "Col. Nowak was a friend and a colleague...we came to the Center together...we knew each other in Warsaw. It makes no sense that I should be a suspect!"

"But you do admit knowing of his death," observed Elliott patiently.

"Of course I do, colonel...it was I who first reported finding him lying in his office," said Hanna contemptuously.

Elliott nodded, "So you are now in Warsaw...to do what, precisely?"

"To alert his family and to extend them my deepest sympathy, of course. I should have imagined it would be obvious."

"And now, you intend to return to Berlin to resume your duties...am I correct?" asked Elliott quietly.

"Of course...I've already told you that is my intention!" she replied testily.

Just then, Sgt. Farrand stepped into the room, "Colonel, we've identified the two security guards...they are both Russian nationals according to their papers."

"Thanks, sergeant," said Elliott, keeping his gaze on Hanna. "So, Hanna, what are we to make of the fact you sought lodging in a building that our investigations have revealed is a safe house for an international espionage ring—a place guarded by two armed Russian nationals?"

Hanna shrugged, "I know nothing about this...and as for those two men you shot...well...I only knew them as resident staff personnel...people living here to look after my needs, or the needs of whoever uses the place."

"All right...let's assume this is all a misunderstanding," began Elliott reasonably, "I'll then have to assume you know the owner of the building...am I right?"

"Of course I do, colonel," said Hanna with a false smile, "since it was the owner who extended me a standing invitation to use the home whenever I find myself in Warsaw on a short visit, such as now."

"And who would that be, Hanna?" asked Elliott softly.

Hanna hesitated for a moment, then said, "His name is Alexandru...he's a Moldovan who lives in Tiraspol. He has business interests that bring him to Warsaw frequently enough that he's chosen to have his own residence here...and to employ household staff to look after the place. The two men you shot were his employees...I should imagine Alexandru will wish to press criminal charges against you...and perhaps also to sue the Berlin Center for its involvement in this violent act!"

Elliott nodded, as if agreeing with her, then asked, "And you and this man Alexandru met...how?"

"Socially, of course...Warsaw is that sort of city...people of all kinds encounter one another rather easily here. But more recently Alexandru chose to employ me...initially as a clerical assistant, then later as his personal assistant during the times he was in Warsaw."

"How did he take it...you know...when you notified him you were leaving for Berlin to take up a post at the NATO Planning Center?" asked Elliott.

Hanna shrugged, "We were friends…he held no grudge…it was after I told him of my plans that he invited me to use this residence."

Elliott nodded again, then turned his gaze on the room and its furnishings, "This is a splendid home…I should think it can easily accommodate several guests…were you the only guest last night?"

"As a matter of fact I wasn't," replied Hanna indignantly, "a business associate of the owner—also Moldovan—slept here last night. I'm sure your Capt. Perez informed you that two of the upstairs bedrooms had been slept in. The man left about a half-hour before you and those other two Americans came busting in."

"Can you identify him for me?" Elliott asked absently, as if it didn't really matter.

"He called himself Marius," she replied casually. "I know nothing about him, nor where he came from."

Elliott rose from his chair and began to pace, "Hanna, I'm afraid your story won't cut it…we know Col. Nowak's body was not discovered by you, as you allege, but by his military aide, Capt. Kowalski. We also know you were summoned by phone to report to Col. Nowak's office at about three o'cock yesterday afternoon, and were seen returning to the secretarial pool less than a half hour later. Then, shortly before the alarm was raised regarding the death of Col. Nowak, you were seen leaving the Center in a hurry. Although all of this can be regarded as merely circumstantial evidence of your involvement, it's been enough for the Berlin Landespolizei to justify launching an investigation, and to ask for assistance from Europol in having you detained for questioning."

Hanna didn't say anything, she kept her gaze away from Elliott—unwilling to acknowledge, even with a glance, the truth of his allegations.

Elliott studied her reaction, then returned to his seat, "As I see it, Hanna, you've got two options. The first is for me to inform the Warsaw police of what you've been accused of, along with evidence currently in the hands of the German Federal Intelligence Agency that you're a professional espionage agent in the employ of an outfit based in Moldova that is working against NATO. Furthermore, I'll inform them that you are in my custody, here in Warsaw, and that they can come arrest you immediately."

Hanna continued to pointedly ignore Elliott.

"Your second option, should you choose to cooperate with my investigation, would resemble the first in all particulars, the only difference being that I would impress upon the German and Polish authorities how helpful you'd been in allowing me to accomplish my mission."

Hanna turned to Elliott, then said in a bitter tone of voice, "What you're asking is that I betray those with whom I work… for what? For a couple of nice words from you…a nobody?"

"It's you, Hanna, that is the "nobody"," countered Elliott evenly. "Had you not panicked and killed Col. Nowak the authorities would have had little interest in punishing you severely, especially if they were successful in rolling up the espionage ring and arresting its leader. Without your help, however, there's a good chance the espionage ring will continue to operate, and its leader permitted to remain free. Unfortunately, under such circumstances I imagine you will, by default, be regarded as the person who perhaps most exemplifies the extremely violent and sinister cadre of which you are a member, and whose mission is to undermine the security of NATO. I'm sure you will agree that should this occur you would most likely become the "treasonous face" of a particularly dangerous espionage ring...one can only imagine how such a person would be treated in Poland."

Hanna gave an involuntary shudder as she imagined her fate, especially while in the custody of the Polish authorities given the importance of NATO to the security of Poland. Regaining her composure, she asked resignedly, "What do you want to know?"

"Before we begin I'd like to have Capt. Perez come in...both to ensure your cooperation is duly corroborated, and to assist me in assessing the value of whatever it is you agree to share with us."

Hanna indicated she understood with a slight nod.

"Capt. Perez!" shouted Elliott, "Can you join us?"

"As you wish, sir," replied Perez some moments later as he stepped into the living room through the doorway that led from the front hall. "Sgt. Farrand is standing watch on the front doorstep," he added, bringing Elliott up to date on the sergeant's whereabouts.

Elliott motioned for Perez to take a seat, then said, "Hanna has agreed to cooperate with our investigation, captain."

Perez nodded, but didn't make a comment.

"Let's begin, Hanna, by having you tell us the identity of the espionage ring we're dealing with," said Elliott.

Hanna gave the question some thought, then said, "The organization goes by the name *Otskry.*"

Before she could elaborate, Capt. Perez turned excitedly to Elliott and said, "Colonel, isn't that the outfit we shut down in that airborne raid on the luxury yacht sailing just off the coast from Odessa?"

"One would think so, captain," replied Elliott, also somewhat taken aback by Hanna's revelation. "It was about a year and half ago, and you'll remember, captain, we placed the leader, a man named Mikhail, in the custody of the Bulgarian authorities. Given the trouble that man caused the Bulgarians I can't believe he's already free and up to his old tricks."

"No, colonel, *Otskry's* leader is the Moldovan I mentioned... the one who owns this residence...a man named Alexandru. I know of no one named Mikhail," interjected Hanna.

Elliott took a moment to absorb this new information...to make sense of it, then said, "Yeah...it's probably the same outfit, but with a new leader. You'll remember, captain, that *Otskry* had just transitioned from specializing in arms smuggling in countries bordering the Black Sea to international espionage when we first encountered the organization. We got involved when the Defense Intelligence Agency became aware of *Otskry's* elaborate attempt to gain possession of highly classified software of interest to the Department of Defense being developed by that start-up in the small port town of Carr's Pt. on Puget Sound."

"Yeah, I do remember...and as I recall, sir, *Otskry* was known to have solid contacts with powerful people in eastern Ukraine, as well as in Russia," said Perez.

"I guess that hasn't changed...it might explain why the security personnel we found ourselves up against this morning were Russian nationals," said Elliott. "Chances are, we'll encounter more of them if we press ahead with our investigation."

"So, *Otskry* is alive and well," said Perez in wonderment. "But how the hell did it end up being based in a place like Transnistria?"

"I don't know...it does kind of makes sense," said Elliott, "A year and a half ago, *Otskry* was based in Odessa. That location was probably fatally compromised as a result of our assault on *Otskry's* vessel, an assault which shined a counter-intelligence spotlight on the outfit...one that Ukrainian and other European governments couldn't ignore. Transnistria offered an outfit like *Otskry* the advantage of being a kind of "no-man's land"...a territory split off from Moldova and outside the embrace of European jurisdictional entities, but at the same time one that enjoys the active support of Russia. And it doesn't hurt that Tiraspol, the capital of Transnistria, is only about a hundred kilometers west of Odessa, and easily accessible from Odessa by car as well as by rail."

"Okay, I get how Transnistria might have become the new base of operations for *Otskry*," said Perez, "but who the hell is Alexandru...and how did he manage to become the new headman?"

"Hanna, can you shed some light on that?" asked Elliott.

"All I know is that the leadership of *Otskry*—not just Alexandru, but all of them, including Marius—are all Moldovans who have links with the territory of Transnistria," replied Hanna. "I know nothing about the Odessa outfit you describe," she added.

"I guess we'll just have to ask Alexandru himself," said Elliott in a voice of steely determination. "Though, I'm willing to bet Alexandru was one of the half-dozen or so high-ranking associates of Mikhail who we left on board Mikhail's luxury yacht after our assault. I'd always supposed the Ukrainian authorities scooped them all up before the vessel had a chance to evade capture, but apparently that wasn't so. One way or another some, most likely including Alexandru, escaped the net."

"Supposing that was the case," added Perez, "maybe Alexandru persuaded the others that relocating to Transnistria offered the best solution for the survival of *Otskry*...an outcome that meant he could put at the organization's disposal all his Transnistrian resources...hell, why wouldn't they agree to his becoming the new chief under such circumstances."

"As I said, we'll have to hope we'll get an opportunity to ask him directly," said Elliott, intent on changing the subject. He then turned to Hanna. "Tell us what you can about Marius... your fellow guest here at the residence."

She hesitated for a moment, gathering her thoughts, then said, "Marius was already here when I arrived. I of course knew him...he was my boss in Berlin. We didn't talk too much the previous evening, though he did indicate it would be best if I followed him to Tiraspol where we could both secure some sort of protection from the European authorities."

"Was that after you told him of your involvement in the killing of Col. Nowak?"

"Yes...he realized I knew enough to jeopardize the sale of the intel I'd stolen from Col. Nowak so he was especially anxious that I elude capture."

"I got the impression Marius was in a hurry to get out of Berlin...can you shed some light on why that might have been the case...was it because he was transporting the intel you had found at Col. Nowak's apartment?"

Hanna nodded.

"Does *Otskry* already have a buyer for the intel?" asked Elliott.

"I don't suppose so...Alexandru would want to assess its value before negotiating a price, and he'd need to read it in order to do that. Marius believed the intel was of very high value...not only to the Russians, but to others as well. He was anxious to get it to Alexandru and to make sure it remained out of the hands of people like yourselves," replied Hanna with some bitterness.

"You said that Marius left about a half-hour before we arrived. Can you tell us where he was heading and how he planned to travel?"

"He was flying to Odessa from the Warsaw-Chopin Airport. I was a little surprised he planned to leave for the airport so early...it's only about eleven kilometers west of the city. But he argued that although the airport was only about thirty minutes away by public transportion, he wasn't sure he'd get a seat on the plane...he needed to leave early enough that he'd be at the top of the queue for a seat on the popular 11:20 am flight should a cancellation arise."

"And why didn't he insist you accompany him?" asked Elliott.

Hanna shrugged, "I suppose he didn't think the chances were particularly good that both of us could manage to land a cancelled seat on that flight; so I took my time this morning, figuring if I left about an hour or so after him I'd at least have a good chance of getting on the 2:40 pm flight this afternoon. I was just about to leave when your Capt. Perez detained me."

"Captain, call Sgt. Farrand in to keep a watch on our guest while you and I talk privately," said Elliott, busily thinking through an improvised plan for the recovery of the Nowak document before Marius could take it to Odessa.

Without a word, Perez left the room to get Farrand.

Elliott used the interval to press his questions, "Let's assume Marius is successful in getting to Odessa, Hanna, would he immediately start out for Tiraspol, and if so, how?"

Hanna thought about it, then said, "If he was successful in getting on the 11:20 flight he'd have plenty of time to connect with the 6:00 pm train to Tiraspol, but if he had to make do with the 2:40 pm flight he'd be unable to make the connection, forcing him to remain in Odessa...that is, unless he went by car. In that case, he'd easily be able to continue on to Tiraspol since the drive takes less than two hours."

"What are the chances he'd have access to a car upon arriving in Odessa?" asked Elliott.

Hanna shrugged, "I'd imagine it's quite likely, colonel. Alexandru would probably insist on it, given the importance of the document Marius is carrying."

Elliott nodded, going over in his mind the various options available to Marius, and how they might impact his mission.

While he was still digesting the logistical information Hanna had supplied, Perez and Farrand entered the room.

"Sergeant, keep an eye on Hanna while Capt. Perez and I step out of the room."

"Yes, sir," said Sgt. Farrand, who chose one of the upholstered chairs across from the couch and sat down.

Elliott led Perez to the rear of the apartment and faced him, "Captain, I think we have a chance to liberate Marius' briefcase while he's on standby in the airport…hopefully in a way that doesn't create too much of a scene."

"Are you thinking of letting him escape custody while he's in Warsaw, sir?" asked Perez in a surprised tone of voice. "Letting him actually board one of the flights to Odessa?"

"I don't see the harm in it, captain, especially if we've taken possession of the intel. We have to continue on to Tiraspol in any case if we intend to shut down *Otskry* for good…we can deal with him there."

"I don't know, sir…we won't have the backing of the local authorities, or any effective recourse to NATO agencies," replied Perez, clearly troubled.

"Okay, I appreciate the merit of your misgivings, captain, so let's proceed as follows, you and Sgt. Farrand take my vehicle and drive to the Warsaw-Chopin Airport. Locate Marius and assess your tactical options. If you and Farrand feel you can take the man into custody right then and there without raising a holy stink, then fine…do it. But if that's not doable then figure a way of separating him from his briefcase. He'll protest, and shout for assistance from airport security personnel, I'm sure, but at least one of you should be able to evade pursuit and get the briefcase safely to the SUV."

"I like that better, colonel," said Capt. Perez, "but there's still the issue of whether or not the intel we're trying to interdict is actually still in the man's briefcase."

"It's a risk we've got to take, captain," said Elliott resignedly. "And given the desperate way Marius was holding the briefcase as he escaped from the brokerage safe house in Berlin I'm betting we'll find the document inside even now."

Perez nodded, seeing the merit in Elliott's point of view. "I read you, sir...we'll head for the airport right away...will you be okay handling this end all by yourself?"

"Not a problem, captain," Elliott replied confidently. "Oh, and while you're at the airport try to book us three seats on the 2:40 pm flight to Odessa. And keep in mind the likelihood Marius could very easily recognize you from when the two of you were on surveillance duty at the travel agency."

"Understood, sir," said Perez crisply. He then turned and headed back to the living room to collect Sgt. Farrand.

Elliott followed, but more slowly, thinking through his final set of questions for Hanna, and how to manage the custody turnover to the Warsaw police. But first, he knew he'd need to bring Col. Appleton up to date since he'd be depending on Appleton to ensure that the Warsaw authorities were fully apprised of Elliott's authorized counter-intelligence mission on behalf of NATO's Berlin operation.

Chapter Twenty-One

Hanna watched Elliott come back into the room. She watched him hesitate at the threshold for a moment, seemingly studying her, before walking over to where she was seated. He nodded to her before quietly settling back in the chair he'd previously occupied. Perez and Farrand had left; it was just the two of them. "So what now, colonel?" she asked.

Elliott sighed, "You should know, Hanna, that our discovery of you...of your identity as a trained espionage agent who'd been cleverly imbedded in Berlin's highly secret NATO Planning Center...was simply a fluke."

"What do you mean?" asked Hanna, clearly puzzled.

"It all came about because we were studying video footage from a surveillance camera targeting the main entrance to the Center. We were looking for pattern disruptions in the behavior of staffers passing through the entrance at midday. Our hope was to identify a small set of employees whose behavior marked them as possible victims of blackmail...an event we believed would have unsettled them...making them partial to altering behavior they suspected might have originally led to their being vulnerable to blackmail in the first place."

"Are you saying I exhibited such behavior?" asked Hanna, incredulous.

"It seems so…though in your case it probably had nothing to do with feelings of guilt, but to more mundane circumstances," replied Elliott sympathetically. "Our interview yesterday morning would have clarified that fact and you would have been free to continue with your more deeply imbedded operation… with us no wiser. But our scheduled interview with you must have triggered some sort of alarm in Col. Nowak's mind…alerting him to the risk he'd been taking—bringing highly classified documents home. He must have realized he'd inadvertently allowed you to possibly gain access to them."

"Jesus Christ!" exclaimed Hanna in frustration.

"Your absolutely right to feel a bit ridiculous…if you'd just dismissed Nowak's suspicions…walked out of his office in indignation then took our interview, all of this would never have happened," said Elliott, reflecting on the matter.

"But he threatened to order a full investigation!" argued Hanna.

"Yes…and he had the authority to make good on his threat… and it's entirely possible that NATO's counter-intelligence operatives would have eventually discovered your true mission," conceded Elliott, "but then again they might not have."

Hanna shook her head in disbelief, then turned to Elliott, "So are we done with the questions?" she asked bitterly.

"Only one more," replied Elliott quietly.

"I suppose you'll then call the police to come for me," she said contemptuously.

"I've already called them...they should be here in a matter of minutes. So let's get this interrogation over with quickly... you okay with that?"

"Ask your question then," she muttered glumly.

"First, let me ask...have you ever visited the *Otskry* headquarters in Tiraspol?"

Hanna shrugged, "Once...about a year ago...I'd been sent there to be be trained."

"But you were recruited in Warsaw...is that right?" asked Elliott.

She nodded.

"So...my final question...actually a request...is for you to supply me with information on how I can best locate that headquarters facility."

Hanna shook her head, "It won't be easy to find, colonel... the building—as best I can recall—has no street address. It's located in a fairly large light-industrial sector west of Kirov Park."

"Can't you give me any details?" asked Elliott, clearly frustrated.

Hanna thought back to her visit, then added, "I remember the area was roughly divided into two precincts—the one to the west exhibited a pronounced amount of manufacturing activity...with lots of cars parked adjacent to the buildings. The *Otskry* headquarters was not in that part of the sector, but rather in the eastern half where the buildings seemed neglected and somewhat dilapidated. Pockets of overgrown trees and shrubs grew haphazardly between the buildings, and there were a number of empty lots where buildings had previously stood. I was particularly struck by the absence of parked cars or trucks as I was driven through the sector."

"Can you remember anything about the building itself?"

"Well...it was probably in better shape than buildings near it...that I remember," she said, then added, "It was a metal building with a roof about two stories high, though there wasn't a proper second floor...only a single elevated office complex in one corner, reached by means of a skeletal metal staircase bolted to the interior wall."

"So...no external windows...not at ground level or in connection with the office inset?" speculated Elliott.

Hanna nodded, "Yes...that's right...access was either through a regular-sized metal door or through one of the two over-sized vehicle doors...all three doors were located on the south side of the building."

"And inside the building...how was it subdivided...or wasn't it?"

"When I was there the floor on the eastern side of the building was subdivided into office cubicles by shoulder-high partitions. Some of the cubicles were actually offices with desks, but others were used to house file cabinets or various kinds of office equipment. A portion of the west side of the interior space was given over to a firing range, and the rest to classrooms."

"So...as best you can remember, there wasn't any sort of barracks-type sleeping arrangement...is that right?"

"No...actually there was...now that I recall," said Hanna. "Back of the classroom configuration was a temporary wall and behind it there were living quarters—with sleeping rooms, a lavatory, and a large kitchen and dining area. I probably forgot about it because only members of the security staff stayed there...agents-in-training, together with the leadership and teaching cadre, lived off-premises in a neighborhood close to the train station. Are we done now, colonel?"

Elliott nodded, "Yeah, I guess we are." He then added, "You've proven to be quite helpful, Hanna...and I'll keep to my word about ensuring your cooperation is properly noted in the report I submit. The police should be arriving about now so you'll want to prepare yourself...I don't think they'll treat you as cordially as I've done. In fact, they'll most likely handle you rather roughly."

Hanna nodded, acknowledging Elliott's words, then sat up straight, shoulders back, and awaited her arrest with calm but militant determination.

* * *

Elliott and Hanna heard them talking among themselves as they threw open the front door and stumbled on the bodies of the two dead Russians. "Police!" shouted whoever was in command.

"We're in here!" Elliott shouted back.

A large, uniformed man stepped into the living room and briskly walked over, "Colonel Stone?" he asked.

Elliott stood, "Yes...I'm the one who called...and this is the woman we've identified as an espionage agent who also happens to be the principal suspect in the murder of Col. Nowak...a murder that took place in Berlin about midday yesterday. Col. Nowak was an officer in the Polish army who'd been assigned to a key NATO planning unit."

"Yes, I'm familiar with the details, colonel...I have a copy of the Europol arrest warrant regarding her," he said, glancing over at Hanna. The officer then turned and shouted, "Corporal Jankowski, bring one of your men and escort this woman to the holding van!"

Two uniformed policemen rushed into the room where their leader, a Capt. Mazur, pointed at Hanna. Hanna stood up without a word and turned to the captain, keeping a haughty expression on her face—all but ignoring the two policemen who had been summoned to remove her from the building. But they quickly seized her, removed the plasticuffs Capt. Perez had placed on her wrists and replaced them with steel cuffs from the corporal's belt. Then, with each taking a firm grip on an upper arm they marched her roughly out of the room.

"So, Col. Stone, perhaps we should begin with you explaining your involvement in the woman's capture...then, of course, there is the matter of the two dead bodies," said Capt. Mazur evenly.

Elliott pulled out his Defense Intelligence Agency card that identified him as a Lt. Colonel in the US Army who was currently assigned to the DIA. "I'm acting under the orders of Col. Appleton, military attaché at the US Embassy in Berlin and director of the NATO Planning Center located in that city," said Elliott crisply, handing the card to the police captain. "Since the killing of Col. Nowak occured at the Planning Center, and the woman you've detained—an employee—was quickly identified as the likely perpetrator, it fell within Col. Appleton's mandate to ensure she was quickly apprehended. Unfortunately, she managed to flee the scene, but intel from espionage agents arrested earlier led us to believe she was headed here. Col. Appleton therefore ordered a rapid pursuit by US special operators already involved in shutting down the espionage operation, given the need to recover critical documents believed to be on their way here."

The police captain nodded, "And you, I suppose, are the person in command of this team of special operators?"

"That is correct, captain."

"And the others…the men you lead…where are they?"

"They are elsewhere in the city carrying out a surveillance operation, the details of which I am not at liberty to disclose at this time."

The policeman stared at Elliott, weighing the possible consequences of challenging Elliott on the matter. Opting to let it go, the captain instead asked, "Am I correct in supposing the subject of your men's current surveillance assignment is somehow connected to the two dead bodies out in the hallway?"

Elliott nodded, "In a way…yes. Placing Hanna in custody was certainly important, but of far greater importance was interdicting the transmission of vital NATO secrets believed to be in the possession of the Berlin chief of operations for the espionage ring. Having good reason to believe this person might possibly be in the building, and aware of the man's skill at evading capture, I felt it best to take out the two security agents preemptively then storm the building. As it turned out, the man had left the residence less than an hour before our arrival. However, the woman revealed certain facts under intense questioning that led me to believe there was a slim chance he could be detained before he left Warsaw."

Capt. Mazur thought about what Elliott had told him, then asked, "Can you assure me that this espionage ring you've been chasing down is not based in Poland?"

"Yes, I believe I can, captain," replied Elliott.

Mazur nodded, "Okay…then we'll leave it at that. I suspect you're anxious to get on with your current operation, colonel, so I'll take care of things at this end…you're free to go."

"Thank you, captain," said Elliott, shaking the man's hand. "I'll send you a detailed report for your records once I'm back in Berlin."

"I'd appreciate that, colonel…now…should I have one of my men drive you somewhere?"

"Thanks anyway, captain, but I'll manage on my own," replied Elliott as he walked out of the living room, heading for the street.

* * *

Elliott quickly called a car service. As he waited to be picked up he watched as the coroner's removal team wheeled out the bodies of the two dead Russians. He couldn't help wondering what role—if any—the Russian government was playing in support of Alexandru's ring—did it have a final say on what entities the outfit chose to target? He'd always assumed *Otskry* was a freelance criminal enterprise, selling to the highest bidder, but the quick reemergence of the outfit in Russia-friendly Transnistria after having been heavily compromised by his own efforts, together with the troubling presence of Russian security personnel, was causing him to rethink his assumptions.

Finally, a car-service vehicle showed up and Elliott climbed in. "The Warsaw-Chopin Airport, driver," he said before settling back in the seat. While the driver made his way west across the Lazienkowski bridge over the Vistula River, Elliott busied himself texting Perez for an update. He waited patiently for a reply, but received nothing. Finally, Elliott's phone rang.

"Colonel, we've got a problem," said Capt. Perez once Elliott picked up.

"What is it?" asked Elliott.

"It's Marius, colonel...we can't seem to locate him."

"What do you mean, captain?"

"Well, Sgt. Farrand and I have thoroughly searched the terminals and haven't been able to spot him. We've checked restaurants, restrooms, shops, boarding stations for imminent flights...everywhere...but he's not to be seen."

"Perhaps he's deliberately staying concealed until it's time to board his flight," suggested Elliott.

"That's the thing, colonel, he's not on the passenger manifest for the ll:20 am flight, and the plane is booked solid."

"What about the 2:40 pm flight?"

"He's doesn't show up on that manifest either."

"Is there still a chance he could get on that flight?" asked Elliott.

"I doubt it, sir...we bought the last three seats," replied Perez.

Elliott didn't comment right away—taking time to rethink the problem. He knew Warsaw had two other airports—but didn't think Marius would have gone to either of them. The Warsaw-Modlin airport—40 kilometers outside the city—handled low-budget flights to popular destinations, which most likely left out Odessa; and the Warsaw-Babice airport, although close in, was used primarily for local recreational flying. No... Marius had to have been heading for the city's international airport—the Warsaw-Chopin where Perez and Farrand were now located.

As Elliott turned the matter over in his mind he tried to look at it from Marius' perspective. Marius needed to get to Odessa, hopefully in time to make some sort of connection that would get him to Tiraspol before the day was up. He was unsuccessful in getting on the morning flight and didn't seem interested in waiting around for the afternoon flight, or for one of the Ukrainian airline flights which had lengthy layovers, so what were his options? Then it came to him—a charter!

"Captain, does the airport have a separate general aviation terminal that handles business jets?" asked Elliott, resuming his phone conversation with Perez.

"Let me ask," replied Perez, who turned and spoke to Farrand. "Sgt. Farrand is going to check, colonel...give us a minute."

Elliott waited patiently, using the time to look out his window at the old city as the driver kept to the Waleska highway which passed through it—heading for Hwy. 634 that would take them south to Warsaw-Chopin airport.

"Okay, colonel, we've got an answer," said Perez, coming back on line. "Sgt. Farrand has learned there's a separate executive jet terminal north of where we are now. We're going to head over."

"I'll meet you there," replied Elliott before breaking the connection.

* * *

After giving the driver his revised destination, Elliott put a call through to Col. Appleton, whom he hadn't yet brought up to date on the mission.

"Colonel, sorry it's taken so long to bring you up to speed on where things stand, but it's been a hectic morning," began Elliott once Appleton's sergeant put him through.

"No problem, Elliott...we've all had days like that...so, what have you got?" replied Appleton.

"Well, the big news is that the outfit we've been chasing is a reconstituted version of *Otskry*...now based in Tiraspol, the capital of breakaway Transnistria."

"I'll be damned! Thought we'd put them out of business over a year ago."

"Yeah, it came as a big surprise to Capt. Perez and myself as well."

"How'd you learn of it?"

"The woman suspect...Hanna...became cooperative once I assured her any assistance on her part with respect to our mission would be duly noted in how she'd be treated by the Polish and Berlin authorities."

"So, she's in custody?"

"Yes, sir…we turned her over to the Warsaw police. My men and I managed to catch her just as she was attempting to leave for Transnistria…unfortunately, however, we were too late to seize Marius, who'd also been in the Warsaw residence…he left about a half-hour before we arrived."

"Any complications I should know about?" asked Appleton.

"One, perhaps…in the course of our forced entry into the building we engaged two security guards—both Russians—who were shot dead. The Warsaw police are handling that situation as well."

"So…good cooperation all around, I take it," commented Appleton.

"That's correct, sir…it seems the Polish authorities had been apprised of the Europol warrant for Hanna, and were grateful we'd been able to assist in placing her in custody."

"So what's your next step?"

"We're still in pursuit of Marius, sir, whom we believe is heading for Odessa where he's likely to look for immediate transportation to Tiraspol."

"How can I help?" asked Appleton.

"Well, sir, we're booked on the 2:40 pm flight to Odessa, which means we're continuing on without our weapons. It would be very helpful if you could call your counterpart at the US Embassy in Ukraine and have him contact the head of the Office of Defense Cooperation. Those people, as you know, have set up a Joint Contact Team involving US Army personnel. Assuming they've a unit in Odessa, I'd be much obliged if they could see their way to having someone meet us at the Odessa airport with the kind of hardware we'd hope to have as we press on with our mission. If they could also loan us a vehicle as well...all the better."

"I'll see what I can do...tell me what you'd like to have?"

"The vehicle should be a nondescript sedan with Odessa plates...the weapons ideally would include several Heckler & Koch 416 assault rifles, a couple of Glock 17's, and a Beretta M9 for me."

"Anything else?"

"Noise suppressors for all of the weapons, for sure, plus maybe some flash-bangs."

"I think that's all doable, colonel...especially since the Joint Contact Team is tasked primarily with familiarizing the Ukrainian military with our tactical assault methods...chances are good they'll have all of that stuff ready at hand. I'll text you what I learn," said Appleton.

"Very good, sir," replied Elliott.

"What about the weapons you'll be leaving behind in Warsaw?"

"I'll have the marines at the US Embassy come pick them up...I'll tell them to hold them in the embassy's armory. We'll arrange to have them given back to us upon our return," replied Elliott.

"Well, good luck, soldier," said Col. Appleton spiritedly, before terminating the call.

Settling back in his seat, Elliott glanced at the driver, wondering how much he'd understood of what had been said... not too much, he hoped.

Chapter Twenty-Two

Elliott rushed out of the car and into the executive jet terminal, looking for his team. He found them talking with an attendant at the counter of one of the air chartering firms operating out of the terminal. They waved him over.

"This man tells us Marius flew out of here on a light jet only minutes ago, colonel," said Capt. Perez once Elliott joined them.

"Was he the sole passenger?" Elliott asked the counter man.

"Actually, no," said the attendant. "The charter was originally intended solely for two employees of a construction company based in Odessa, but after learning of the urgency expressed by the man you people are interested in the two men agreed to share the charter, providing, of course, that he bear a third of the cost."

"Well, that solves the mystery of where Marius has kept himself," said Elliott resignedly.

"Can I interest the three of you in a charter of your own?" asked the attendant.

Both Perez and Farrand looked inquiringly at Elliott.

"I'm afraid not...but thanks anyway," said Elliott. "We've got tickets on the afternoon flight to Odessa."

The three of them walked away, but once they were out of earshot of the attendant Perez stopped Elliott and said, "Colonel, we can probably nail the guy right at the Odessa airport if we fly out now...what's the problem?"

Elliott shook his head, "A couple of things, captain. First, getting the Army to execute travel orders of that sort...even with the assistance of Col. Appleton...would take the better part of a day; second, even if we had the necessary travel documents there's no guarantee a craft and a couple of pilots could be made ready for departure within a time frame that would give us a greater than even chance we'd catch up with Marius."

"What are you saying, sir?" asked Sgt. Farrand, worriedly.

"I'm saying our immediate objective can no longer be recovery of the documents being carried by Marius...that option has passed. Now, what we must do is ensure we reach Tiraspol—and *Otskry's* headquarters—before Alexandru has had a chance to sell the intel Marius will have brought with him."

"You think flying out this afternoon is soon enough, colonel?" asked Farrand.

"I surely hope so, sergeant," replied Elliott. "Towards that end I've put in motion an arrangement whereby a vehicle and replacements for our existing weaponry will be waiting for us upon our arrival at the Odessa airport. The drive to Tiraspol is said to take less than two hours, so if we arrive at the airport on schedule, at about 1730 hours, we should make it to Tiraspol by about 1930 hours."

"Yes, but Marius will most likely have made it to Tiraspol hours earlier," protested Capt. Perez. "Wouldn't that give *Otskry* ample time to assess the intel and line up buyers well before we could possibly launch an assault on the *Otskry* facility—even assuming we knew where it was?"

Elliott shrugged, "You're right, captain, it may turn out that we arrive too late, but there's also a chance they'll still be working the phones and the internet in search for one or more paying customers despite the fact it's early evening."

They resumed walking back to where Elliott's SUV was parked outside the executive jet terminal. As they climbed in Sgt. Farrand said, in his inimitable laconic style, "Colonel, I'm thinking if we had eyes on *Otskry* closer to when Marius is expected to arrive we'd be better positioned to react, whatever the circumstances."

"What are you saying, sergeant?" asked Elliott.

"Well…earlier I noticed there's a 11:15 am flight non-stop to Chisinau. Now, what if we could get one of us on that flight, which would put that person in Chisinau by about 1400 hours, making it possible for him to reach Tiraspol by taxi only a little more than an hour later—at least that's what I learned from an internet search."

"Go on," urged Elliott.

"What I'm thinking, sir, is if you'd authorize me to take the flight it would put me on-site by about 1500 hours whereas the earliest Marius could show up would be closer to 1400 hours… only an hour earlier."

"That may be, sergeant, but we'd still have to factor in the time needed to accurately locate the outfit's headquarters, even assuming we knew where it was," argued Perez.

"As it happens, we do know where their headquarters is," said Elliott. "Hanna gave me a fairly good description...I don't think it'll take long to zero in on the precise building once the sergeant is in its immediate vicinity."

"And, captain, we can't overlook the fact Marius might not have all his ducks in a row...hell, he might be delayed at the Odessa airport waiting for a car dispatched from Tiraspol—over highways that might not be the most car-worthy," observed Farrand, hoping to lend the colonel some support.

"So...what, colonel? You going with the Farrand's proposal?" asked Capt. Perez skeptically.

Elliott shrugged, "I can't see the harm in it...and from a tactical point of view it makes a hell of a lot of sense...having Sgt. Farrand on target to evaluate Alexandru's security and to work out the best approach."

"Let me give the airline a call, colonel...see if there's even a seat available," said Farrand.

While they waited for Farrand's call to be put through, Perez pressed further, "If the Chisinau flight isn't already full, why didn't Marius take it? Hell, it would have made it possible for him to reach Tiraspol two hours earlier than if he'd been able to get on the 11:20 am Odessa flight."

"It's the destination, captain," said Elliott patiently, "Moldova and Transnistria are in an awkward relationship, and since Marius most likely carries a passport that shows him to be a resident of Transnistria...it's likely he worried he'd be delayed in Chisinau by unsympathetic Moldovan customs authorities... or worse yet, he might have feared they'd express some interest in the documents he was carrying. No, I don't think Marius regarded the flight Sgt. Farrand is referring to as even an option."

"We're in luck, colonel," said Farrand as he got off his phone. "The flight isn't fully booked."

Elliott looked at his watch, "It's just about 9:30 am…they probably won't start boarding until 10:15 am at the earliest… once we drop you off, sergeant, you should have plenty of time to buy a ticket and get over to the departure gate."

"That's about what I figured, colonel," replied Farrand quietly, before reaching for the sketch map Elliott had prepared of the Tiraspol location of *Otskry's* headquarters.

"You won't be armed," cautioned Capt. Perez. "You will take care until we arrive…right sergeant?"

"You better believe it, sir," said Farrand soberly.

* * *

"Where now, colonel?" asked Perez as they watched Farrand disappear into the terminal building.

"Let's put the SUV into overnight parking then give the embassy our location," replied Elliott, pulling away from the curb and joining the stream of traffic moving slowly through the arrival/departure lane.

Signs guided them to Parking Lot P-4 where Elliott found a spot just to the left of the entrance kiosk. He put a call through to the US Embassy, "Military Attaché's office please, operator," he said, once the call was picked up.

"This is Sgt. Abernathy…who should I say is calling?" asked the woman handling incoming calls for the office of the Attaché.

"This is Lt. Col. Elliott Stone of the US Army, currently assigned to the Defense Intelligence Agency…any chance there's someone in the office I can talk to?"

"Major Braithwaite is in…let me connect you with her," she said.

"Major Braithwaite here," said a disciplined female voice, "How can I help you, colonel?"

"Major, I'm currently at the Warsaw-Chopin airport, in transit to Odessa, and ultimately to Tiraspol, in connection with a counter-intelligence mission that originated in Berlin, Germany. Since I'm flying out, I need to leave my SUV behind in the overnight parking lot of the airport. The problem is I've several assault rifles, three handguns, and a couple of flash-bangs that can't be left in the vehicle and that I can't take with me. I'm hoping you can arrange for a couple of the embassy's marines to come pick up the weapons and take them for safekeeping back to the embassy's armory."

There was a pause in the conversation as the major mentally processed Elliott's request. "I assume you've got military identification with you, colonel…is that the case?"

"Yes, major…not only for me, but for my aide, Capt. Perez. You can verify the particulars of my mission with Col. Appleton, military attaché at the US Embassy in Berlin who serves as my commanding officer."

"Very good, colonel…I'll dispatch a car immediately…can you give me your precise location?"

Elliott did so, then thanked the major. But before terminating the call he inquired whether the major knew anything about plans to have the US Army contingent of the Joint Contact Team stationed in Odessa supply him and his men equivalent weapons upon their arrival at the Odessa airport later that afternoon.

"I'm sorry, colonel, but I've no personal knowledge of those arrangements...let me check with the officer handling liaison with the Office of Defense Cooperation...can I get back to you?"

"I'd appreciate it...thanks," replied Elliott, giving her his cell phone number.

Elliott terminated the call, then gave Perez a thumbs-up, "The marines should show up in about a half-hour...the major will call back regarding the status of our request for weapons and a vehicle once she talks with someone who knows about it."

A good twenty minutes elapsed before Elliott's phone rang.

"It's Maj. Braithwaite, colonel," she said once Elliott picked up. "The word is that your request for replacement weapons and a vehicle has been approved. I've also been informed that the timing of the delivery is workable, so I believe you can count on the assistance you requested."

"That's great news, major...thanks."

"I should also mention I contacted Col. Appleton in Berlin who vouched for you and impressed upon me the importance of your mission. If there's any further way the embassy can be of assistance just let me know."

"I'll do that, major...though at the moment I think we're okay."

"Good luck, sir," she said before breaking the connection.

Elliott had barely put away his phone when a plain sedan of American manufacture pulled up to the entrance kiosk with two marines in uniform seated inside. Perez waved at them.

Elliott and Perez walked up to the embassy vehicle as it pulled alongside Elliott's SUV, holding their ID-creds up for the marines to see. The marines nodded, then stepped out of their vehicle.

"What do you have for us, sir?" asked the lead marine.

"Take a look," said Elliott, opening the rear hatch of the SUV.

"Okay, we've got it," said the marine, motioning for his partner to retrieve the weapons and take them to their vehicle.

"Tell the armorer we'll pick up the weapons on our way back," said Elliott as he locked the SUV."

"Very well, sir," said the lead marine. "You going to be okay going forward on your mission without them?"

"We'll be resupplied once we land in Odessa," replied Elliott.

"Good to know, sir...and good luck!" said the lead marine as he climbed into the passenger seat of the embassy vehicle. His partner, who was already seated behind the wheel, started up the motor and gave Elliott and Perez a wave as he headed for the Lot P-4 exit.

"Well, let's hoof it back to the main terminal," said Elliott once he watched the embassy vehicle pass through the exit and turn onto the arrival/departure lane.

"You think we'll need our weapons on the return drive, colonel?" asked Perez as they walked towards the terminal complex.

"We probably won't, captain, but your unit back at Stuttgart will need to have those assault weapons returned or be given a damned good reason why not. No…if things go as we hope we'll look for an opportunity to destroy any NATO documents encountered, together with any written or digital records of high value intel obtained illicitly from the staff at the NATO Planning Center. So my guess is we'll be traveling back without anything that would be of any interest to an outfit like *Otskry*."

"You don't think we'll need to return with at least some documentary evidence, colonel?" asked Perez, who was clearly puzzled.

Elliott shrugged, "We'll use our smart phones to photograph and video record what we encounter, captain, then encrypt and upload the evidence directly to Col. Appleton's technical staff—it's a lot safer that way."

"So, the plan is for us to withdraw from the scene once our mission is completed having full deniability we were ever involved…that right, sir?" queried Perez.

"Something like that, captain…though it might be hard to pull off given that we'll be driving back to Odessa heavily-armed and without any legitimate reason for being inside a breakaway enclave not entirely welcoming to NATO personnel."

* * *

The afternoon flight landed at Odessa's international airport at around 1730 hours in the evening. Elliott and Perez walked briskly into the arrival terminal carrying their day packs, then began looking around for any sign of US Army personnel from the Joint Contact Team. Not seeing anyone that even remotely fit the bill, they headed for the main doors that led to the street. Once outside, they spotted a US Military Humvee parked at the curb just to the right of the entrance, its diesel engine idling noisily. Two men in ACU's (U.S. Army combat uniforms) were seated inside.

"You men here to meet up with us, lieutenant?" asked Elliott through the open window on the passenger side, holding up his ID-creds so the officer seated there could get a good glimpse.

"Yes, sir!" said the lieutenant as he hurriedly opened his door and climbed out. "We thought it best to remain outside—being in uniform and all."

"I understand…now what have you brought for us?" asked Elliott.

"Sir…the weapons are stashed in the rear compartment of the vehicle we've brought along. We figured it would be preferable to make the handoff in the parking lot…it's less congested… more private."

"Makes good sense, lieutenant…Capt. Perez, why don't you and I climb into the back seat so these men can take us to the car."

Perez nodded, then walked around to the other side of the vehicle, opened the door and climbed in, dropping his day pack on the floor next to his feet. Elliott followed suit. The driver—a sergeant—turned around to check they were properly seated, then put the vehicle in gear and pulled away from the curb.

The parking lot was adjacent to the terminal, requiring the driver merely to pull around to the north end of the arrival/

departure roundabout, then drive straight in through the un-manned entrance. The lot was less than a half full, and the car the soldiers had brought along was parked by itself at the far end.

"That's it, sir," said the lieutenant, pointing to a sedan of French manufacture.

Elliott studied the vehicle as they drove closer. The body was painted a subdued non-metallic gray, and it was clear there'd been no effort made to run the vehicle through a carwash before turning it over. For this, Elliott was grateful—it meant the car wouldn't stand out among the other vehicles on the highway to Tiraspol. Similarly, Elliott noted with satisfaction the vehicle's license plate: it was a local Odessa plate.

"It looks quite satisfactory, lieutenant," said Elliott as he climbed out of the Humvee.

The lieutenant also climbed out, then went around to the trunk of the parked car, opened it and pointed to the weapons placed carefully in the rear compartment. "I think we brought everything requested, sir, with the exception of a Beretta M9… couldn't locate one so we substituted another Glock 17…hope that's all right."

"It'll be fine…thanks," said Elliott as he did a mental inventory of the weaponry: three Glock 17's; three Heckler & Koch 416 assault rifles, suppressors for all six firearms; multiple ammo clips and magazines; two M84 stun grenades.

"Captain, why don't you get the ignition keys from the lieutenant and check out the engine and fuel gages while I transfer these items to the rear seating area," said Elliott.

"The vehicle is only a year old and we made sure it's got a full tank, captain," said the lieutenant as he handed Perez the keys. "You shouldn't have any problems with it."

"Good to know, lieutenant," replied Perez as he stepped over to the car, unlocked the driver's side door and climbed in. Once in, Perez unlocked the doors to the rear seating area so that Elliott could make the transfer.

"I was also asked to give you these," said the lieutenant as he handed Elliott three maps: a highway map covering the roads between Odessa and Tiraspol, and two city maps— one of Odessa, with the route from the airport to the main highway clearly marked, and one of Tiraspol. "Place names on the highway map and the Odessa map are in Ukrainian, those on the Tiraspol map are in Romanian—it's about the best we could come up with in the short time available to us," he added apologetically.

"It's okay, lieutenant, I've a good working knowledge of Ukrainian, and the captain has fluency in Spanish which—he tells me—makes deciphering Romanian words a manageable challenge," said Elliott with a smile.

"Well, if you feel everything is in order we'll take our leave," said the lieutenant.

"Yeah, I think we can handle it from here...thanks lieutenant...appreciate all you and the sergeant have done to facilitate our mission."

"Thank you, sir...and good luck!" With that, the lieutenant climbed back in the Humvee, motioned for the sergeant to start the engine. Once the sergeant put the vehicle in reverse and began turning around, the lieutenant gave Elliott a final wave. Elliott waved back, then watched as the Humvee headed for the lot exit.

"Everything on the instrument panel looks okay, colonel," said Perez as Elliott climbed into the passenger seat.

"Glad to hear it, captain," said Elliott absently, as he studied the Odessa street map. "Okay...I think I see how to get us out of town."

Chapter Twenty-Three

A little over an hour later they crossed the Ukraine/Moldova border and Perez slowed as they approached the international border security outpost manned by forces loyal to Transnistria.

"Let me do the talking, captain," said Elliott.

There were two cars ahead, and Elliott watched to see how burdensome the vetting would be. It was still light, but the sun was almost beyond the horizon. It was getting close to time for the evening meal. Elliott was hoping that meant the border guards were about to end their shift. It had been his experience that often at such times security personnel tended to perform their duties rather more casually than if they were just coming on duty. As he continued to study the scene he noticed that the officer interrogating the persons in the cars ahead looked to be young—perhaps a junior grade officer. He thought it might work to their advantage.

"Seems as if they're mostly interested in identity papers, colonel," said Perez, who'd also been studying the interaction between the travelers in the cars ahead and the officer.

"I see that," replied Elliott quietly. "Let's just hope it stays that way when it's our turn."

The travelers in the two vehicles appeared to have satisfactory papers and were allowed to proceed on their way. The officer then motioned for Perez to drive up to where he was standing.

Once Perez brought the car to a stop Elliott immediately climbed out and walked over to the officer, "I'm sorry, officer," said Elliott in fluent Ukrainian, but my driver doesn't speak anything but English and Spanish…perhaps I can answer your questions."

The officer looked at Elliott suspiciously, "Your papers!" he demanded brusquely in Ukrainian.

Elliott handed him his passport and military ID, purposely concealing his counter-intelligence creds, then said in a casual tone, "Capt. Perez and I are temporarily assigned to the US/Ukrainian Joint Contact Team based in Odessa…being so close to Transnistria we thought we'd take the opportunity of driving over here…maybe see the sights…who knows when we'll be back in this area again."

The officer immediately stiffened his posture upon learning Elliott was a Lt. Colonel in the US Army. "You come as a tourist, sir?" he asked.

"Yes…both Capt. Perez—captain, show the officer your papers—and I are on temporary duty in Odessa…probably for no more than a week…and with only a limited amount of free time we figured we'd learn more about your part of the world by coming here rather than sticking around Odessa."

"You know much about Transnistria, colonel?" asked the officer, somewhat suspiciously.

Elliott shrugged, "Hell, officer, we're combat infantry...they don't send our kind to theatre-specific cultural affairs briefings unless there's a chance we'll be pointed in a particular direction. And I'm not speaking out of turn if I tell you the Joint Contact Team exercises we're here to participate in point north and east from Odessa...not west!"

The officer nodded absently as he took Perez' documents in hand and began to read.

"So, your plan is to return to Odessa tomorrow, colonel?" asked the officer.

"Yup...probably in the late afternoon after the captain and I have a leisurely lunch in one of your nicer restaurants and we've finished checking out Tiraspol's cultural highlights."

"Have you made hotel reservations?" asked the officer, who Elliott figured was now trying to be helpful.

Elliott shrugged, "Haven't given it a thought...why? Are the hotels likely to be booked up this time of year?"

"No...but you should probably try getting into Tiraspol's best hotel...here...let me write down the hotel's name and street address for you."

"Thanks, officer," said Elliott as he took the scrap of paper with the hotel information from the man's outstretched hand. "Are we free to go now?"

"Yes, of course...have a pleasant stay, colonel," he replied, offering a quick salute.

Elliott acknowledged the military courtesy with a nod, then climbed back into the car. Perez put the vehicle in gear and drove out of the covered border-control facility and onto the M14 Highway.

"According to the map, captain, Tiraspol is only about 35 kilometers distant…we should be there in about a half-hour," said Elliott as he pulled out his cell phone and put a call through to Sgt. Farrand.

"Sergeant, we've just passed through border security and are now no more than a half-hour away…give me an update on what's happening on your end," said Elliott once Farrand picked up.

"I'm on site, colonel…the sector is just as you described…a cluster of dilapidated light-industrial buildings and empty lots just west of Kirov Park."

"Have you been able to identify the building being used by *Otskry?*" asked Elliott.

"I think so, colonel…the building fits the description given by Hanna."

"Is there anything else that's making you feel you've got the right building?"

"Well, sir, it's the only building resembling the description that has cars parked nearby. Currently, there are four vehicles, and one of them is a high priced German model. Earlier, there were more cars, but they were eventually driven away by persons who I observed leaving the building. Also, whatever outfit is in there seems a little uptight with regard to security."

"Okay, I guess the call—whether it's *Otskry* or not—will have to be made once we get there…any chance you can guide us in...we'll be entering the city from the east on *Strada 9-January*, according to my map," said Elliott.

"That should work perfectly, colonel...the street you'll be coming in on borders the south edge of the park. Stay on it past the intersection with the street forming the west side of the park, then take the first lane on the right...it'll give you access to the interior cluster of buildings. I'll watch for you...can you give me a description of your vehicle?"

'It's a late-model, gray sedan of French manufacture," replied Elliott.

"Roger that," said Farrand before breaking the connection.

* * *

It was growing dark as Perez turned into the lane. He switched on his brights, hoping to catch a glimpse of Farrand. "There he is!" said Elliott, pointing to the shadowy figure off to their left. Perez shut off his headlights then slowed down and rolled to a stop. Farrand climbed into the back seat.

"We haven't far to go," said Farrand quietly. "Make a left at the cross-street just ahead, then immediately pull over...next to those trees."

"How far away is the building?" asked Perez as he followed Farrand's instructions.

"It's just on the other side of that clump of trees—less than a hundred feet."

Perez shut off the motor, and as the vehicle settled—ticking faintly in the background against the deep silence of the darkening evening—Elliott turned to Farrand, "Okay, sergeant, give us a full report of what you've learned."

"To begin with, colonel, as I said earlier, I'm inclined to believe we've targeted the right building. I've observed that every hour on the half-hour a security guard steps out through the small entrance door, does a perimeter inspection then goes back inside. Over the four plus hours I've watched the building four different guards pulled the duty…and on the last circuit it was the guard who'd pulled the first inspection, making me believe the security team inside consists of no more than four men."

"Go on," urged Elliott.

"Well, sir, there seems to be something of a business-like character to whatever is going on inside. I say that because at about 1800 hours—quitting time at most business here in Moldova—a stream of people left the building, climbed into their cars then drove off."

"Can you say anything about them, sergeant?" asked Elliott.

Farrand shrugged, "They seemed fairly non-descript… certainly none that I'd take as being military in their bearing, or persons evidencing a heightened sense of awareness of their surroundings as you would imagine a veteran spy might exhibit. No…a handful looked like regular clerical staffers…others, like young adult trainees—not unlike the young women who served as eavesdroppers in Berlin. I counted twenty-two in all…a mix of men and women."

"What about Marius…did you see him leave?" asked Elliott.

Farrand shook his head, "No, sir...and I was keeping a sharp lookout for him. No...if he was in the building he's still there...as is Alexandru, who I believe owns that luxury German sedan parked in the lot on the east side of the building. As for the other three cars still parked in the lot I'd wager one is the vehicle driven by Marius; one, a car owned by a staffer working overtime...it looks like the other cars that were parked there; and one—a large SUV—that's most likely shared by the four security guards. I say that because I know they're all still inside."

"Okay, so according to your assessment we're dealing with an after-hours skeleton staff of four security guards, a single staffer, and the two principals: Alexandru and Marius...is that right?" asked Elliott.

Farrand shrugged, "That's the way it seems to me, sir... assuming it's *Otskry's* headquarters."

"What do you think," captain?" asked Elliott.

"I'd go along with the sergeant's take on the scene, colonel. And if we think about the guards...it seems to me that we've got to assume the four of them actually live on the premises— certainly that option exists since Hanna described built-in living facilities behind the rear wall of the classroom complex."

"Okay...the consensus seems to be that the building is the *Otskry* headquarters...so we'll go with that," said Elliott.

"How do you want to proceed, colonel?" asked Perez.

Elliott took a moment to gather his thoughts, then said, "Sergeant, during your visual inspection of the building did you happen to spot any surveillance cameras?"

Farrand shook his head, "No, sir...and that surprised me. It was only after I caught the pattern of perimeter inspection by the guards that I understood Alexandru seemed to want more than a visual scan of the building's immediate exterior... something more like the kind of full-on assessment that only an eyes-on patrol can produce."

"So, if the sergeant, here, were to approach the building and clumsily try to force open one of the two large drive-through doors it's likely at least one of the guards still on duty would hear the disturbance and step outside to see what was going on," mused Elliott.

"But once the guard spotted the sergeant wouldn't he be likely to report it to his partner who would then probably rush out to join him?" queried Perez.

Elliott shrugged, "Perhaps, captain, but there's no reason we couldn't prepare for either contingency...for example, if only the first guard elected to brace Sgt. Farrand, the sergeant could quietly subdue him; on the other hand, if a second guard joined the first, and the two of them approached Sgt. Farrand, then the sergeant could find someway of distracting them while the captain and I rushed over to lend assistance."

Sgt. Farrand nodded, "It works for me, sir...shall I head over?"

Elliott turned to Perez, inquiringly.

"Let's do it, sir," said Perez.

"Okay...gear up...let's get this show on the road," said Elliott as he attached a sound suppressor to his Glock 17 and also one to his Heckler & Koch 416 assault rifle. The assault rifle he attached to the side of his day pack before strapping it to his back; the Glock he snapped into a suppressor-compatible belt holster.

Farrand and Perez followed suit, then the three of them climbed out of the car and walked stealthily through the irregular grove of trees and shrubs to a point where they remained concealed but could clearly observe the front of the building— now less than thirty feet away.

With a faint nod of acknowledgement to his companions, Farrand stepped clear of the trees, walked across the narrow road and over to the large drive-through metal door closest to the center of the building. The door was the kind that rolled up along overhead tracks, and was secured with a single hasp-type assembly locked to a bracket imbedded in the concrete floor with the aid of a padlock. Farrand bent over and gave the padlock a vigorous shake, then let it drop, creating a loud metallic sound that he hoped reverberated through the interior of the building.

Only moments later, one of the guards opened the walk-through door and leaned out. Farrand continued to crouch down, appearing absorbed in figuring out how to overcome the lock, his back to the guard. The guard turned and said something to whoever was just inside the door, then he began to walk purposively towards Farrand, holding a heavy-duty flashlight in his hand. A second guard stepped through the door and hurried to join him. Both had sidearms, but they were holstered.

Farrand looked up at them, then seemingly dismissing them, continued to shake the padlock obsessively.

"Hey...you there!" shouted the lead guard as he shown a light on Farrand, "stand up!"

Farrand meekly stood up facing them at a slight angle so that the assault rifle attached to his day pack was not visible from their direction. His Glock was hidden beneath his jacket.

"What the hell do you think you're doing!" shouted the lead guard, menacingly.

Farrand pretended to shrink in terror as the two guards came close. Then, as the lead guard made a lunge to grab him, Farrand lashed out with his right elbow, hitting the guard on the side of the head, stunning him, and causing him to drop the flashlight. Instantly, the second guard reached for his sidearm, but before he could pull it free Perez came up from behind and put a chokehold on him. Simultaneously, Elliott grabbed the man's weapon.

Meanwhile, Farrand had kicked the lead guard's feet out from under him, then kept him from getting up by putting a knee on his chest, his Glock pointed at the man's head, "Don't move or say a thing," he said in German.

Elliott quickly bound the two guards with plasticuffs on both their wrists and their ankles while Farrand and Perez kept them subdued. Next, he pulled off the men's shoes and socks. He balled up the socks and forced them into their mouths, then taped each of their mouth with duct tape that Farrand had enterprisingly bought after landing in Chisinau.

"Get the keys to the doors of the building, and to the big SUV," whispered Elliott to Farrand. The sergeant nodded, then proceeded to empty all the pockets of the two guards. He found, and tossed to Elliott, a set of keys that seemed to be for the building. Elliott tried the keys on the padlock securing the drive-through door and found one that worked. He removed the padlock but didn't attempt to slide open the large metal door. Confident now that he had the right keys, Elliott quickly walked over to the small walk-through door and unlocked it with one of the other keys. Propping it open a crack with a handy rock, Elliott motioned for Perez and Farrand to drag the two men over.

"Found the keys to the SUV, colonel," whispered Farrand as he showed Elliott the distinctive vehicle icon on the remote keys.

"Keep them, sergeant," whispered Elliott.

"Okay...let's get inside," added Elliott. "I'll lead...captain, you follow. Sergeant, you keep an eye on our prisoners until it's safe to drag them inside."

"Roger that, sir!" said Farrand in a subdued voice.

Having been advised by Hanna that much of the interior space on the right side of the building was subdivided by shoulder-high cubicle walls, Elliott and Perez entered the the reception area in a crouch. They listened for sounds of activity from within the six cubicles comprising the front portion of that side of the building. Hearing nothing, Elliott stood up and advanced stealthily down the hallway towards the rear portion—an area partitioned off by a much taller and more solidly built free-standing wall, with access made possible by way of a doorway located at the end of the hallway. Meanwhile, Perez slipped out the front door and helped Farrand drag the two bound guards into the reception area, laying them carefully on the floor and checking to see they were having no difficulty breathing.

Elliott passed a closed door on his left that he figured led to the classrooms Hanna had described. He stopped and waited for Perez and Farrand to catch up. Eventually, he caught sight of them as they entered the central hallway. As they approached, Elliott motioned for them to be aware of the door, then—using hand signs—signalled for one of them to peel off and check out that part of the building. Perez picked up on his meaning and whispered instructions to Farrand.

Farrand lingered next to the doorway while Perez hurried forward to join up with Elliott. As Elliott and Perez watched, Farrand reached for the door's handle—testing to see if the door was locked. It wasn't. Elliott gave him a nod, which Farrand acknowledged before carefully opening the door and disappearing through it. Once Elliott and Perez were satisfied Farrand hadn't met with any immediate resistance they unslung their assault rifles and readied themselves to force their way into the rear area where they hoped to find *Otskry's* leadership.

Chapter Twenty-Four

Elliott and Perez burst through the door and took a moment to make sense of what they saw: four people—two men and two women—seated around a long work table that was piled high with paper documents arranged in neatly marked folders. Elliott put a finger to his lips, signaling for them to remain quiet, but the two women began to scream.

Suddenly, a window in the elevated office complex high above them was slid open and a male figure leaned out holding an assault rifle. Perez got off a short burst before backing through the doorway he and Elliott had just come out of. Elliott, for his part, made a dash for the area immediately below the office module. And the man upstairs, despite no longer having a direct target, still let loose with a burst of his own.

Silence reigned for a few seconds as all parties took stock of the situation, then the four staffers at the table dropped from their seats and crawled under the table. Perez, leaning out from the doorway, took more careful aim and fired a tight pattern of rounds through the open office window, forcing whoever was up there to back away. Elliott took that opportunity to step to the center of the room from where he was able to lob one of the two

270

M84 stun grenades through the open window. As the grenade detonated, Elliott rushed over to the metal staircase leading up to the office module and began to climb.

A dazed figure reappeared at the open office window and began to fire his weapon wildly at the workroom below, but Perez instantly responded with a lethal three-shot burst. Just then, Elliott managed to reach the top of the staircase where he kicked open the office door, then dropped defensively into a prone position. Gunshots from a handgun greeted him, but did no damage as they passed high over their intended target. But the shots did help Elliott spot the shooter who was crouched behind a metal desk. Elliott aimed his assault rifle at the desk, sprayed multiple rounds into it and immediately above it. Some of the rounds managed to catch the man just as he was getting up to rest his handgun on the desk surface, hoping to get off a more accurate second round of shots.

Sensing there was no longer a threat from that quarter, Elliott stood and walked carefully into the office. As he was about to bend down to examine the body of the man Perez had shot, Perez yells from below "Get to cover!" Then all hell broke loose as firing from a new hostile source was met by return fire from Perez.

Elliott crawled to the open window and peeked out. There, on the wall directly across from his vantage point, he saw that someone had opened a door—one he figured probably led to the building's sleeping quarters. And from it, Elliott could see a man—crouched protectively—firing towards Perez. Elliott was about to raise his Heckler & Koch 416 and deliver suppressive fire when the man spotted him and shifted his aim upward—toward this new target. Elliott ducked back down just as a burst of shots ripped through the window, shattering what remained of the window's frame.

Perez reengaged the new shooter, giving Elliott a brief opportunity to reestablish the hostile target by quickly standing up and directing sustained fire on the man whom he supposed was probably one of the off-duty security guards, killing him.

But as the man slumped to the floor, a second shooter took his place, forcing Elliott to take cover again. It looked as if a standoff might ensue, with all three combatants primed to shoot but safe from any hurried fusillade. Then, a burst of gunfire from one of the back rooms behind the wall separating the two sections of the building felled the second shooter.

"Don't fire...it's me...Sgt. Farrand!" shouted Farrand from behind the doorway where the bodies of the two dead guards lay inert.

"We hear you!" Elliott shouted back. "Come on out!"

Farrand stepped through the doorway and into the large workroom, holding his Heckler & Koch 416 at the ready. Perez stepped forward to join him. Elliott, however, remained at the upstairs office window looking down.

"You can stand up now!" Elliott shouted in Ukrainian, addressing the four staffers huddled together under the long table.

Tentatively, the four crawled out from beneath the table and stood up—their fear palpable. Farrand and Perez quickly searched them for weapons, then gestured for them to return to their seats.

"Do any of you speak English?" asked Elliott.

All four raised their hands. "We are working with mostly English and German documents...knowing English was required for employment," said one of the female staffers.

"So, what are all these documents...the ones piled on the table? What is it about them that is so important you've all been kept working after business hours?" asked Elliott.

A tall, slender man of middle age, whom Elliott figured was the lead clerk replied, "They are copies of intelligence transcripts delivered here from our Berlin headquarters. We've been ordered to go through all of these files, then identify and pull those transcripts that deal with topics covered in the document delivered by Marius. I've been told this needs to be done in order to supplement the intel package brought here by Marius."

"So Marius is here...is he one of the persons lying dead in the office module where I'm now standing?"

The man nodded.

"And the other man killed up here...is he Alexandru?" asked Elliott.

The man nodded again, then asked shakily, "Are you Americans?"

"It doesn't matter what our nationality is...all you and the others have to know is that this is a NATO counter-intelligence operation," said Elliott dismissively. "Captain, escort these people from the building, together with the two guards in the reception area. Hold them until we're ready to leave."

"Yes, sir," said Perez who, using his Heckler & Koch 416, gestured for the four staffers to walk towards the hallway.

"Sergeant...you've still got the keys to the SUV, I take it?" said Elliott.

Farrand nodded.

"Okay, what I want you to do is to open that unlocked drive-through door, then drive the SUV into the building...crashing through all the free-standing walls until you make it into this area."

"Then what, sir?" asked Farrand.

"Then go back outside, lock the drive-through door, and after that's done, assist the captain in keeping the others from leaving."

"Roger that, sir," said Farrand with a grin before hurrying down the hallway.

Elliott figured he'd used up most of the time he could safely assume was available to him before the local authorities descended on the building, having been alerted by someone nearby who probably couldn't help hearing the sharp report of the M84 stun grenade, or the loud firings emanating from the weapons of the *Otskry* team—weapons that had not been fixed with noise suppressors.

As he waited for Farrand to reappear in the SUV, he bent down and examined the two bodies lying on the floor of the upstairs office. He wasn't at all sure he could personally identify Marius, and knew for certain he wouldn't be able to identify Alexandru. So, he went through their pockets looking for some sort of documentary corroboration. Both had ID's with photographs that reassured him the two dead bodies were the men he was intent on finding. He also discovered it was Alexandru who had been the one behind the desk, firing at him. He shook his head at the futility of it all, then took his smart phone and quickly photographed the two dead men before hurrying out of the office complex and down the stairs.

Moments later, Elliott heard the roar of the SUV's big engine as Farrand pressed the accelerator and drove the heavy vehicle through the open drive-through entrance. Almost immediately, the sound of crashing furniture and collapsing walls filled the building as the SUV, with its 4-wheel drive fully engaged, dug its way forward. Finally, Elliott watched as the big vehicle emerged from the shambles it had caused, coming to a stop only feet from where the documents table was located, its front end torn and dented.

Farrand climbed out, still grinning, then gave a nod to Elliott before heading back out to team up with Perez.

Elliott took a last look at all the copies of intel transcriptions that had accumulated over the duration of the eavesdropping operation run out of the bookstore in Berlin. He imagined there were also an untold number of documents scattered among the files that had been handed over to *Otskry* operatives by Planning Center employees coerced through threats of exposure. Finally—before turning to his final task—he allowed himself a weary sense of satisfaction as he entertained the irony of it all: the image of Marius desperately rushing to deliver that packet of breakthrough documents only to have them end up being burned to ashes in the heart of *Otskry's* main headquarters.

"They're coming!" shouted Perez from down the hallway.

Elliott nodded, then unslung his Heckler & Koch 416, backed away from the table and towards the hallway leading outside. When he felt he had a relatively clear view of the elevated undercarriage of the SUV he got down into a prone firing position, aimed carefully at the fuel line just forward of the fuel tank and fired.

Fuel began to spill out of the severed line onto the concrete floor of the building. When enough fuel had spread Elliott pulled out the second M84 stun grenade, activated it, then tossed it under the SUV.

Elliott was halfway to the entrance of the building when the grenade went off, and fully through the outside door when he heard the muffled explosion of the fuel tank. Shutting the door quickly, he shouted, "Let's get out of here!"

The six *Otskry* employees abandoned any thought of getting into one of the cars parked in the lot on the east side of the building, fearing the imminent arrival of the police, and instead ran headlong down the interior lane that led to a scatter of derelict buildings to the west where they could hide. Elliott and his team jogged across the road, through the thickly wooded patch of land, over to where their car was parked.

Just before they climbed in, they looked back the way they had come and saw a bright glow emanating from the fire. "Looks like the SUV's fuel tank exploding ruptured some part of the metal building," said Elliott. "Hell, with all that fresh air fueling the flames that fire's likely to thoroughly incinerate every combustible thing it touches."

Perez took the wheel, Elliott climbed into the passenger seat, and Farrand was busy in the back seat stashing all of their packs and assault rifles on the floor where they'd be out of sight.

"Let's go!" shouted Elliott.

Perez started up the engine, did a tight U-turn and headed back towards *Strada 9-January.* Once there, he pulled a left and headed east—toward Odessa.

* * *

Throughout the thirty-some minutes of the drive to the Moldova/Ukrainian border, Elliott and his two teammates kept a nervous watch to their rear, worried the authorities in Tiraspol had somehow managed to identify them as the men who perpetrated the attack on *Otskry's* headquarters. They were both relieved and freshly worried as the lights of the roofed border police facility came into view—relieved because there had been no pursuit, but freshly worried by the thought it was because arrangements had been made to have them arrested at the border that explained the absence of any attempt at stopping them in transit.

"Should I just power through...without stopping?" asked Perez grimly.

Elliott thought about it, then said, "Let's slow down as we come closer...check out the scene...if it looks like there are an unusual number of armed border agents in sight, and some sort of temporary barrier across the road, then I think we may want to do precisely what you suggest, captain…no way we're going to want to allow ourselves to be detained by the Transnistrian authorities—it'd create a hell of an international incident!"

"I hear you, sir!" said Perez as he studied the activity at the border control complex, now just a short distance ahead.

There were no cars in front of them, just two trucks. The drivers of both trucks seemed to know the drill and pulled off onto a lane at the extreme right which curved away from the main highway pass-through towards the truck inspection lanes further to the side.

Perez drove forward at a modest speed once the trucks were out of the way, expecting to pull up under the roofed inspection complex where he could see what appeared to be an officer and two armed enlisted men idly awaiting the next vehicle. The man who Perez presumed was the officer motioned for Perez to drive up to where he was standing. Perez looked over at Elliott, inquiringly. "Go ahead, captain…let's let it play out," said Elliott.

Perez nodded, then slowly brought the car to a halt directly where the officer had instructed. As he had on the way in, Elliott quickly climbed out of the car and walked over to the officer, "My companions speak mostly English, officer," said Elliott in Ukrainian, "perhaps I can assist in answering your questions."

The officer shook his head dismissively, "It is no problem…I speak English," then, ignoring Elliott, he motioned for Perez to lower his window. "Papers!" he commanded brusquely.

Perez lowered his window and handed the officer his passport. While the officer inspected the document, Elliott shrugged, then stepped back around the car, opened the door to the passenger seat, but remained standing next to the vehicle.

"Your entry stamp indicates that you entered Transnistria earlier this evening, but now you are leaving already? How do you explain this?" asked the officer, clearly suspicious.

The tone of his voice alerted the two armed sentries that there was something irregular about this car and its occupants. They became alert, gripping their assault rifles with extra care.

"We are members of the US Army, attached to the US/ Ukrainian Joint Contact Team based in Odessa, officer," said Elliott firmly, ignoring the officer's preference for speaking with Perez. "I am the senior officer...a Lt. Colonel. Capt. Perez, with whom you are speaking, is my second in command. And in the back seat is Sgt. Farrand. We have all been called back to Odessa unexpectedly...that is why we have been obliged to suspend our visit to Tiraspol...we plan to attempt a second visit when our military schedule allows it."

The officer looked angrily at Elliott, sensing he'd been given a stinging reprimand by this American colonel. "Well, we'll see...won't we," said the officer contemptuously as he handed Perez back his passport. "Pull your car over there," he ordered, pointing to a parking zone next to the border control office.

"I'm afraid that's not going to happen, officer," said Elliott forcefully. "You're free to have your superiors file a complaint, but under no circumstances are you going to detain three American soldiers... even temporarily!" Unseen by the border police, Farrand had slipped Elliott his Heckler & Koch 416. Elliott now pointed it at the officer. "We're prepared to use force…so unless you and your guards want to create an international incident I suggest all three of you step away."

The officer was clearly out of his depth. He wasn't sure what to do. That was even more true of the two ordinary rank-and-file guards who had no inkling what had been said, or why this passenger was pointing a gun at their officer.

"Step away!" Elliott shouted, repeating his command in Ukrainian so the two guards could understand. At the same moment, Sgt. Farrand opened his door and slipped out, holding his Heckler & Koch 416 and pointing it at the two guards.

The officer looked around for support, but none of the others working that evening were near enough to observe what was going on.

"Tell your men to shoulder their weapons, then walk away!" ordered Elliott in Ukrainian.

The two guards, having understood Elliott's command, looked at their leader. After a moment of hesitation he nodded in the affirmative.

All three backed away from the car, the officer hardly able to conceal his rage.

Perez, who had kept the motor running, barely allowed Farrand and Elliott enough time to jump in before hitting the accelerator, then racing full speed towards the highway bridge spanning a broad expanse of wetlands that served as the official border separating Moldova from the Ukraine. Elliott breathed a sigh of relief as Farrand reported that there had been no following shots fired.

"But we're not out of trouble yet," said Elliott, eyeing the brightly lit Ukrainian border control complex coming into view less than 500 meters ahead.

"They just passed us through as we left the country, colonel... you think it'll be different coming back?" asked Perez.

"Yeah...I do, captain. They're a bit sensitive when it comes to trade relations with Transnistria...wanting to make sure whatever comes into the Ukraine from there has the stamp of approval from the government in Chisinau...even private citizens are scrutinized for purchases that don't make the cut."

"Looks like you're right, colonel," said Farrand from the back seat. "They're signaling us to pull into an inspection lane."

Perez drove towards the third inspection kiosk under the roofed complex where a handful of Ukrainian border officials were standing—some in uniform, others in civilian attire. Once Perez brought the car to a halt and rolled down his window, he was asked to step out of the car. The man giving the orders was not one of the uniformed border police, and unlike most officials they'd dealt with he spoke good English. "The others in your car are also required to leave the vehicle...all of you will follow me, please."

Perez glanced over at Elliott, who gave him an affirmative nod. Once all three of them were out of the car, the man in charge again motioned for them to follow him, then began walking towards one of the glassed-in offices beyond the first kiosk. Elliott and the two others fell in behind him. Elliott looked back and was surprised to see they were not being escorted by any armed border agents, and their vehicle was not being searched.

Once they reached the office, the man held open the door and motioned for the three of them to enter. The office was furnished more like what an executive might require than that of a police command post, with a large desk, multiple phones, an upholstered desk chair, a sitting area, and a conference table. He gestured for them to take seats at the table.

He then began to speak, "My name is Pavlo Kushnir...I represent the Ukrainian foreign office...in what capacity and in what rank is of no importance. What is important is that the three of you have created something of a problem for us. We have received urgent phone calls from our counterpart border facility across the bridge claiming you used the threat of armed violence to evade proper vetting. We've been asked to place all of you in custody then return you to their jurisdiction without delay."

Elliott began to reply, but Kushnir held up his hand, "Please let me finish. Our colleagues across the bridge say that the three of you claim to be US Army personnel attached to the US-Ukrainian Joint Contact Team based in Odessa and hold the ranks of colonel, captain, and sergeant, respectively. My task is to ascertain the truth of these allegations, then figure out how my government should respond. Now, perhaps whichever of you is the lead officer may wish to identify himself so that we may begin."

"That would be me, sir...I'm Lt. Col. Elliott Stone...and the man to my right is Capt. Perez. The man to my left is Sgt. Farrand. We are all members of the US Army special forces detachment based near Stuttgart, Germany. Currently, we are on an assigned counter-intelligence mission for NATO that is led by Col. Appleton, military attaché at the US Embassy in Berlin. This mission was just concluded during an operation in Tiraspol. We are now on our way back to Odessa to return weaponry loaned to us by the Joint Contact Team, then to catch a flight back to Warsaw where our vehicle is currently parked. Our final destination is Germany."

Kushnir leaned back in his chair and quietly thought about what Elliott had divulged. Then he spoke, "That operation in Tiraspol…I probably shouldn't ask whether it had anything to do with the reports we've been receiving of a large incendiary event at a building in an under-used light industrial precinct within the city."

Elliott shrugged, but said nothing.

Kushnir nodded knowingly, then said, "Well, let me see if I can confirm your account. He walked over to the desk, picked up one of the phones, pressed a preset number then waited. "Connect me with the emergency number of a Col. Appleton at the US Embassy in Berlin…yes, hurry."

Several minutes went by without anyone saying anything. Kushnir continued to study his guests.

Finally the phone on the desk rang, and Kushnir picked it up. "Yes…thank you, colonel, for getting back to me so quickly. I have three men in my office at the international border station on Highway E-58, leading to Moldova/Transnistria. They identify themselves as Lt. Col. Stone, Capt. Perez, and Sgt. Farrand, respectively, and say they are on a NATO counter-intelligence mission authorized by yourself."

Kushnir listened attentively as Appleton not only confirmed the account provided by Elliott, but also impressed upon Kushnir how the mission was deemed a crucial one, especially for countries such as the Ukraine—countries that hope ultimately to find themselves west of the protective shield formed by the Eastern Flank of NATO's defensive perimeter.

"Yes, that's right, colonel, we encountered the team as it was leaving Transnistria. And yes, they do report their mission has ended, and that they were on their way back to Germany via Odessa and Warsaw when we encountered them."

Kushnir put the phone down and turned to Elliott and his team, "I must say, your colonel paints a compelling picture of the importance of your mission." Then, after a short pause, he added, "I don't suppose you'll tell me whether your mission was successful or not."

Elliott smiled briefly, then said, "We're special forces operators, Mr. Kushnir, completing a mission is a big part of who we are."

Kushnir thought about that, then said, "Well, I guess that answers my question." He got up from the desk and walked over to the conference table. "You three are free to go...it's been an honor to meet you," he added as he shook the hand of each in turn.

"And the protests from Transnistria...how will you deal with them?" asked Elliott.

Kushnir smiled, "Why...we are entirely mystified by such claims...we've no record of any party such as they describe as having crossed our border—either coming in or going out."

Elliott smiled, "I can see the merit of having a diplomat like yourself available to run interference for operators such as ourselves...good luck with it."

Kushnir nodded, "Well...let's get you on your way. From what Col. Appleton said over the phone, there's a lot of very important people eagerly awaiting your debriefing."

The End

CPSIA information can be obtained
at www.ICGtesting.com
Printed in the USA
BVHW032129090120
569156BV00001B/7/P

9 781532 078415